I0831452

THE PHANTOM OF THE OPERA

The Phantom of the Opera
Leroux, Gaston 1865 – 1927
Published in French in 1910 by Gaston Leroux
Translated by Alexander Teixeira de Mattos
de Mattos, Alexander Teixeira 1865 – 1921
First Published by published by Grosset & Dunlap in 1911

Text set in 18 point Helvetica.
Chapter headings set in Helvetica Neue.

ISBN: 978-1-83412-286-1

THE PHANTOM OF THE OPERA

GASTON LEROUX

GRAND TYPE CLASSICS

CONTENTS

The Phantom of the Opera

PROLOGUE

In which the author of this singular work informs the reader how he acquired the certainty that the Opera Ghost really existed.

THE OPERA GHOST really existed. He was not, as was long believed, a creature of the imagination of the artists, the superstition of the managers, or a product of the absurd and impressionable brains of the young ladies of the ballet, their mothers, the box-keepers, the cloakroom attendants or the concierge. Yes, he existed in flesh and blood, although he assumed the complete appearance of a real phantom; that is to say, of a spectral shade.

When I began to ransack the archives of the National Academy of Music I was at once struck by the surprising coincidences between the phenomena ascribed to the "ghost" and the most extraordinary and fantastic tragedy that ever excited the Paris upper classes; and I soon conceived the idea that this tragedy might reasonably be explained by the phenomena in question. The events do not date more than thirty years back; and it would not be difficult to find at the present day, in the foyer of the ballet, old men of the highest respectability, men upon whose word one could absolutely rely, who would remember as though they happened yesterday the mysterious and dramatic conditions that attended the kidnapping of Christine Daaé, the disappearance of the Vicomte de Chagny and the death of his elder brother, Count Philippe, whose body was found on the bank of the lake that exists in the lower cellars of the Opera on the Rue-Scribe side. But none of those witnesses had until that day thought that there was any reason for connecting the more or less legendary figure of the Opera ghost with that terrible story.

The truth was slow to enter my mind, puzzled by an inquiry that at every moment was complicated by events which, at first sight, might be looked upon as superhuman; and more than once I was within an ace of abandoning a task in which I was exhausting myself in the hopeless pursuit of a vain image. At last, I received the proof that my presentiments had not deceived me, and I was rewarded for all my efforts on the day when I acquired the certainty that the Opera ghost was more than a mere shade.

On that day, I had spent long hours over **The Memoirs of a Manager**, the light and frivolous work of the too-skeptical Moncharmin, who, during his term at the Opera, understood nothing of the mysterious behavior of the ghost and who was making all the fun of it that he could at the very moment when he became the first victim of the curious financial operation that went on inside the "magic envelope."

I had just left the library in despair, when I met the delightful acting-manager of our National Academy, who stood chatting on a landing with a lively and well-groomed little old man, to whom he introduced me gaily. The acting-manager knew all about my investigations and how eagerly and unsuccessfully I had been trying to discover the whereabouts of the examining magistrate in the famous Chagny case, M. Faure. Nobody knew what had become of him, alive or dead; and here he was back from Canada, where he had spent fifteen years, and the first thing he had done, on his return to Paris, was to come to the secretarial offices at the Opera and ask for a free seat. The little old man was M. Faure himself.

We spent a good part of the evening together and he told me the whole Chagny case as he had understood it at the time. He was bound to conclude in favor of the madness of the viscount and the accidental death of the elder brother, for lack of evidence to the contrary; but he was nevertheless persuaded that a terrible tragedy had taken place between the two brothers in connection with Christine Daaé. He could not tell me what became of Christine or the viscount. When I mentioned the ghost, he only laughed. He, too, had been told of the curious manifestations that seemed to point to the existence of an abnormal being, residing in one of the most mysterious corners of the Opera, and he knew the story of the envelope; but he had never seen anything in it worthy of his attention as magistrate in charge of the Chagny case, and it was as much as he had done to listen to the evidence of a witness who appeared of his own accord and declared that he had often met the ghost. This witness was none other than the man whom all Paris called the "Persian" and who was well-known to every subscriber to the Opera. The magistrate took him for a visionary.

I was immensely interested by this story of the Persian. I wanted, if there were still time, to find this valuable and eccentric witness. My luck began to improve and I discovered him in his little flat in the Rue de Rivoli, where he had lived ever since and where he died five months after my visit. I was at first inclined to be suspicious; but when the Persian had told me, with childlike candor, all that he knew about the ghost and had handed me the proofs of the ghost's existence – including the strange correspondence of Christine Daaé –

to do as I pleased with, I was no longer able to doubt. No, the ghost was not a myth!

I have, I know, been told that this correspondence may have been forged from first to last by a man whose imagination had certainly been fed on the most seductive tales; but fortunately I discovered some of Christine's writing outside the famous bundle of letters and, on a comparison between the two, all my doubts were removed. I also went into the past history of the Persian and found that he was an upright man, incapable of inventing a story that might have defeated the ends of justice.

This, moreover, was the opinion of the more serious people who, at one time or other, were mixed up in the Chagny case, who were friends of the Chagny family, to whom I showed all my documents and set forth all my inferences. In this connection, I should like to print a few lines which I received from General D – – :

Sir:

I can not urge you too strongly to publish the results of your inquiry. I remember perfectly that, a few weeks before the disappearance of that great singer, Christine Daaé, and the tragedy which threw the whole of the Faubourg Saint-Germain into mourning, there was a great deal of talk, in the foyer of the ballet, on the subject of the "ghost;" and I believe that it only ceased to be discussed in consequence of the later affair that excited us all so greatly. But, if it be possible – as, after hearing you, I believe – to explain the tragedy through the ghost, then I beg you, sir, to talk to us about the ghost again. Mysterious though the ghost may at first appear, he will always be more easily explained than the dismal story in which malevolent people have tried to picture two brothers killing each other who had worshiped each other all their lives.

Believe me, etc.

Lastly, with my bundle of papers in hand,

I once more went over the ghost's vast domain, the huge building which he had made his kingdom. All that my eyes saw, all that my mind perceived, corroborated the Persian's documents precisely; and a wonderful discovery crowned my labors in a very definite fashion. It will be remembered that, later, when digging in the substructure of the Opera, before burying the phonographic records of the artist's voice, the workmen laid bare a corpse. Well, I was at once able to prove that this corpse was that of the Opera ghost. I made the acting-manager put this proof to the test with his own hand; and it is now a matter of supreme indifference to me if the papers pretend that the body was that of a victim of the Commune.

The wretches who were massacred, under the Commune, in the cellars of the Opera, were not buried on this side; I will tell where their skeletons can be found in a spot not very far from that immense crypt which was stocked during the siege with all sorts of provisions. I came upon this track just when I was looking for the remains of the Opera ghost, which I should never have discovered but for the unheard-of chance described above.

But we will return to the corpse and what ought to be done with it. For the present, I must conclude this very necessary introduction by thanking M. Mifroid (who was the commissary of police called in for the first investigations after the disappearance of Christine Daaé), M. Rémy, the late secretary, M. Mercier, the late acting-manager, M. Gabriel, the late chorus-master, and more particularly Mme. la Baronne de Castelot-Barbezac, who was once the "little Meg" of the story (and who is not ashamed of it), the most charming star of our admirable **corps de ballet**, the eldest daughter of the worthy Mme. Giry, now deceased, who had charge of the ghost's private box. All these were of the greatest assistance to me; and, thanks to them, I shall be able to reproduce those hours of sheer love and terror, in their smallest details, before the reader's eyes.

And I should be ungrateful indeed if I omitted, while standing on the threshold of this dreadful and veracious story, to thank the present management of the Opera, which has so kindly assisted me in all my inquiries, and M. Messager in particular, together with M. Gabion, the acting-manager, and that most amiable of men, the architect entrusted with the preservation of the building, who did not hesitate to lend me the works of Charles Garnier, although he was almost sure that I would never return them to him. Lastly, I must pay a public tribute to the generosity of my friend and former collaborator, M. J. Le Croze, who allowed me to dip into his splendid theatrical library and to borrow the rarest editions of books by which he set great store.

Gaston Leroux

CHAPTER ONE

Is It the Ghost?

IT WAS THE EVENING on which MM. Debienne and Poligny, the managers of the Opera, were giving a last gala performance to mark their retirement. Suddenly the dressing-room of La Sorelli, one of the principal dancers, was invaded by half-a-dozen young ladies of the ballet, who had come up from the stage after "dancing" **Polyeucte**. They rushed in amid great confusion, some giving vent to forced and unnatural laughter, others to cries of terror. Sorelli, who wished to be alone for a moment to "run through" the speech which she was to make to the resigning managers, looked around angrily at the mad and tumultuous crowd. It was little Jammes – the girl with the tip-tilted nose, the forget-me-not eyes, the rose-red cheeks and the lily-white neck and shoulders – who gave the explanation in a trembling voice:

"It's the ghost!" And she locked the door.

Sorelli's dressing-room was fitted up with official, commonplace elegance. A pier-glass, a sofa, a dressing-table and a cupboard or two provided the necessary furniture. On the walls hung a few engravings, relics of the mother, who had known the glories of the old Opera in the Rue le Peletier; portraits of Vestris, Gardel, Dupont, Bigottini. But the room seemed a palace to the brats of the **corps de ballet**, who were lodged in common dressing-rooms where they spent their time singing, quarreling, smacking the dressers and hairdressers and buying one another glasses of cassis, beer, or even rum, until the call-boy's bell rang.

Sorelli was very superstitious. She shuddered when she heard little Jammes speak of the ghost, called her a "silly little fool" and then, as she was the first to believe in ghosts in general, and the Opera ghost in particular, at once asked for details:

"Have you seen him?"

"As plainly as I see you now!" said little Jammes, whose legs were giving way beneath her, and she dropped with a moan into a chair.

Thereupon little Giry – the girl with eyes black as sloes, hair black as ink, a swarthy complexion and a poor little skin stretched over poor little bones – little Giry added:

"If that's the ghost, he's very ugly!"

"Oh, yes!" cried the chorus of ballet-girls.

And they all began to talk together. The

ghost had appeared to them in the shape of a gentleman in dress-clothes, who had suddenly stood before them in the passage, without their knowing where he came from. He seemed to have come straight through the wall.

"Pooh!" said one of them, who had more or less kept her head. "You see the ghost everywhere!"

And it was true. For several months, there had been nothing discussed at the Opera but this ghost in dress-clothes who stalked about the building, from top to bottom, like a shadow, who spoke to nobody, to whom nobody dared speak and who vanished as soon as he was seen, no one knowing how or where. As became a real ghost, he made no noise in walking. People began by laughing and making fun of this specter dressed like a man of fashion or an undertaker; but the ghost legend soon swelled to enormous proportions among the **corps de ballet**. All the girls pretended to have met this supernatural being more or less often. And those who laughed the loudest were not the most at ease. When he did not show himself, he betrayed his presence or his passing by accident, comic or serious, for which the general superstition held him responsible. Had anyone met with a fall, or suffered a practical joke at the hands of one of the other girls, or lost a powder-puff, it was at once the fault of the ghost, of the Opera ghost.

After all, who had seen him? You meet so many men in dress-clothes at the Opera who are not ghosts. But this dress-suit had a peculiarity of its own. It covered a skeleton. At least, so the ballet-girls said. And, of course, it had a death's head.

Was all this serious? The truth is that the idea of the skeleton came from the description of the ghost given by Joseph Buquet, the chief scene-shifter, who had really seen the ghost. He had run up against the ghost on the little staircase, by the footlights, which leads to "the cellars." He had seen him for a second – for the ghost had fled – and to anyone who cared to listen to him he said:

"He is extraordinarily thin and his dress-coat hangs on a skeleton frame. His eyes are so deep that you can hardly see the fixed pupils. You just see two big black holes, as in a dead man's skull. His skin, which is stretched across his bones like a drumhead, is not white, but a nasty yellow. His nose is so little worth talking about that you can't see it side-face; and **the absence** of that nose is a horrible thing **to look at**. All the hair he has is three or four long dark locks on his forehead and behind his ears."

This chief scene-shifter was a serious, sober, steady man, very slow at imagining things. His words were received with interest and amazement; and soon there were other people to say that they too had met a man in dress-clothes with a death's head on his shoulders. Sensible men who had wind of the story began by saying that Joseph Buquet had been the victim of a joke played by one of his assistants. And then, one after the other, there came a series of incidents so curious and so inexplicable that the very shrewdest people began to feel uneasy.

For instance, a fireman is a brave fellow! He fears nothing, least of all fire! Well, the fireman in question, who had gone to make a round of inspection in the cellars and who, it seems, had ventured a little farther than usual, suddenly reappeared on the stage, pale, scared, trembling, with his eyes starting out of his head, and practically fainted in the arms of the proud mother of little Jammes.[1] And why? Because he had seen coming toward him, **at the level of his head, but without a body attached to it, a head of fire**! And, as I said, a fireman is not afraid of fire.

The fireman's name was Pampin.

---

[1] I have the anecdote, which is quite authentic, from M. Pedro Gailhard himself, the late manager of the Opera.

The **corps de ballet** was flung into consternation. At first sight, this fiery head in no way corresponded with Joseph Buquet's description of the ghost. But the young ladies soon persuaded themselves that the ghost had several heads, which he changed about as he pleased. And, of course, they at once imagined that they were in the greatest danger. Once a fireman did not hesitate to faint, leaders and front-row and back-row girls alike had plenty of excuses for the fright that made them quicken their pace when passing some dark corner or ill-lighted corridor. Sorelli herself, on the day after the adventure of the fireman, placed a horseshoe on the table in front of the stage-door-keeper's box, which everyone who entered the Opera otherwise than as a spectator must touch before setting foot on the first tread of the staircase. This horseshoe was not invented by me – any more than any other part of this story, alas! – and may still be seen on the table in the passage outside the stage-door-keeper's box, when you enter the Opera through the court known as the Cour de l'Administration.

To return to the evening in question.

"It's the ghost!" little Jammes had cried.

An agonizing silence now reigned in the dressing-room. Nothing was heard but the hard breathing of the girls. At last, Jammes, flinging herself upon the farthest corner of the wall, with every mark of real terror on her face, whispered:

"Listen!"

Everybody seemed to hear a rustling outside the door. There was no sound of footsteps. It was like light silk sliding over the panel. Then it stopped.

Sorelli tried to show more pluck than the others. She went up to the door and, in a quavering voice, asked:

"Who's there?"

But nobody answered. Then feeling all eyes upon her, watching her last movement, she made an effort to show courage, and said very loudly:

"Is there anyone behind the door?"

"Oh, yes, yes! Of course there is!" cried that little dried plum of a Meg Giry, heroically holding Sorelli back by her gauze skirt. "Whatever you do, don't open the door! Oh, Lord, don't open the door!"

But Sorelli, armed with a dagger that never left her, turned the key and drew back the door, while the ballet-girls retreated to the inner dressing-room and Meg Giry sighed:

"Mother! Mother!"

Sorelli looked into the passage bravely. It was empty; a gas-flame, in its glass prison, cast a red and suspicious light into the surrounding darkness, without succeeding in dispelling it. And the dancer slammed the door again, with a deep sigh.

"No," she said, "there is no one there."

"Still, we saw him!" Jammes declared, returning with timid little steps to her place beside Sorelli. "He must be somewhere prowling about. I shan't go back to dress. We had better all go down to the foyer together, at once, for the 'speech,' and we will come up again together."

And the child reverently touched the little coral finger-ring which she wore as a charm against bad luck, while Sorelli, stealthily, with the tip of her pink right thumbnail, made a St. Andrew's cross on the wooden ring which adorned the fourth finger of her left hand. She said to the little ballet-girls:

"Come, children, pull yourselves together! I dare say no one has ever seen the ghost."

"Yes, yes, we saw him – we saw him just now!" cried the girls. "He had his death's head and his dress-coat, just as when he appeared to Joseph Buquet!"

"And Gabriel saw him too!" said Jammes. "Only yesterday! Yesterday afternoon – in broad daylight – "

"Gabriel, the chorus-master?"

"Why, yes, didn't you know?"

"And he was wearing his dress-clothes, in broad daylight?"

"Who? Gabriel?"

"Why, no, the ghost!"

"Certainly! Gabriel told me so himself. That's what he knew him by. Gabriel was in the stage-manager's office. Suddenly the door opened and the Persian entered. You know the Persian has the evil eye – "

"Oh, yes!" answered the little ballet-girls in chorus, warding off ill-luck by pointing their forefinger and little finger at the absent Persian, while their second and third fingers were bent on the palm and held down by the thumb.

"And you know how superstitious Gabriel is," continued Jammes. "However, he is always polite. When he meets the Persian, he just puts his hand in his pocket and touches his keys. Well, the moment the Persian appeared in the doorway, Gabriel gave one jump from his chair to the lock of the cupboard, so as to touch iron! In doing so, he tore a whole skirt of his overcoat on a nail. Hurrying to get out of the room, he banged his forehead against a hat-peg and gave himself a huge bump; then, suddenly stepping back, he skinned his arm on the screen, near the piano; he tried to lean on the piano, but the lid fell on his hands and crushed his fingers; he rushed out of the office like a madman, slipped on the staircase and came down the whole of the first flight on his back. I was just passing with mother. We picked him up. He was covered with bruises and his face was all over blood. We were frightened out of our lives, but, all at once, he began to thank Providence that he had got off so cheaply. Then he told us what had frightened him. He had seen the ghost behind the Persian, **the ghost with the death's head**, just like Joseph Buquet's description!"

Jammes had told her story ever so quickly, as though the ghost were at her heels, and was quite out of breath at the finish. A silence followed, while Sorelli polished her nails in great excitement. It was broken by little Giry, who said:

"Joseph Buquet would do better to hold his tongue."

"Why should he hold his tongue?" asked somebody.

"That's mother's opinion," replied Meg, lowering her voice and looking all about her as though fearing lest other ears than those present might overhear.

"And why is it your mother's opinion?"

"Hush! Mother says the ghost doesn't like being talked about."

"And why does your mother say so?"

"Because – because – nothing – "

This reticence exasperated the curiosity of the young ladies, who crowded round little Giry, begging her to explain herself. They were there, side by side, leaning forward simultaneously in one movement of entreaty and fear, communicating their terror to one another, taking a keen pleasure in feeling their blood freeze in their veins.

"I swore not to tell!" gasped Meg.

But they left her no peace and promised to keep the secret, until Meg, burning to say all she knew, began, with her eyes fixed on the door:

"Well, it's because of the private box."

"What private box?"

"The ghost's box!"

"Has the ghost a box? Oh, do tell us, do tell us!"

"Not so loud!" said Meg. "It's Box Five, you know, the box on the grand tier, next to the stage-box, on the left."

"Oh, nonsense!"

"I tell you it is. Mother has charge of it. But you swear you won't say a word?"

"Of course, of course."

"Well, that's the ghost's box. No one has had it for over a month, except the ghost, and orders have been given at the box-office that it must never be sold."

"And does the ghost really come there?"

"Yes."

"Then somebody does come?"

"Why, no! The ghost comes, but there is nobody there."

The little ballet-girls exchanged glances. If the ghost came to the box, he must be seen, because he wore a dress-coat and a death's head. This was what they tried to make Meg understand, but she replied:

"That's just it! The ghost is not seen. And he has no dress-coat and no head! All that talk about his death's head and his head of fire is nonsense! There's nothing in it. You only hear him when he is in the box. Mother has never seen him, but she has heard him. Mother knows, because she gives him his program."

Sorelli interfered.

"Giry, child, you're getting at us!"

Thereupon little Giry began to cry.

"I ought to have held my tongue – if mother ever came to know! But I was quite right, Joseph Buquet had no business to talk of things that don't concern him – it will bring him bad luck – mother was saying so last night – ”

There was a sound of hurried and heavy footsteps in the passage and a breathless voice cried:

“Cecile! Cecile! Are you there?”

“It’s mother’s voice,” said Jammes. “What’s the matter?”

She opened the door. A respectable lady, built on the lines of a Pomeranian grenadier, burst into the dressing-room and dropped groaning into a vacant armchair. Her eyes rolled madly in her brick-dust colored face.

“How awful!” she said. “How awful!”

“What? What?”

“Joseph Buquet – ”

“What about him?”

“Joseph Buquet is dead!”

The room became filled with exclamations, with astonished outcries, with scared requests for explanations.

“Yes, he was found hanging in the third-floor cellar!”

“It’s the ghost!” little Giry blurted, as

though in spite of herself; but she at once corrected herself, with her hands pressed to her mouth: "No, no! – I didn't say it! – I didn't say it! – "

All around her, her panic-stricken companions repeated under their breaths:

"Yes – it must be the ghost!"

Sorelli was very pale.

"I shall never be able to recite my speech," she said.

Ma Jammes gave her opinion, while she emptied a glass of liqueur that happened to be standing on a table; the ghost must have something to do with it.

The truth is that no one ever knew how Joseph Buquet met his death. The verdict at the inquest was "natural suicide." In his **Memoirs of a Manager**, M. Moncharmin, one of the joint managers who succeeded MM. Debienne and Poligny, describes the incident as follows:

A grievous accident spoiled the little party which MM. Debienne and Poligny gave to celebrate their retirement. I was in the manager's office, when Mercier, the acting-manager, suddenly came darting in. He seemed half mad and told me that the body of a scene-shifter had been found hanging in the third cellar under the stage, between a farmhouse and a scene from the **Roi de Lahore**. I shouted:

"Come and cut him down!"

By the time I had rushed down the staircase and the Jacob's ladder, the man was no longer hanging from his rope!

So this is an event which M. Moncharmin thinks natural. A man hangs at the end of a rope; they go to cut him down; the rope has disappeared. Oh, M. Moncharmin found a very simple explanation! Listen to him:

It was just after the ballet; and leaders and dancing-girls lost no time in taking their precautions against the evil eye.

There you are! Picture the **corps de ballet** scuttling down the Jacob's ladder and dividing the suicide's rope among themselves in less time than it takes to write! When, on the other hand, I think of the exact spot where the body was discovered – the third cellar underneath the stage – I imagine that **somebody** must have been interested in seeing that the rope disappeared after it had effected its purpose; and time will show if I am wrong.

The horrid news soon spread all over the Opera, where Joseph Buquet was very popular. The dressing-rooms emptied and the ballet-girls, crowding around Sorelli like timid sheep around their shepherdess, made for the foyer through the ill-lit passages and staircases, trotting as fast as their little pink legs could carry them.

CHAPTER TWO

The New Margarita

ON THE FIRST LANDING, Sorelli ran against the Comte de Chagny, who was coming upstairs. The count, who was generally so calm, seemed greatly excited.

"I was just going to you," he said, taking off his hat. "Oh, Sorelli, what an evening! And Christine Daaé: what a triumph!"

"Impossible!" said Meg Giry. "Six months ago, she used to sing like a **crock**! But do let us get by, my dear count," continues the brat, with a saucy curtsey. "We are going to inquire after a poor man who was found hanging by the neck."

Just then the acting-manager came fussing past and stopped when he heard this remark.

"What!" he exclaimed roughly. "Have you girls heard already? Well, please forget about it for tonight – and above all don't let M. Debienne and M. Poligny hear; it would upset them too much on their last day."

They all went on to the foyer of the ballet, which was already full of people. The Comte de Chagny was right; no gala performance ever equalled this one. All the great composers of the day had conducted their own works in turns. Faure and Krauss had sung; and, on that evening, Christine Daaé had revealed her true self, for the first time, to the astonished and enthusiastic audience. Gounod had conducted the "Funeral March of a Marionnette;" Reyer, his beautiful overture to **Siguar**; Saint Saëns, the "Danse Macabre" and a "Rêverie Orientale;" Massenet, an unpublished Hungarian march; Guiraud, his "Carnaval;" Delibes, the "Valse lente" from **Sylvia** and the "Pizzicati" from **Coppelia**. Mlle. Krauss had sung the bolero in the **Vespri Siciliani**; and Mlle. Denise Bloch the drinking song in **Lucrezia Borgia**.

But the real triumph was reserved for Christine Daaé, who had begun by singing a few passages from **Romeo and Juliet**. It was the first time that the young artist sang in this work of Gounod, which had not been transferred to the Opera and which was revived at the Opéra Comique after it had been produced at the old Theatre Lyrique by Mme. Carvalho. Those who heard her say that her voice, in these passages, was seraphic; but this was nothing to the superhuman notes that she gave forth in the prison scene and the final trio in **Faust**, which she sang in the place of La Carlotta, who was ill. No one had ever heard or seen anything like it.

Daaé revealed a new Margarita that night, a Margarita of a splendor, a radiance hitherto unsuspected. The whole house went mad, rising to its feet, shouting, cheering, clapping, while Christine sobbed and fainted in the arms of her fellow-singers and had to be carried to her dressing-room. A few subscribers, however, protested. Why had so great a treasure been kept from them all that time? Till then, Christine Daaé had played a good Siebel to Carlotta's rather too splendidly material Margarita. And it had needed Carlotta's incomprehensible and inexcusable absence from this gala night for the little Daaé, at a moment's warning, to show all that she could do in a part of the program reserved for the Spanish diva! Well, what the subscribers wanted to know was, why had Debienne and Poligny applied to Daaé, when Carlotta was taken ill? Did they know of her hidden genius? And, if they knew of it, why had they kept it hidden? And why had she kept it hidden? Oddly enough, she was not known to have a professor of singing at that moment. She had often said she meant to practise alone for the future. The whole thing was a mystery.

The Comte de Chagny, standing up in his box, listened to all this frenzy and took part in it by loudly applauding. Philippe Georges Marie Comte de Chagny was just forty-one years of age. He was a great aristocrat and a good-looking man, above middle height and with attractive features, in spite of his hard forehead and his rather cold eyes. He was exquisitely polite to the women and a little haughty to the men, who did not always forgive him for his successes in society. He had an excellent heart and an irreproachable conscience. On the death of old Count Philibert, he became the head of one of the oldest and most distinguished families in France, whose arms dated back to the fourteenth century. The Chagnys owned a great deal of property; and, when the old count, who was a widower, died, it was no easy task for Philippe to accept the management of so large an estate. His two sisters and his brother, Raoul, would not hear of a division and waived their claim to their shares, leaving themselves entirely in Philippe's hands, as though the right of primogeniture had never ceased to exist. When the two sisters married, on the same day, they received their portion from their brother, not as a thing rightfully belonging to them, but as a dowry for which they thanked him.

The Comtesse de Chagny, **née** de Moerogis de La Martyniere, had died in giving birth to Raoul, who was born twenty years after his elder brother. At the time of the old count's death, Raoul was twelve years of age. Philippe busied himself actively with the youngster's education. He was admirably assisted in this work first by his sisters and afterward by an old aunt, the widow of a naval officer, who lived at Brest and gave young Raoul a taste for the sea. The lad entered the **Borda** training-ship, finished his course with honors and quietly made his trip round the world. Thanks to powerful influence, he had just been appointed a member of the official expedition on board the **Requin**, which was to be sent to the Arctic Circle in search of the survivors of the D'Artoi's expedition, of whom nothing had been heard for three years. Meanwhile, he was enjoying a long furlough which would not be over for six months; and already the dowagers of the Faubourg Saint-Germain were pitying the handsome and apparently delicate stripling for the hard work in store for him.

The shyness of the sailor-lad – I was almost saying his innocence – was remarkable. He seemed to have but just left the women's apron-strings. As a matter of fact, petted as he was by his two sisters and his old aunt, he had retained from this purely feminine education manners that were almost candid and stamped with a charm that nothing had yet been able to sully. He was a little over twenty-one years of age and looked eighteen. He had a small, fair mustache, beautiful blue eyes and a complexion like a girl's.

Philippe spoiled Raoul. To begin with, he was very proud of him and pleased to foresee a glorious career for his junior in the navy in which one of their ancestors, the famous Chagny de La Roche, had held the rank of admiral. He took advantage of the young man's leave of absence to show him Paris, with all its luxurious and artistic delights. The count considered that, at Raoul's age, it is not good to be too good. Philippe himself had a character that was very well-balanced in work and pleasure alike; his demeanor was always faultless; and he was incapable of setting his brother a bad example. He took him with him wherever he went. He even introduced him to the foyer of the ballet. I know that the count was said to be “on terms” with Sorelli. But it could hardly be reckoned as a crime for this nobleman, a bachelor, with plenty of leisure, especially since his sisters were settled, to come and spend an hour or two after dinner in the company of a dancer, who, though not so very, very witty, had the finest eyes that ever were seen! And, besides, there are places where a true Parisian, when he has the rank of the Comte de Chagny, is bound to show himself; and at that time the foyer of the ballet at the Opera was one of those places.

Lastly, Philippe would perhaps not have taken his brother behind the scenes of the Opera if Raoul had not been the first to ask him, repeatedly renewing his request with a gentle obstinacy which the count remembered at a later date.

On that evening, Philippe, after applauding the Daaé, turned to Raoul and saw that he was quite pale.

"Don't you see," said Raoul, "that the woman's fainting?"

"You look like fainting yourself," said the count. "What's the matter?"

But Raoul had recovered himself and was standing up.

"Let's go and see," he said, "she never sang like that before."

The count gave his brother a curious smiling glance and seemed quite pleased. They were soon at the door leading from the house to the stage. Numbers of subscribers were slowly making their way through. Raoul tore his gloves without knowing what he was doing and Philippe had much too kind a heart to laugh at him for his impatience. But he now understood why Raoul was absentminded when spoken to and why he always tried to turn every conversation to the subject of the Opera.

They reached the stage and pushed through the crowd of gentlemen, scene-shifters, supers and chorus-girls, Raoul leading the way, feeling that his heart no longer belonged to him, his face set with passion, while Count Philippe followed him with difficulty and continued to smile. At the back of the stage, Raoul had to stop before the inrush of the little troop of ballet-girls who blocked the passage which he was trying to enter. More than one chaffing phrase darted from little made-up lips, to which he did not reply; and at last he was able to pass, and dived into the semidarkness of a corridor ringing with the name of "Daaé! Daaé!" The count was surprised to find that Raoul knew the way. He had never taken him to Christine's himself and came to the conclusion that Raoul must have gone there alone while the count stayed talking in the foyer with Sorelli, who often asked him to wait until it was her time to "go on" and sometimes handed him the little gaiters in which she ran down from her dressing-room to preserve the spotlessness of her satin dancing-shoes and her flesh-colored tights. Sorelli had an excuse; she had lost her mother.

Postponing his usual visit to Sorelli for a few minutes, the count followed his brother down the passage that led to Daaé's dressing-room and saw that it had never been so crammed as on that evening, when the whole house seemed excited by her success and also by her fainting fit. For the girl had not yet come to; and the doctor of the theater had just arrived at the moment when Raoul entered at his heels. Christine, therefore, received the first aid of the one, while opening her eyes in the arms of the other. The count and many more remained crowding in the doorway.

"Don't you think, Doctor, that those gentlemen had better clear the room?" asked Raoul coolly. "There's no breathing here."

"You're quite right," said the doctor.

And he sent everyone away, except Raoul and the maid, who looked at Raoul with eyes of the most undisguised astonishment. She had never seen him before and yet dared not question him; and the doctor imagined that the young man was only acting as he did because he had the right to. The viscount, therefore, remained in the room watching Christine as she slowly returned to life, while even the joint managers, Debienne and Poligny, who had come to offer their sympathy and congratulations, found themselves thrust into the passage among the crowd of dandies. The Comte de Chagny, who was one of those standing outside, laughed:

"Oh, the rogue, the rogue!" And he added, under his breath: "Those youngsters with their schoolgirl airs! So he's a Chagny after all!"

He turned to go to Sorelli's dressing-room, but met her on the way, with her little troop of trembling ballet-girls, as we have seen.

Meanwhile, Christine Daaé uttered a deep sigh, which was answered by a groan. She turned her head, saw Raoul and started. She looked at the doctor, on whom she bestowed a smile, then at her maid, then at Raoul again.

"Monsieur," she said, in a voice not much above a whisper, "who are you?"

"Mademoiselle," replied the young man, kneeling on one knee and pressing a fervent kiss on the diva's hand, "**I am the little boy who went into the sea to rescue your scarf.**"

Christine again looked at the doctor and the maid; and all three began to laugh.

Raoul turned very red and stood up.

"Mademoiselle," he said, "since you are pleased not to recognize me, I should like to say something to you in private, something very important."

"When I am better, do you mind?" And her voice shook. "You have been very good."

"Yes, you must go," said the doctor, with his pleasantest smile. "Leave me to attend to mademoiselle."

"I am not ill now," said Christine suddenly, with strange and unexpected energy.

She rose and passed her hand over her eyelids.

"Thank you, Doctor. I should like to be alone. Please go away, all of you. Leave me. I feel very restless this evening."

The doctor tried to make a short protest, but, perceiving the girl's evident agitation, he thought the best remedy was not to thwart her. And he went away, saying to Raoul, outside:

"She is not herself tonight. She is usually so gentle."

Then he said good night and Raoul was left alone. The whole of this part of the theater was now deserted. The farewell ceremony was no doubt taking place in the foyer of the ballet. Raoul thought that Daaé might go to it and he waited in the silent solitude, even hiding in the favoring shadow of a doorway. He felt a terrible pain at his heart and it was of this that he wanted to speak to Daaé without delay.

Suddenly the dressing-room door opened and the maid came out by herself, carrying bundles. He stopped her and asked how her mistress was. The woman laughed and said that she was quite well, but that he must not disturb her, for she wished to be left alone. And she passed on. One idea alone filled Raoul's burning brain: of course, Daaé wished to be left alone **for him**! Had he not told her that he wanted to speak to her privately?

Hardly breathing, he went up to the dressing-room and, with his ear to the door to catch her reply, prepared to knock. But his hand dropped. He had heard **a man's voice** in the dressing-room, saying, in a curiously masterful tone:

"Christine, you must love me!"

And Christine's voice, infinitely sad and trembling, as though accompanied by tears, replied:

"How can you talk like that? **When I sing**

only for you!"

Raoul leaned against the panel to ease his pain. His heart, which had seemed gone forever, returned to his breast and was throbbing loudly. The whole passage echoed with its beating and Raoul's ears were deafened. Surely, if his heart continued to make such a noise, they would hear it inside, they would open the door and the young man would be turned away in disgrace. What a position for a Chagny! To be caught listening behind a door! He took his heart in his two hands to make it stop.

The man's voice spoke again:

"Are you very tired?"

"Oh, tonight I gave you my soul and I am dead!" Christine replied.

"Your soul is a beautiful thing, child," replied the grave man's voice, "and I thank you. No emperor ever received so fair a gift. **The angels wept tonight.**"

Raoul heard nothing after that. Nevertheless, he did not go away, but, as though he feared lest he should be caught, he returned to his dark corner, determined to wait for the man to leave the room. At one and the same time, he had learned what love meant, and hatred. He knew that he loved. He wanted to know whom he hated. To his great astonishment, the door opened and Christine Daaé appeared, wrapped in furs, with her face hidden in a lace veil, alone. She closed the door behind her, but Raoul observed that she did not lock it. She passed him. He did not even follow her with his eyes, for his eyes were fixed on the door, which did not open again.

When the passage was once more deserted, he crossed it, opened the door of the dressing-room, went in and shut the door. He found himself in absolute darkness. The gas had been turned out.

"There is someone here!" said Raoul, with his back against the closed door, in a quivering voice. "What are you hiding for?"

All was darkness and silence. Raoul heard

only the sound of his own breathing. He quite failed to see that the indiscretion of his conduct was exceeding all bounds.

"You shan't leave this until I let you!" he exclaimed. "If you don't answer, you are a coward! But I'll expose you!"

And he struck a match. The blaze lit up the room. There was no one in the room! Raoul, first turning the key in the door, lit the gas-jets. He went into the dressing-closet, opened the cupboards, hunted about, felt the walls with his moist hands. Nothing!

"Look here!" he said, aloud. "Am I going mad?"

He stood for ten minutes listening to the gas flaring in the silence of the empty room; lover though he was, he did not even think of stealing a ribbon that would have given him the perfume of the woman he loved. He went out, not knowing what he was doing nor where he was going. At a given moment in his wayward progress, an icy draft struck him in the face. He found himself at the bottom of a staircase, down which, behind him, a procession of workmen were carrying a sort of stretcher, covered with a white sheet.

"Which is the way out, please?" he asked of one of the men.

"Straight in front of you, the door is open. But let us pass."

Pointing to the stretcher, he asked mechanically:

"What's that?"

The workmen answered:

"'That' is Joseph Buquet, who was found in the third cellar, hanging between a farmhouse and a scene from the **Roi de Lahore**."

He took off his hat, fell back to make room for the procession and went out.

CHAPTER THREE

The Mysterious Reason

DURING THIS TIME, the farewell ceremony was taking place. I have already said that this magnificent function was being given on the occasion of the retirement of M. Debienne and M. Poligny, who had determined to "die game," as we say nowadays. They had been assisted in the realization of their ideal, though melancholy, program by all that counted in the social and artistic world of Paris. All these people met, after the performance, in the foyer of the ballet, where Sorelli waited for the arrival of the retiring managers with a glass of champagne in her hand and a little prepared speech at the tip of her tongue. Behind her, the members of the **corps de ballet**, young and old, discussed the events of the day in whispers or exchanged discreet signals with their friends, a noisy crowd of whom surrounded the supper-tables arranged along the slanting floor.

A few of the dancers had already changed into ordinary dress; but most of them wore their skirts of gossamer gauze; and all had thought it the right thing to put on a special face for the occasion: all, that is, except little Jammes, whose fifteen summers – happy age! – seemed already to have forgotten the ghost and the death of Joseph Buquet. She never ceased to laugh and chatter, to hop about and play practical jokes, until MM. Debienne and Poligny appeared on the steps of the foyer, when she was severely called to order by the impatient Sorelli.

Everybody remarked that the retiring managers looked cheerful, as is the Paris way. None will ever be a true Parisian who has not learned to wear a mask of gaiety over his sorrows and one of sadness, boredom or indifference over his inward joy. You know that one of your friends is in trouble; do not try to console him: he will tell you that he is already comforted; but, should he have met with good fortune, be careful how you congratulate him: he thinks it so natural that he is surprised that you should speak of it. In Paris, our lives are one masked ball; and the foyer of the ballet is the last place in which two men so "knowing" as M. Debienne and M. Poligny would have made the mistake of betraying their grief, however genuine it might be. And they were already smiling rather too broadly upon Sorelli, who had begun to recite her speech, when an exclamation from that little madcap of a Jammes broke the smile of the managers so brutally that the expression of distress and dismay that lay beneath it became apparent to all eyes:

"The Opera ghost!"

Jammes yelled these words in a tone of unspeakable terror; and her finger pointed, among the crowd of dandies, to a face so pallid, so lugubrious and so ugly, with two such deep black cavities under the straddling eyebrows, that the death's head in question immediately scored a huge success.

"The Opera ghost! The Opera ghost!"

Everybody laughed and pushed his neighbor and wanted to offer the Opera ghost a drink, but he was gone. He had slipped through the crowd; and the others vainly hunted for him, while two old gentlemen tried to calm little Jammes and while little Giry stood screaming like a peacock.

Sorelli was furious; she had not been able to finish her speech; the managers had kissed her, thanked her and run away as fast as the ghost himself. No one was surprised at this, for it was known that they were to go through the same ceremony on the floor above, in the foyer of the singers, and that finally they were themselves to receive their personal friends, for the last time, in the great lobby outside the managers' office, where a regular supper would be served.

Here they found the new managers, M. Armand Moncharmin and M. Firmin Richard, whom they hardly knew; nevertheless, they were lavish in protestations of friendship and received a thousand flattering compliments in reply, so that those of the guests who had feared that they had a rather tedious evening in store for them at once put on brighter faces. The supper was almost gay and a particularly clever speech of the representative of the government, mingling the glories of the past with the successes of the future, caused the greatest cordiality to prevail.

The retiring managers had already handed over to their successors the two tiny master-keys which opened all the doors – thousands of doors – of the Opera house. And those little keys, the object of general curiosity, were being passed from hand to hand, when the attention of some of the guests was diverted by their discovery, at the end of the table, of that strange, wan and fantastic face, with the hollow eyes, which had already appeared in the foyer of the ballet and been greeted by little Jammes' exclamation:

"The Opera ghost!"

There sat the ghost, as natural as could be, except that he neither ate nor drank. Those who began by looking at him with a smile ended by turning away their heads, for the sight of him at once provoked the most funereal thoughts. No one repeated the joke of the foyer, no one exclaimed:

"There's the Opera ghost!"

He himself did not speak a word and his

very neighbors could not have stated at what precise moment he had sat down between them; but everyone felt that if the dead did ever come and sit at the table of the living, they could not cut a more ghastly figure. The friends of Firmin Richard and Armand Moncharmin thought that this lean and skinny guest was an acquaintance of Debienne's or Poligny's, while Debienne's and Poligny's friends believed that the cadaverous individual belonged to Firmin Richard and Armand Moncharmin's party.

The result was that no request was made for an explanation; no unpleasant remark; no joke in bad taste, which might have offended this visitor from the tomb. A few of those present who knew the story of the ghost and the description of him given by the chief scene-shifter – they did not know of Joseph Buquet's death – thought, in their own minds, that the man at the end of the table might easily have passed for him; and yet, according to the story, the ghost had no nose and the person in question had. But M. Moncharmin declares, in his **Memoirs**, that the guest's nose was transparent: "long, thin and transparent" are his exact words. I, for my part, will add that this might very well apply to a false nose. M. Moncharmin may have taken for transparency what was only shininess. Everybody knows that orthopaedic science provides beautiful false noses for those who have lost their noses naturally or as the result of an operation.

Did the ghost really take a seat at the managers' supper-table that night, uninvited? And can we be sure that the figure was that of the Opera ghost himself? Who would venture to assert as much? I mention the incident, not because I wish for a second to make the reader believe – or even to try to make him believe – that the ghost was capable of such a sublime piece of impudence; but because, after all, the thing is impossible.

M. Armand Moncharmin, in chapter eleven of his **Memoirs**, says:

When I think of this first evening, I can not separate the secret confided to us by MM. Debienne and Poligny in their office from the presence at our supper of that **ghostly** person whom none of us knew.

What happened was this: MM. Debienne and Poligny, sitting at the center of the table, had not seen the man with the death's head. Suddenly he began to speak.

"The ballet-girls are right," he said. "The death of that poor Buquet is perhaps not so natural as people think."

Debienne and Poligny gave a start.

"Is Buquet dead?" they cried.

"Yes," replied the man, or the shadow of a man, quietly. "He was found, this evening, hanging in the third cellar, between a farmhouse and a scene from the **Roi de Lahore**."

The two managers, or rather ex-managers, at once rose and stared strangely at the speaker. They were more excited than they need have been, that is to say, more excited than anyone need be by the announcement of the suicide of a chief scene-shifter. They looked at each other. They had both turned whiter than the tablecloth. At last, Debienne made a sign to MM. Richard and Moncharmin; Poligny muttered a few words of excuse to the guests; and all four went into the managers' office. I leave M. Moncharmin to complete the story. In his **Memoirs**, he says:

MM. Debienne and Poligny seemed to grow more and more excited, and they appeared to have something very difficult to tell us. First, they asked us if we knew the man, sitting at the end of the table, who had told them of the death of Joseph Buquet; and, when we answered in the negative, they looked still more concerned. They took the master-keys from our hands, stared at them for a moment and advised us to have new locks made, with the greatest secrecy, for the rooms, closets and presses that we might wish to have hermetically closed. They said this so funnily that we began to laugh and to ask if there were thieves at the Opera. They replied that there was something worse, which was the **ghost**. We began to laugh again, feeling sure that they were indulging in some joke that was intended to crown our little entertainment. Then, at their request, we became "serious," resolving to humor them and to enter into the spirit of the game. They told us that they never would have spoken to us of the ghost, if they had not received formal orders from the ghost himself to ask us to be pleasant to him and to grant any request that he might make. However, in their relief at leaving a domain where that tyrannical shade held sway, they had hesitated until the last moment to tell us this curious story, which our skeptical minds were certainly not prepared to entertain. But the announcement of the death of Joseph Buquet had served them as a brutal reminder that, whenever they had disregarded the ghost's wishes, some fantastic or disastrous event had brought them to a sense of their dependence.

During these unexpected utterances made in a tone of the most secret and important confidence, I looked at Richard. Richard, in his student days, had acquired a great reputation for practical joking, and he seemed to relish the dish which was being served up to him in his turn. He did not miss a morsel of it, though the seasoning was a little gruesome because of the death of Buquet. He nodded his head sadly, while the others spoke, and his features assumed the air of a man who bitterly regretted having taken over the Opera, now that he knew that there was a ghost mixed up in the business. I could think of nothing better than to give him a servile imitation of this attitude of despair. However, in spite of all our efforts, we could not, at the finish, help bursting out laughing in the faces of MM. Debienne and Poligny, who, seeing us pass straight from the gloomiest state of mind to one of the most insolent merriment, acted as though they thought that we had gone mad.

The joke became a little tedious; and Richard asked half-seriously and half in jest:

"But, after all, what does this ghost of yours want?"

M. Poligny went to his desk and returned with a copy of the memorandum-book. The memorandum-book begins with the well-known words saying that "the management of the Opera shall give to the performance of the National Academy of Music the splendor that becomes the first lyric stage in France" and ends with Clause 98, which says that the privilege can be withdrawn if the manager infringes the conditions stipulated in the memorandum-book. This is followed by the conditions, which are four in number.

The copy produced by M. Poligny was written in black ink and exactly similar to that in our possession, except that, at the end, it contained a paragraph in red ink and in a queer, labored handwriting, as though it had been produced by dipping the heads of matches into the ink, the writing of a child that has never got beyond the downstrokes and has not learned to join its letters. This paragraph ran, word for word, as follows:

5. Or if the manager, in any month, delay for more than a fortnight the payment of the allowance which he shall make to the Opera ghost, an allowance of twenty thousand francs a month, say two hundred and forty thousand francs a year.

M. Poligny pointed with a hesitating finger to this last clause, which we certainly did not expect.

"Is this all? Does he not want anything else?" asked Richard, with the greatest coolness.

"Yes, he does," replied Poligny.

And he turned over the pages of the memorandum-book until he came to the clause specifying the days on which certain private boxes were to be reserved for the free use of the president of the republic, the ministers and so on. At the end of this clause, a line had been added, also in red ink:

"Box Five on the grand tier shall be placed at the disposal of the Opera ghost for every performance."

When we saw this, there was nothing else for us to do but to rise from our chairs, shake our two predecessors warmly by the hand and congratulate them on thinking of this charming little joke, which proved that the old French sense of humor was never likely to become extinct. Richard added that he now understood why MM. Debienne and Poligny were retiring from the management of the National Academy of Music. Business was impossible with so unreasonable a ghost.

"Certainly, two hundred and forty thousand francs are not to be picked up for the asking," said M. Poligny, without moving a muscle of his face. "And have you considered what the loss over Box Five meant to us? We did not sell it once; and not only that, but we had to return the subscription: why, it's awful! We really can't work to keep ghosts! We prefer to go away!"

"Yes," echoed M. Debienne, "we prefer to go away. Let us go."

And he stood up. Richard said: "But, after all, it seems to me that you were much too kind to the ghost. If I had such a troublesome ghost as that, I should not hesitate to have him arrested – "

"But how? Where?" they cried, in chorus. "We have never seen him!"

"But when he comes to his box?"

"**We have never seen him in his box.**"

"Then sell it."

"Sell the Opera ghost's box! Well,

gentlemen, try it."

Thereupon we all four left the office. Richard and I had "never laughed so much in our lives."

CHAPTER FOUR

Box Five

ARMAND MONCHARMIN WROTE SUCH voluminous **Memoirs** during the fairly long period of his co-management that we may well ask if he ever found time to attend to the affairs of the Opera otherwise than by telling what went on there. M. Moncharmin did not know a note of music, but he called the minister of education and fine arts by his Christian name, had dabbled a little in society journalism and enjoyed a considerable private income. Lastly, he was a charming fellow and showed that he was not lacking in intelligence, for, as soon as he made up his mind to be a sleeping partner in the Opera, he selected the best possible active manager and went straight to Firmin Richard.

Firmin Richard was a very distinguished composer, who had published a number of successful pieces of all kinds and who liked nearly every form of music and every sort of musician. Clearly, therefore, it was the duty of every sort of musician to like M. Firmin Richard. The only things to be said against him were that he was rather masterful in his ways and endowed with a very hasty temper.

The first few days which the partners spent at the Opera were given over to the delight of finding themselves the head of so magnificent an enterprise; and they had forgotten all about that curious, fantastic story of the ghost, when an incident occurred that proved to them that the joke – if joke it were – was not over. M. Firmin Richard reached his office that morning at eleven o'clock. His secretary, M. Rémy, showed him half a dozen letters which he had not opened because they were marked "private." One of the letters had at once attracted Richard's attention not only because the envelope was addressed in red ink, but because he seemed to have seen the writing before. He soon remembered that it was the red handwriting in which the memorandum-book had been so curiously completed. He recognized the clumsy childish hand. He opened the letter and read:

Dear Mr. Manager:

I am sorry to have to trouble you at a time when you must be so very busy, renewing important engagements, signing fresh ones and generally displaying your excellent taste. I know what you have done for Carlotta, Sorelli and little Jammes and for a few others whose admirable qualities of talent or genius you have suspected.

Of course, when I use these words, I do not mean to apply them to La Carlotta, who sings like a squirt and who ought never to have been allowed to leave the Ambassadeurs and the Café Jacquin; nor to La Sorelli, who owes her success mainly to the coach-builders; nor to little Jammes, who dances like a calf in a field. And I am not speaking of Christine Daaé either, though her genius is certain, whereas your jealousy prevents her from creating any important part. When all is said, you are free to conduct your little business as you think best, are you not?

All the same, I should like to take advantage of the fact that you have not yet turned Christine Daaé out of doors by hearing her this evening in the part of Siebel, as that of Margarita has been forbidden her since her triumph of the other evening; and I will ask you not to dispose of my box today nor on the **following days**, for I can not end this letter without telling you how disagreeably surprised I have been once or twice, to hear, on arriving at the Opera, that my box had been sold, at the box-office, by your orders.

I did not protest, first, because I dislike scandal, and, second, because I thought that your predecessors, MM. Debienne and Poligny, who were always charming to me, had neglected, before leaving, to mention my little fads to you. I have now received a reply from those gentlemen to my letter asking for an explanation, and this reply proves that you know all about my memorandum-book and, consequently, that you are treating me with outrageous contempt. **If you wish to live in peace, you must not begin by taking away my private box.**

Believe me to be, dear Mr. Manager, without prejudice to these little observations,

Your Most Humble and Obedient Servant,

Opera Ghost.

The letter was accompanied by a cutting

from the agony-column of the **Revue Théâtrale**, which ran:

O. G. – There is no excuse for R. and M. We told them and left your memorandum-book in their hands. Kind regards.

M. Firmin Richard had hardly finished reading this letter when M. Armand Moncharmin entered, carrying one exactly similar. They looked at each other and burst out laughing.

"They are keeping up the joke," said M. Richard, "but I don't call it funny."

"What does it all mean?" asked M. Moncharmin. "Do they imagine that, because they have been managers of the Opera, we are going to let them have a box for an indefinite period?"

"I am not in the mood to let myself be laughed at long," said Firmin Richard.

"It's harmless enough," observed Armand Moncharmin. "What is it they really want? A box for tonight?"

M. Firmin Richard told his secretary to

send Box Five on the grand tier to MM. Debienne and Poligny, if it was not sold. It was not. It was sent off to them. Debienne lived at the corner of the Rue Scribe and the Boulevard des Capucines; Poligny, in the Rue Auber. O. Ghost's two letters had been posted at the Boulevard des Capucines post-office, as Moncharmin remarked after examining the envelopes.

"You see!" said Richard.

They shrugged their shoulders and regretted that two men of that age should amuse themselves with such childish tricks.

"They might have been civil, for all that!" said Moncharmin. "Did you notice how they treat us with regard to Carlotta, Sorelli and Little Jammes?"

"Why, my dear fellow, these two are mad with jealousy! To think that they went to the expense of an advertisement in the **Revue Théâtrale**! Have they nothing better to do?"

"By the way," said Moncharmin, "they seem to be greatly interested in that little

Christine Daaé!"

"You know as well as I do that she has the reputation of being quite good," said Richard.

"Reputations are easily obtained," replied Moncharmin. "Haven't I a reputation for knowing all about music? And I don't know one key from another."

"Don't be afraid: you never had that reputation," Richard declared.

Thereupon he ordered the artists to be shown in, who, for the last two hours, had been walking up and down outside the door behind which fame and fortune – or dismissal – awaited them.

The whole day was spent in discussing, negotiating, signing or cancelling contracts; and the two overworked managers went to bed early, without so much as casting a glance at Box Five to see whether M. Debienne and M. Poligny were enjoying the performance.

Next morning, the managers received a card of thanks from the ghost:

Dear Mr. Manager:

Thanks. Charming evening. Daaé exquisite. Choruses want waking up. Carlotta a splendid commonplace instrument. Will write you soon for the 240,000 francs, or 233,424 fr. 70 c., to be correct. MM. Debienne and Poligny have sent me the 6,575 fr. 30 c. representing the first ten days of my allowance for the current year; their privileges finished on the evening of the tenth inst.

Kind regards.

O. G.

On the other hand, there was a letter from MM. Debienne and Poligny:

Gentlemen:

We are much obliged for your kind thought of us, but you will easily understand that the prospect of again hearing **Faust**, pleasant though it is to ex-managers of the Opera, can not make us forget that we have no right to occupy Box Five on the grand tier, which is the exclusive property of **him** of whom we spoke to you when we went through the memorandum-book with you for the last time. See Clause 98, final paragraph.

Accept, gentlemen, etc.

"Oh, those fellows are beginning to annoy me!" shouted Firmin Richard, snatching up the letter.

And that evening Box Five was sold.

The next morning, MM. Richard and Moncharmin, on reaching their office, found an inspector's report relating to an incident that had happened, the night before, in Box Five. I give the essential part of the report:

I was obliged to call in a municipal guard twice, this evening, to clear Box Five on the grand tier, once at the beginning and once in the middle of the second act. The occupants, who arrived as the curtain rose on the second act, created a regular scandal by their laughter and their ridiculous observations. There were cries of "Hush!" all around them and the whole house was beginning to protest, when the box-keeper came to fetch me. I entered the box and said what I thought necessary. The people did not seem to me to be in their right mind; and they made stupid remarks. I said that, if the noise was repeated, I should be compelled to clear the box. The moment I left, I heard the laughing again, with fresh protests from the house. I returned with a municipal guard, who turned them out. They protested, still laughing, saying they would not go unless they had their money back. At last, they became quiet and I allowed them to enter the box again. The laughter at once recommenced; and, this time, I had them turned out definitely.

"Send for the inspector," said Richard to his secretary, who had already read the report and marked it with blue pencil.

M. Rémy, the secretary, had foreseen the order and called the inspector at once.

"Tell us what happened," said Richard bluntly.

The inspector began to splutter and referred to the report.

"Well, but what were those people laughing at?" asked Moncharmin.

"They must have been dining, sir, and seemed more inclined to lark about than to listen to good music. The moment they entered the box, they came out again and called the box-keeper, who asked them what they wanted. They said, 'Look in the box: there's no one there, is there?' 'No,' said the woman. 'Well,' said they, 'when we went in, we heard a voice saying **that the box was taken**!'"

M. Moncharmin could not help smiling as he looked at M. Richard; but M. Richard did not smile. He himself had done too much in that way in his time not to recognize, in the inspector's story, all the marks of one of those practical jokes which begin by amusing and end by enraging the victims. The inspector, to curry favor with M. Moncharmin, who was smiling, thought it best to give a smile too. A most unfortunate smile! M. Richard glared at his subordinate, who thenceforth made it his business to display a face of utter consternation.

"However, when the people arrived," roared Richard, "there was no one in the box, was there?"

"Not a soul, sir, not a soul! Nor in the box on the right, nor in the box on the left: not a soul, sir, I swear! The box-keeper told it me often enough, which proves that it was all a joke."

"Oh, you agree, do you?" said Richard. "You agree! It's a joke! And you think it funny, no doubt?"

"I think it in very bad taste, sir."

"And what did the box-keeper say?"

"Oh, she just said that it was the Opera ghost. That's all she said!"

And the inspector grinned. But he soon found that he had made a mistake in grinning, for the words had no sooner left his mouth than M. Richard, from gloomy, became furious.

"Send for the box-keeper!" he shouted. "Send for her! This minute! This minute! And bring her in to me here! And turn all those people out!"

The inspector tried to protest, but Richard closed his mouth with an angry order to hold his tongue. Then, when the wretched man's lips seemed shut forever, the manager commanded him to open them once more.

"Who is this 'Opera ghost?'" he snarled.

But the inspector was by this time incapable of speaking a word. He managed to convey, by a despairing gesture, that he knew nothing about it, or rather that he did not wish to know.

"Have you ever seen him, have you seen the Opera ghost?"

The inspector, by means of a vigorous shake of the head, denied ever having seen the ghost in question.

"Very well!" said M. Richard coldly.

The inspector's eyes started out of his head, as though to ask why the manager had uttered that ominous "Very well!"

"Because I'm going to settle the account of anyone who has not seen him!" explained the manager. "As he seems to be everywhere, I can't have people telling me that they see him nowhere. I like people to work for me when I employ them!"

Having said this, M. Richard paid no attention to the inspector and discussed various matters of business with his acting-manager, who had entered the room meanwhile. The inspector thought he could go and was gently – oh, so gently! – sidling toward the door, when M. Richard nailed the man to the floor with a thundering:

"Stay where you are!"

M. Rémy had sent for the box-keeper to the Rue de Provence, close to the Opera, where she was engaged as a porteress. She soon made her appearance.

"What's your name?"

"Mame Giry. You know me well enough, sir; I'm the mother of little Giry, little Meg, what!"

This was said in so rough and solemn a tone that, for a moment, M. Richard was impressed. He looked at Mame Giry, in her faded shawl, her worn shoes, her old taffeta dress and dingy bonnet. It was quite evident from the manager's attitude, that he either did not know or could not remember having met Mame Giry, nor even little Giry, nor even "little Meg!" But Mame Giry's pride was so great that the celebrated box-keeper imagined that everybody knew her.

"Never heard of her!" the manager declared. "But that's no reason, Mame Giry, why I shouldn't ask you what happened last night to make you and the inspector call in a municipal guard..."

"I was just wanting to see you, sir, and talk to you about it, so that you mightn't have the same unpleasantness as M. Debienne and M. Poligny. They wouldn't listen to me either, at first."

"I'm not asking you about all that. I'm asking what happened last night."

Mame Giry turned purple with indignation. Never had she been spoken to like that. She rose as though to go, gathering up the folds of her skirt and waving the feathers of her dingy bonnet with dignity, but, changing her mind, she sat down again and said, in a haughty voice:

"I'll tell you what happened. The ghost was annoyed again!"

Thereupon, as M. Richard was on the point of bursting out, M. Moncharmin interfered and conducted the interrogatory, whence it appeared that Mame Giry thought it quite natural that a voice should be heard to say that a box was taken, when there was nobody in the box. She was unable to explain this phenomenon, which was not new to her, except by the intervention of the ghost. Nobody could see the ghost in his box, but everybody could hear him. She had often heard him; and they could believe her, for she always spoke the truth. They could ask M. Debienne and M. Poligny, and anybody who knew her; and also M. Isidore Saack, who had had a leg broken by the ghost!

"Indeed!" said Moncharmin, interrupting her. "Did the ghost break poor Isidore Saack's leg?"

Mame Giry opened her eyes with astonishment at such ignorance. However, she consented to enlighten those two poor innocents. The thing had happened in M. Debienne and M. Poligny's time, also in Box Five and also during a performance of **Faust**. Mame Giry coughed, cleared her throat – it sounded as though she were preparing to sing the whole of Gounod's score – and began:

"It was like this, sir. That night, M. Maniera and his lady, the jewelers in the Rue Mogador, were sitting in the front of the box, with their great friend, M. Isidore Saack, sitting behind Mme. Maniera. Mephistopheles was singing"

– Mame Giry here burst into song herself – "'Catarina, while you play at sleeping,' and then M. Maniera heard a voice in his right ear (his wife was on his left) saying, 'Ha, ha! Julie's not playing at sleeping!' His wife happened to be called Julie. So M. Maniera turns to the right to see who was talking to him like that. Nobody there! He rubs his ear and asks himself if he's dreaming. Then Mephistopheles went on with his serenade.... But, perhaps I'm boring you gentlemen?"

"No, no, go on."

"You are too good, gentlemen," with a smirk. "Well, then, Mephistopheles went on with his serenade" – Mame Giry burst into song again – "'Saint, unclose thy portals holy and accord the bliss, to a mortal bending lowly, of a pardon-kiss.' And then M. Maniera again hears the voice in his right ear, saying, this time, 'Ha, ha! Julie wouldn't mind according a kiss to Isidore!' Then he turns round again, but, this time, to the left; and what do you think he sees? Isidore, who had taken his lady's hand and was covering it with kisses through the little round place in the glove – like this, gentlemen" – rapturously kissing the bit of palm left bare in the middle of her thread gloves. "Then they had a lively time between them! Bang! Bang! M. Maniera, who was big and strong, like you, M. Richard, gave two blows to M. Isidore Saack, who was small and weak like M. Moncharmin, saving his presence. There was a great uproar. People in the house shouted, 'That will do! Stop them! He'll kill him!' Then, at last, M. Isidore Saack managed to run away."

"Then the ghost had not broken his leg?" asked M. Moncharmin, a little vexed that his figure had made so little impression on Mame Giry.

"He did break it for him, sir," replied Mame Giry haughtily. "He broke it for him on the grand staircase, which he ran down too fast, sir, and it will be long before the poor gentleman will be able to go up it again!"

"Did the ghost tell you what he said in M.

Maniera's right ear?" asked M. Moncharmin, with a gravity which he thought exceedingly humorous.

"No, sir, it was M. Maniera himself. So – "

"But you have spoken to the ghost, my good lady?"

"As I'm speaking to you now, my good sir!" Mame Giry replied.

"And, when the ghost speaks to you, what does he say?"

"Well, he tells me to bring him a footstool!"

This time, Richard burst out laughing, as did Moncharmin and Rémy, the secretary. Only the inspector, warned by experience, was careful not to laugh, while Mame Giry ventured to adopt an attitude that was positively threatening.

"Instead of laughing," she cried indignantly, "you'd do better to do as M. Poligny did, who found out for himself."

"Found out about what?" asked Moncharmin, who had never been so much amused in his life.

"About the ghost, of course!... Look here..."

She suddenly calmed herself, feeling that this was a solemn moment in her life:

"**Look here**," she repeated. "They were playing **La Juive**. M. Poligny thought he would watch the performance from the ghost's box.... Well, when Léopold cries, 'Let us fly!' – you know – and Eléazer stops them and says, 'Whither go ye?'... well, M. Poligny – I was watching him from the back of the next box, which was empty – M. Poligny got up and walked out quite stiffly, like a statue, and before I had time to ask him, 'Whither go ye?' like Eléazer, he was down the staircase, but without breaking his leg...."

"Still, that doesn't let us know how the Opera ghost came to ask you for a footstool," insisted M. Moncharmin.

"Well, from that evening, no one tried to take the ghost's private box from him. The manager gave orders that he was to have it at each performance. And, whenever he came, he asked me for a footstool."

"Tut, tut! A ghost asking for a footstool! Then this ghost of yours is a woman?"

"No, the ghost is a man."

"How do you know?"

"He has a man's voice, oh, such a lovely man's voice! This is what happens: When he comes to the opera, it's usually in the middle of the first act. He gives three little taps on the door of Box Five. The first time I heard those three taps, when I knew there was no one in the box, you can think how puzzled I was! I opened the door, listened, looked; nobody! And then I heard a voice say, 'Mame Jules' – my poor husband's name was Jules – 'a footstool, please.' Saving your presence, gentlemen, it made me feel all-overish like. But the voice went on, 'Don't be frightened, Mame Jules, I'm the Opera ghost!' And the voice was so soft and kind that I hardly felt frightened. **The voice was sitting in the corner chair, on**

the right, in the front row."

"Was there anyone in the box on the right of Box Five?" asked Moncharmin.

"No; Box Seven, and Box Three, the one on the left, were both empty. The curtain had only just gone up."

"And what did you do?"

"Well, I brought the footstool. Of course, it wasn't for himself he wanted it, but for his lady! But I never heard her nor saw her."

"Eh? What? So now the ghost is married!" The eyes of the two managers traveled from Mame Giry to the inspector, who, standing behind the box-keeper, was waving his arms to attract their attention. He tapped his forehead with a distressful forefinger, to convey his opinion that the widow Jules Giry was most certainly mad, a piece of pantomime which confirmed M. Richard in his determination to get rid of an inspector who kept a lunatic in his service. Meanwhile, the worthy lady went on about her ghost, now painting his generosity:

"At the end of the performance, he always gives me two francs, sometimes five, sometimes even ten, when he has been many days without coming. Only, since people have begun to annoy him again, he gives me nothing at all...."

"Excuse me, my good woman," said Moncharmin, while Mame Giry tossed the feathers in her dingy hat at this persistent familiarity, "excuse me, how does the ghost manage to give you your two francs?"

"Why, he leaves them on the little shelf in the box, of course. I find them with the program, which I always give him. Some evenings, I find flowers in the box, a rose that must have dropped from his lady's bodice... for he brings a lady with him sometimes; one day, they left a fan behind them."

"Oh, the ghost left a fan, did he? And what did you do with it?"

"Well, I brought it back to the box next night."

Here the inspector's voice was raised.

"You've broken the rules; I shall have to fine you, Mame Giry."

"Hold your tongue, you fool!" muttered M. Firmin Richard.

"You brought back the fan. And then?"

"Well, then, they took it away with them, sir; it was not there at the end of the performance; and in its place they left me a box of English sweets, which I'm very fond of. That's one of the ghost's pretty thoughts."

"That will do, Mame Giry. You can go."

When Mame Giry had bowed herself out, with the dignity that never deserted her, the manager told the inspector that they had decided to dispense with that old madwoman's services; and, when he had gone in his turn, they instructed the acting-manager to make up the inspector's accounts. Left alone, the managers told each other of the idea which they both had in mind, which was that they should look into that little matter of Box Five themselves.

CHAPTER FIVE

The Enchanted Violin

CHRISTINE DAAÉ, owing to intrigues to which I will return later, did not immediately continue her triumph at the Opera. After the famous gala night, she sang once at the Duchess de Zurich's; but this was the last occasion on which she was heard in private. She refused, without plausible excuse, to appear at a charity concert to which she had promised her assistance. She acted throughout as though she were no longer the mistress of her own destiny and as though she feared a fresh triumph.

She knew that the Comte de Chagny, to please his brother, had done his best on her behalf with M. Richard; and she wrote to thank him and also to ask him to cease speaking in her favor. Her reason for this curious attitude was never known. Some pretended that it was due to overweening pride; others spoke of her heavenly modesty. But people on the stage are not so modest as all that; and I think that I shall not be far from the truth if I ascribe her action simply to fear. Yes, I believe that Christine Daaé was frightened by what had happened to her. I have a letter of Christine's (it forms part of the Persian's collection), relating to this period, which suggests a feeling of absolute dismay:

"I don't know myself when I sing," writes the poor child.

She showed herself nowhere; and the

Vicomte de Chagny tried in vain to meet her. He wrote to her, asking to call upon her, but despaired of receiving a reply when, one morning, she sent him the following note:

Monsieur:

I have not forgotten the little boy who went into the sea to rescue my scarf. I feel that I must write to you today, when I am going to Perros, in fulfilment of a sacred duty. Tomorrow is the anniversary of the death of my poor father, whom you knew and who was very fond of you. He is buried there, with his violin, in the graveyard of the little church, at the bottom of the slope where we used to play as children, beside the road where, when we were a little bigger, we said goodbye for the last time.

The Vicomte de Chagny hurriedly consulted a railway guide, dressed as quickly as he could, wrote a few lines for his valet to take to his brother and jumped into a cab which brought him to the Gare Montparnasse just in time to miss the morning train. He spent a dismal day in town and did not recover his spirits until the evening, when he was seated in his compartment in the Brittany express. He read Christine's note over and over again, smelling its perfume, recalling the sweet pictures of his childhood, and spent the rest of that tedious night journey in feverish dreams that began and ended with Christine Daaé. Day was breaking when he alighted at Lannion. He hurried to the diligence for Perros-Guirec. He was the only passenger. He questioned the driver and learned that, on the evening of the previous day, a young lady who looked like a Parisian had gone to Perros and put up at the inn known as the Setting Sun.

The nearer he drew to her, the more fondly he remembered the story of the little Swedish singer. Most of the details are still unknown to the public.

There was once, in a little market-town not far from Upsala, a peasant who lived there with his family, digging the earth during the week and singing in the choir on Sundays. This peasant had a little daughter to whom he taught the musical alphabet before she knew how to read. Daaé's father was a great musician, perhaps without knowing it. Not a fiddler throughout the length and breadth of Scandinavia played as he did. His reputation was widespread and he was always invited to set the couples dancing at weddings and other festivals. His wife died when Christine was entering upon her sixth year. Then the father, who cared only for his daughter and his music, sold his patch of ground and went to Upsala in search of fame and fortune. He found nothing but poverty.

He returned to the country, wandering from fair to fair, strumming his Scandinavian melodies, while his child, who never left his side, listened to him in ecstasy or sang to his playing. One day, at Ljimby Fair, Professor Valérius heard them and took them to

Gothenburg. He maintained that the father was the first violinist in the world and that the daughter had the making of a great artist. Her education and instruction were provided for. She made rapid progress and charmed everybody with her prettiness, her grace of manner and her genuine eagerness to please.

When Valérius and his wife went to settle in France, they took Daaé and Christine with them. "Mamma" Valérius treated Christine as her daughter. As for Daaé, he began to pine away with homesickness. He never went out of doors in Paris, but lived in a sort of dream which he kept up with his violin. For hours at a time, he remained locked up in his bedroom with his daughter, fiddling and singing, very, very softly. Sometimes Mamma Valérius would come and listen behind the door, wipe away a tear and go downstairs again on tiptoe, sighing for her Scandinavian skies.

Daaé seemed not to recover his strength

until the summer, when the whole family went to stay at Perros-Guirec, in a faraway corner of Brittany, where the sea was of the same color as in his own country. Often he would play his saddest tunes on the beach and pretend that the sea stopped its roaring to listen to them. And then he induced Mamma Valérius to indulge a queer whim of his. At the time of the "pardons," or Breton pilgrimages, the village festival and dances, he went off with his fiddle, as in the old days, and was allowed to take his daughter with him for a week. They gave the smallest hamlets music to last them for a year and slept at night in a barn, refusing a bed at the inn, lying close together on the straw, as when they were so poor in Sweden. At the same time, they were very neatly dressed, made no collection, refused the halfpence offered them; and the people around could not understand the conduct of this rustic fiddler, who tramped the roads with that pretty child who sang like an angel from

Heaven. They followed them from village to village.

One day, a little boy, who was out with his governess, made her take a longer walk than he intended, for he could not tear himself from the little girl whose pure, sweet voice seemed to bind him to her. They came to the shore of an inlet which is still called Trestraou, but which now, I believe, harbors a casino or something of the sort. At that time, there was nothing but sky and sea and a stretch of golden beach. Only, there was also a high wind, which blew Christine's scarf out to sea. Christine gave a cry and put out her arms, but the scarf was already far on the waves. Then she heard a voice say:

"It's all right, I'll go and fetch your scarf out of the sea."

And she saw a little boy running fast, in spite of the outcries and the indignant protests of a worthy lady in black. The little boy ran into the sea, dressed as he was, and brought her back her scarf. Boy and scarf were both soaked through. The lady in black made a great fuss, but Christine laughed merrily and kissed the little boy, who was none other than the Vicomte Raoul de Chagny, staying at Lannion with his aunt.

During the season, they saw each other and played together almost every day. At the aunt's request, seconded by Professor Valérius, Daaé consented to give the young viscount some violin lessons. In this way, Raoul learned to love the same airs that had charmed Christine's childhood. They also both had the same calm and dreamy little cast of mind. They delighted in stories, in old Breton legends; and their favorite sport was to go and ask for them at the cottage-doors, like beggars:

"Ma'am…" or, "Kind gentleman… have you a little story to tell us, please?"

And it seldom happened that they did not have one "given" them; for nearly every old Breton grandame has, at least once in her life, seen the “korrigans” dance by moonlight on the heather.

But their great treat was, in the twilight, in the great silence of the evening, after the sun had set in the sea, when Daaé came and sat down by them on the roadside and, in a low voice, as though fearing lest he should frighten the ghosts whom he evoked, told them the legends of the land of the North. And, the moment he stopped, the children would ask for more.

There was one story that began:

“A king sat in a little boat on one of those deep, still lakes that open like a bright eye in the midst of the Norwegian mountains...”

And another:

“Little Lotte thought of everything and nothing. Her hair was golden as the sun’s rays and her soul as clear and blue as her eyes. She wheedled her mother, was kind to her doll, took great care of her frock and her little red shoes and her fiddle, but most of all loved, when she went to sleep, to hear the Angel of Music."

While the old man told this story, Raoul looked at Christine's blue eyes and golden hair; and Christine thought that Lotte was very lucky to hear the Angel of Music when she went to sleep. The Angel of Music played a part in all Daddy Daaé's tales; and he maintained that every great musician, every great artist received a visit from the Angel at least once in his life. Sometimes the Angel leans over their cradle, as happened to Lotte, and that is how there are little prodigies who play the fiddle at six better than men at fifty, which, you must admit, is very wonderful. Sometimes, the Angel comes much later, because the children are naughty and won't learn their lessons or practise their scales. And, sometimes, he does not come at all, because the children have a bad heart or a bad conscience.

No one ever sees the Angel; but he is heard by those who are meant to hear him. He often comes when they least expect him, when they are sad and disheartened. Then their ears suddenly perceive celestial harmonies, a divine voice, which they remember all their lives. Persons who are visited by the Angel quiver with a thrill unknown to the rest of mankind. And they can not touch an instrument, or open their mouths to sing, without producing sounds that put all other human sounds to shame. Then people who do not know that the Angel has visited those persons say that they have genius.

Little Christine asked her father if he had heard the Angel of Music. But Daddy Daaé shook his head sadly; and then his eyes lit up, as he said:

"You will hear him one day, my child! When I am in Heaven, I will send him to you!"

Daddy was beginning to cough at that time.

Three years later, Raoul and Christine met again at Perros. Professor Valérius was dead, but his widow remained in

France with Daddy Daaé and his daughter, who continued to play the violin and sing, wrapping in their dream of harmony their kind patroness, who seemed henceforth to live on music alone. The young man, as he now was, had come to Perros on the chance of finding them and went straight to the house in which they used to stay. He first saw the old man; and then Christine entered, carrying the tea-tray. She flushed at the sight of Raoul, who went up to her and kissed her. She asked him a few questions, performed her duties as hostess prettily, took up the tray again and left the room. Then she ran into the garden and took refuge on a bench, a prey to feelings that stirred her young heart for the first time. Raoul followed her and they talked till the evening, very shyly. They were quite changed, cautious as two diplomatists, and told each other things that had nothing to do with their budding sentiments. When they took leave of each other by the roadside, Raoul, pressing a kiss on Christine's trembling hand, said:

"Mademoiselle, I shall never forget you!"

And he went away regretting his words, for he knew that Christine could not be the wife of the Vicomte de Chagny.

As for Christine, she tried not to think of him and devoted herself wholly to her art. She made wonderful progress and those who heard her prophesied that she would be the greatest singer in the world. Meanwhile, the father died; and, suddenly, she seemed to have lost, with him, her voice, her soul and her genius. She retained just, but only just, enough of this to enter the **conservatoire**, where she did not distinguish herself at all, attending the classes without enthusiasm and taking a prize only to please old Mamma Valérius, with whom she continued to live.

The first time that Raoul saw Christine at the Opera, he was charmed by the girl's beauty and by the sweet images of the past which it evoked, but was rather surprised at the negative side of her art. He returned to listen to her. He followed her in the wings. He waited for her behind a Jacob's ladder. He tried to attract her attention. More than once, he walked after her to the door of her box, but she did not see him. She seemed, for that matter, to see nobody. She was all indifference. Raoul suffered, for she was very beautiful and he was shy and dared not confess his love, even to himself. And then came the lightning-flash of the gala performance: the heavens torn asunder and an angel's voice heard upon earth for the delight of mankind and the utter capture of his heart.

And then... and then there was that man's voice behind the door – "You must love me!" – and no one in the room....

Why did she laugh when he reminded her of the incident of the scarf? Why did she not recognize him? And why had she written to him?...

Perros was reached at last. Raoul walked into the smoky sitting-room of the Setting Sun and at once saw Christine standing before him, smiling and showing no astonishment.

"So you have come," she said. "I felt that I should find you here, when I came back from mass. Someone told me so, at the church."

"Who?" asked Raoul, taking her little hand in his.

"Why, my poor father, who is dead."

There was a silence; and then Raoul asked:

"Did your father tell you that I love you, Christine, and that I can not live without you?"

Christine blushed to the eyes and turned away her head. In a trembling voice, she said:

"Me? You are dreaming, my friend!"

And she burst out laughing, to put herself in countenance.

"Don't laugh, Christine; I am quite serious," Raoul answered.

And she replied gravely: "I did not make

you come to tell me such things as that."

"You 'made me come,' Christine; you knew that your letter would not leave me indignant and that I should hasten to Perros. How can you have thought that, if you did not think I loved you?"

"I thought you would remember our games here, as children, in which my father so often joined. I really don't know what I thought.... Perhaps I was wrong to write to you.... This anniversary and your sudden appearance in my room at the Opera, the other evening, reminded me of the time long past and made me write to you as the little girl that I then was...."

There was something in Christine's attitude that seemed to Raoul not natural. He did not feel any hostility in her; far from it: the distressed affection shining in her eyes told him that. But why was this affection distressed? That was what he wished to know and what was irritating him.

"When you saw me in your dressing-room, was that the first time you noticed me, Christine?"

She was incapable of lying.

"No," she said, "I had seen you several times in your brother's box. And also on the stage."

"I thought so!" said Raoul, compressing his lips. "But then why, when you saw me in your room, at your feet, reminding you that I had rescued your scarf from the sea, why did you answer as though you did not know me and also why did you laugh?"

The tone of these questions was so rough that Christine stared at Raoul without replying. The young man himself was aghast at the sudden quarrel which he had dared to raise at the very moment when he had resolved to speak words of gentleness, love and submission to Christine. A husband, a lover with all rights, would talk no differently to a wife, a mistress who had offended him. But he had gone too far and saw no other way out of the ridiculous position than to behave odiously.

"You don't answer!" he said angrily and unhappily. "Well, I will answer for you. It was because there was someone in the room who was in your way, Christine, someone that you did not wish to know that you could be interested in anyone else!"

"If anyone was in my way, my friend," Christine broke in coldly, "if anyone was in my way, that evening, it was yourself, since I told you to leave the room!"

"Yes, so that you might remain with the other!"

"What are you saying, monsieur?" asked the girl excitedly. "And to what other do you refer?"

"To the man to whom you said, 'I sing only for you!... Tonight I gave you my soul and I am dead!'"

Christine seized Raoul's arm and clutched it with a strength which no one would have suspected in so frail a creature.

"Then you were listening behind the door?"

"Yes, because I love you… and I heard everything…."

"You heard what?"

And the young girl, becoming strangely calm, released Raoul's arm.

"He said to you, 'Christine, you must love me!'"

At these words, a deathly pallor spread over Christine's face, dark rings formed round her eyes, she staggered and seemed on the point of swooning. Raoul darted forward, with arms outstretched, but Christine had overcome her passing faintness and said, in a low voice:

"Go on! Go on! Tell me all you heard!"

At an utter loss to understand, Raoul answered: "I heard him reply, when you said you had given him your soul, 'Your soul is a beautiful thing, child, and I thank you. No emperor ever received so fair a gift. The angels wept tonight.'"

Christine carried her hand to her heart,

a prey to indescribable emotion. Her eyes stared before her like a madwoman's. Raoul was terror-stricken. But suddenly Christine's eyes moistened and two great tears trickled, like two pearls, down her ivory cheeks.

"Christine!"

"Raoul!"

The young man tried to take her in his arms, but she escaped and fled in great disorder.

While Christine remained locked in her room, Raoul was at his wit's end what to do. He refused to breakfast. He was terribly concerned and bitterly grieved to see the hours, which he had hoped to find so sweet, slip past without the presence of the young Swedish girl. Why did she not come to roam with him through the country where they had so many memories in common? He heard that she had had a mass said, that morning, for the repose of her father's soul and spent a long time praying in the little church and on the fiddler's tomb. Then, as she seemed to have nothing more to do at Perros and, in fact, was doing nothing there, why did she not go back to Paris at once?

Raoul walked away, dejectedly, to the graveyard in which the church stood and was indeed alone among the tombs, reading the inscriptions; but, when he turned behind the apse, he was suddenly struck by the dazzling note of the flowers that straggled over the white ground. They were marvelous red roses that had blossomed in the morning, in the snow, giving a glimpse of life among the dead, for death was all around him. It also, like the flowers, issued from the ground, which had flung back a number of its corpses. Skeletons and skulls by the hundred were heaped against the wall of the church, held in position by a wire that left the whole gruesome stack visible. Dead men's bones, arranged in rows, like bricks, to form the first course upon which the walls of the sacristy had been built. The door of the sacristy opened in the middle of that bony structure, as is often seen in old Breton churches.

Raoul said a prayer for Daaé and then, painfully impressed by all those eternal smiles on the mouths of skulls, he climbed the slope and sat down on the edge of the heath overlooking the sea. The wind fell with the evening. Raoul was surrounded by icy darkness, but he did not feel the cold. It was here, he remembered, that he used to come with little Christine to see the Korrigans dance at the rising of the moon. He had never seen any, though his eyes were good, whereas Christine, who was a little shortsighted, pretended that she had seen many. He smiled at the thought and then suddenly gave a start. A voice behind him said:

"Do you think the Korrigans will come this evening?"

It was Christine. He tried to speak. She put her gloved hand on his mouth.

"Listen, Raoul. I have decided to tell you something serious, very serious.... Do you remember the legend of the Angel of Music?"

"I do indeed," he said. "I believe it was here that your father first told it to us."

"And it was here that he said, 'When I am in Heaven, my child, I will send him to you.' Well, Raoul, my father is in Heaven, and I have been visited by the Angel of Music."

"I have no doubt of it," replied the young man gravely, for it seemed to him that his friend, in obedience to a pious thought, was connecting the memory of her father with the brilliancy of her last triumph.

Christine appeared astonished at the Vicomte de Chagny's coolness:

"How do you understand it?" she asked, bringing her pale face so close to his that he might have thought that Christine was going to give him a kiss; but she only wanted to read his eyes in spite of the dark.

"I understand," he said, "that no human

being can sing as you sang the other evening without the intervention of some miracle. No professor on earth can teach you such accents as those. You have heard the Angel of Music, Christine."

"Yes," she said solemnly, "**in my dressing-room**. That is where he comes to give me my lessons daily."

"In your dressing-room?" he echoed stupidly.

"Yes, that is where I have heard him; and I have not been the only one to hear him."

"Who else heard him, Christine?"

"You, my friend."

"I? I heard the Angel of Music?"

"Yes, the other evening, it was he who was talking when you were listening behind the door. It was he who said, 'You must love me.' But I then thought that I was the only one to hear his voice. Imagine my astonishment when you told me, this morning, that you could hear him too."

Raoul burst out laughing. The first rays

of the moon came and shrouded the two young people in their light. Christine turned on Raoul with a hostile air. Her eyes, usually so gentle, flashed fire.

"What are you laughing at? **You** think you heard a man's voice, I suppose?"

"Well!..." replied the young man, whose ideas began to grow confused in the face of Christine's determined attitude.

"It's you, Raoul, who say that? You, an old playfellow of my own! A friend of my father's! But you have changed since those days. What are you thinking of? I am an honest girl, M. le Vicomte de Chagny, and I don't lock myself up in my dressing-room with men's voices. If you had opened the door, you would have seen that there was nobody in the room!"

"That's true! I did open the door, when you were gone, and I found no one in the room."

"So you see!... Well?"

The viscount summoned up all his courage.

"Well, Christine, I think that somebody is

making game of you."

She gave a cry and ran away. He ran after her, but, in a tone of fierce anger, she called out: "Leave me! Leave me!" And she disappeared.

Raoul returned to the inn feeling very weary, very low-spirited and very sad. He was told that Christine had gone to her bedroom saying that she would not be down to dinner. Raoul dined alone, in a very gloomy mood. Then he went to his room and tried to read, went to bed and tried to sleep. There was no sound in the next room.

The hours passed slowly. It was about half-past eleven when he distinctly heard someone moving, with a light, stealthy step, in the room next to his. Then Christine had not gone to bed! Without troubling for a reason, Raoul dressed, taking care not to make a sound, and waited. Waited for what? How could he tell? But his heart thumped in his chest when he heard Christine's door turn slowly on its hinges. Where could she be going, at this hour, when everyone was fast asleep at Perros? Softly opening the door, he saw Christine's white form, in the moonlight, slipping along the passage. She went down the stairs and he leaned over the baluster above her. Suddenly he heard two voices in rapid conversation. He caught one sentence: "Don't lose the key."

It was the landlady's voice. The door facing the sea was opened and locked again. Then all was still.

Raoul ran back to his room and threw back the window. Christine's white form stood on the deserted quay.

The first floor of the Setting Sun was at no great height and a tree growing against the wall held out its branches to Raoul's impatient arms and enabled him to climb down unknown to the landlady. Her amazement, therefore, was all the greater when, the next morning, the young man was brought back to her half frozen, more dead than alive, and when she learned that he had been found stretched at full length on the steps of the high altar of the little church. She ran at once to tell Christine, who hurried down and, with the help of the landlady, did her best to revive him. He soon opened his eyes and was not long in recovering when he saw his friend's charming face leaning over him.

A few weeks later, when the tragedy at the Opera compelled the intervention of the public prosecutor, M. Mifroid, the commissary of police, examined the Vicomte de Chagny touching the events of the night at Perros. I quote the questions and answers as given in the official report pp. 150 **et seq.**:

Q. Did Mlle. Daaé not see you come down from your room by the curious road which you selected?

R. No, monsieur, no, although, when walking behind her, I took no pains to deaden the sound of my footsteps. In fact, I was anxious that she should turn round and see me. I realized that I had no excuse for following her and that this way of spying on her was unworthy of me. But she seemed not to hear me and acted exactly as though I were not there. She quietly left the quay and then suddenly walked quickly up the road. The church-clock had struck a quarter to twelve and I thought that this must have made her hurry, for she began almost to run and continued hastening until she came to the church.

Q. Was the gate open?

R. Yes, monsieur, and this surprised me, but did not seem to surprise Mlle. Daaé.

Q. Was there no one in the churchyard?

R. I did not see anyone; and, if there had been, I must have seen him. The moon was shining on the snow and made the night quite light.

Q. Was it possible for anyone to hide behind the tombstones?

R. No, monsieur. They were quite small, poor tombstones, partly hidden under the snow, with their crosses just above the level of the ground. The only shadows were those of the crosses and ourselves. The church stood out quite brightly. I never saw so clear a night. It was very fine and very cold and one could see everything.

Q. Are you at all superstitious?

R. No, monsieur, I am a practising Catholic.

Q. In what condition of mind were you?

R. Very healthy and peaceful, I assure you. Mlle. Daaé's curious action in going out at that hour had worried me at first; but, as soon as I saw her go to the churchyard, I thought that she meant to fulfil some pious duty on her father's grave and I considered this so natural that I recovered all my calmness. I was only surprised that she had not heard me walking behind her, for my footsteps were quite audible on the hard snow. But she must have been taken up with her intentions and I resolved not to disturb her. She knelt down by her father's grave, made the sign of the cross and began to pray. At that moment, it struck midnight. At the last stroke, I saw Mlle. Daaé lift her eyes to the sky and stretch out her arms as though in ecstasy. I was wondering what the reason could be, when I myself raised my head and everything within me seemed drawn toward the invisible, **which was playing the most perfect music**! Christine and I knew that music; we had heard it as children. But it had never been executed with such divine art, even by M. Daaé. I remembered all that Christine had told me of the Angel of Music. The air was "The Resurrection of Lazarus," which old M. Daaé used to play to us in his hours of melancholy and of faith. If Christine's Angel had existed, he could not have played better, that night, on the late musician's violin. When the music stopped, I seemed to hear a noise from the skulls in the heap of bones; it was as though they were chuckling and I could not help shuddering.

Q. Did it not occur to you that the musician might be hiding behind that very heap of bones?

R. It was the one thought that did occur to me, monsieur, so much so that I omitted to follow Mlle. Daaé, when she stood up and walked slowly to the gate. She was so much absorbed just then that I am not surprised that she did not see me.

Q. Then what happened that you were found in the morning lying half-dead on the steps of the high altar?

R. First a skull rolled to my feet… then another… then another…. It was as if I were the mark of that ghastly game of bowls. And I had an idea that false step must have destroyed the balance of the structure behind which our musician was concealed. This surmise seemed to be confirmed when I saw a shadow suddenly glide along the sacristy wall. I ran up. The shadow had already pushed open the door and entered the church. But I was quicker than the shadow and caught hold of a corner of its cloak. At that moment, we were just in front of the high altar; and the moonbeams fell straight upon us through the stained-glass windows of the apse. As I did not let go of the cloak, the shadow turned round; and I saw a terrible death's head, which darted a look at me from a pair of scorching eyes. I felt as if I were face to face with Satan; and, in the presence of this unearthly apparition, my heart gave way, my courage failed me… and I remember nothing more until I recovered consciousness at the Setting Sun.

CHAPTER SIX

A Visit to Box Five

WE LEFT M. Firmin Richard and M. Armand Moncharmin at the moment when they were deciding "to look into that little matter of Box Five."

Leaving behind them the broad staircase which leads from the lobby outside the managers' offices to the stage and its dependencies, they crossed the stage, went out by the subscribers' door and entered the house through the first little passage on the left. Then they made their way through the front rows of stalls and looked at Box Five on the grand tier. They could not see it well, because it was half in darkness and because great covers were flung over the red velvet of the ledges of all the boxes.

They were almost alone in the huge, gloomy house; and a great silence surrounded them. It was the time when most of the stagehands go out for a drink. The staff had left the boards for the moment, leaving a scene half set. A few rays of light, a wan, sinister light, that seemed to have been stolen from an expiring luminary, fell through some opening or other upon an old tower that raised its pasteboard battlements on the stage; everything, in this deceptive light, adopted a fantastic shape. In the orchestra stalls, the drugget covering them looked like an angry sea, whose glaucous waves had been suddenly rendered stationary by a secret order from the storm phantom, who, as everybody knows, is called Adamastor. MM. Moncharmin and Richard were the shipwrecked mariners amid this motionless turmoil of a calico sea. They made for the left boxes, plowing their way like sailors who leave their ship and try to struggle to the shore. The eight great polished columns stood up in the dusk like so many huge piles supporting the threatening, crumbling, big-bellied cliffs whose layers were represented by the circular, parallel, waving lines of the balconies of the grand, first and second tiers of boxes. At the top, right on top of the cliff, lost in M. Lenepveu's copper ceiling, figures grinned and grimaced, laughed and jeered at MM. Richard and Moncharmin's distress. And yet these figures were usually very serious. Their names were Isis, Amphitrite, Hebe, Pandora, Psyche, Thetis, Pomona, Daphne, Clytie, Galatea and Arethusa. Yes, Arethusa herself and Pandora, whom we all know by her box, looked down upon the two new managers of the Opera, who ended by clutching at some piece of wreckage and from there stared silently at Box Five on the grand tier.

I have said that they were distressed. At least, I presume so. M. Moncharmin, in any case, admits that he was impressed. To quote his own words, in his **Memoirs**:

"This moonshine about the Opera ghost in which, since we first took over the duties of MM. Poligny and Debienne, we had been so nicely steeped" – Moncharmin's style is not always irreproachable – "had no doubt ended by blinding my imaginative and also my visual faculties. It may be that the exceptional surroundings in which we found ourselves, in the midst of an incredible silence, impressed us to an unusual extent. It may be that we were the sport of a kind of hallucination brought about by the semidarkness of the theater and the partial gloom that filled Box Five. At any rate, I saw and Richard also saw a shape in the box. Richard said nothing, nor I either. But we spontaneously seized each other's hand. We stood like that for some minutes, without moving, with our eyes fixed on the same point; but the figure had disappeared. Then we went out and, in the lobby, communicated our impressions to each other and talked about 'the shape.' The misfortune was that my shape was not in the least like Richard's. I had seen a thing like a death's head resting on the ledge of the box, whereas Richard saw the shape of an old woman who looked like Mame Giry. We soon discovered that we had really been the victims of an illusion, whereupon, without further delay and laughing like madmen, we ran to Box Five on the grand tier, went inside and found no shape of any kind."

Box Five is just like all the other grand tier boxes. There is nothing to distinguish it from any of the others. M. Moncharmin and M. Richard, ostensibly highly amused and laughing at each other, moved the furniture of the box, lifted the cloths and the chairs and particularly examined the armchair in which “the man’s voice” used to sit. But they saw that it was a respectable armchair, with no magic about it. Altogether, the box was the most ordinary box in the world, with its red hangings, its chairs, its carpet and its ledge covered in red velvet. After feeling the carpet in the most serious manner possible, and discovering nothing more here or anywhere else, they went down to the corresponding box on the pit tier below. In Box Five on the pit tier, which is just inside the first exit from the stalls on the left, they found nothing worth mentioning either.

“Those people are all making fools of us!” Firmin Richard ended by exclaiming. “It will be **Faust** on Saturday: let us both see the performance from Box Five on the grand tier!”

CHAPTER SEVEN

Faust and What Followed

ON THE SATURDAY MORNING, on reaching their office, the joint managers found a letter from O. G. worded in these terms:

My Dear Managers:

So it is to be war between us?

If you still care for peace, here is my ultimatum. It consists of the four following conditions:

You must give me back my private box; and I wish it to be at my free disposal from henceforward.

The part of Margarita shall be sung this evening by Christine Daaé. Never mind about Carlotta; she will be ill.

I absolutely insist upon the good and loyal services of Mme. Giry, my box-keeper, whom you will reinstate in her functions forthwith.

Let me know by a letter handed to Mme. Giry, who will see that it reaches me, that you accept, as your predecessors did, the conditions in my memorandum-book relating to my monthly allowance. I will inform you later how you are to pay it to me.

If you refuse, you will give **Faust** tonight in a house with a curse upon it.

Take my advice and be warned in time.

O. G.

"Look here, I'm getting sick of him, sick of him!" shouted Richard, bringing his fists down on his office-table.

Just then, Mercier, the acting-manager,

entered.

"Lachenel would like to see one of you gentlemen," he said. "He says that his business is urgent and he seems quite upset."

"Who's Lachenel?" asked Richard.

"He's your stud-groom."

"What do you mean? My stud-groom?"

"Yes, sir," explained Mercier, "there are several grooms at the Opera and M. Lachenel is at the head of them."

"And what does this groom do?"

"He has the chief management of the stable."

"What stable?"

"Why, yours, sir, the stable of the Opera."

"Is there a stable at the Opera? Upon my word, I didn't know. Where is it?"

"In the cellars, on the Rotunda side. It's a very important department; we have twelve horses."

"Twelve horses! And what for, in Heaven's name?"

"Why, we want trained horses for the processions in the **Juive**, the **Profeta** and so on; horses 'used to the boards.' It is the grooms' business to teach them. M. Lachenel is very clever at it. He used to manage Franconi's stables."

"Very well… but what does he want?"

"I don't know; I never saw him in such a state."

"He can come in."

M. Lachenel came in, carrying a riding-whip, with which he struck his right boot in an irritable manner.

"Good morning, M. Lachenel," said Richard, somewhat impressed. "To what do we owe the honor of your visit?"

"Mr. Manager, I have come to ask you to get rid of the whole stable."

"What, you want to get rid of our horses?"

"I'm not talking of the horses, but of the stablemen."

"How many stablemen have you, M. Lachenel?"

"Six."

"Six stablemen! That's at least two too many."

"These are 'places,'" Mercier interposed, "created and forced upon us by the undersecretary for fine arts. They are filled by protégées of the government and, if I may venture to..."

"I don't care a hang for the government!" roared Richard. "We don't need more than four stablemen for twelve horses."

"Eleven," said the head riding-master, correcting him.

"Twelve," repeated Richard.

"Eleven," repeated Lachenel.

"Oh, the acting-manager told me that you had twelve horses!"

"I did have twelve, but I have only eleven since César was stolen."

And M. Lachenel gave himself a great smack on the boot with his whip.

"Has César been stolen?" cried the acting-manager. "César, the white horse in the

Profeta?"

"There are not two Césars," said the stud-groom dryly. "I was ten years at Franconi's and I have seen plenty of horses in my time. Well, there are not two Césars. And he's been stolen."

"How?"

"I don't know. Nobody knows. That's why I have come to ask you to sack the whole stable."

"What do your stablemen say?"

"All sorts of nonsense. Some of them accuse the supers. Others pretend that it's the acting-manager's doorkeeper..."

"My doorkeeper? I'll answer for him as I would for myself!" protested Mercier.

"But, after all, M. Lachenel," cried Richard, "you must have some idea."

"Yes, I have," M. Lachenel declared. "I have an idea and I'll tell you what it is. There's no doubt about it in my mind." He walked up to the two managers and whispered. "It's the ghost who did the trick!"

Richard gave a jump.

"What, you too! You too!"

"How do you mean, I too? Isn't it natural, after what I saw?"

"What did you see?"

"I saw, as clearly as I now see you, a black shadow riding a white horse that was as like César as two peas!"

"And did you run after them?"

"I did and I shouted, but they were too fast for me and disappeared in the darkness of the underground gallery."

M. Richard rose. "That will do, M. Lachenel. You can go.... We will lodge a complaint against **the ghost**."

"And sack my stable?"

"Oh, of course! Good morning."

M. Lachenel bowed and withdrew. Richard foamed at the mouth.

"Settle that idiot's account at once, please."

"He is a friend of the government representative's!" Mercier ventured to say.

"And he takes his vermouth at Tortoni's

with Lagréné, Scholl and Pertuiset, the lion-hunter," added Moncharmin. "We shall have the whole press against us! He'll tell the story of the ghost; and everybody will be laughing at our expense! We may as well be dead as ridiculous!"

"All right, say no more about it."

At that moment the door opened. It must have been deserted by its usual Cerberus, for Mame Giry entered without ceremony, holding a letter in her hand, and said hurriedly:

"I beg your pardon, excuse me, gentlemen, but I had a letter this morning from the Opera ghost. He told me to come to you, that you had something to…"

She did not complete the sentence. She saw Firmin Richard's face; and it was a terrible sight. He seemed ready to burst. He said nothing, he could not speak. But suddenly he acted. First, his left arm seized upon the quaint person of Mame Giry and made her describe so unexpected a semicircle that she uttered a despairing cry. Next, his right foot imprinted its sole on the black taffeta of a skirt which certainly had never before undergone a similar outrage in a similar place. The thing happened so quickly that Mame Giry, when in the passage, was still quite bewildered and seemed not to understand. But, suddenly, she understood; and the Opera rang with her indignant yells, her violent protests and threats.

About the same time, Carlotta, who had a small house of her own in the Rue du Faubourg St. Honoré, rang for her maid, who brought her letters to her bed. Among them was an anonymous missive, written in red ink, in a hesitating, clumsy hand, which ran:

If you appear tonight, you must be prepared for a great misfortune at the moment when you open your mouth to sing… a misfortune worse than death.

The letter took away Carlotta's appetite for

breakfast. She pushed back her chocolate, sat up in bed and thought hard. It was not the first letter of the kind which she had received, but she never had one couched in such threatening terms.

She thought herself, at that time, the victim of a thousand jealous attempts and went about saying that she had a secret enemy who had sworn to ruin her. She pretended that a wicked plot was being hatched against her, a cabal which would come to a head one of those days; but she added that she was not the woman to be intimidated.

The truth is that, if there was a cabal, it was led by Carlotta herself against poor Christine, who had no suspicion of it. Carlotta had never forgiven Christine for the triumph which she had achieved when taking her place at a moment's notice. When Carlotta heard of the astounding reception bestowed upon her understudy, she was at once cured of an incipient attack of bronchitis and a bad fit of sulking against the management and lost the slightest inclination to shirk her duties. From that time, she worked with all her might to "smother" her rival, enlisting the services of influential friends to persuade the managers not to give Christine an opportunity for a fresh triumph. Certain newspapers which had begun to extol the talent of Christine now interested themselves only in the fame of Carlotta. Lastly, in the theater itself, the celebrated, but heartless and soulless diva made the most scandalous remarks about Christine and tried to cause her endless minor unpleasantnesses.

When Carlotta had finished thinking over the threat contained in the strange letter, she got up.

"We shall see," she said, adding a few oaths in her native Spanish with a very determined air.

The first thing she saw, when looking out of her window, was a hearse. She was very superstitious; and the hearse and the letter convinced her that she was running the most serious dangers that evening. She collected all her supporters, told them that she was threatened at that evening's performance with a plot organized by Christine Daaé and declared that they must play a trick upon that chit by filling the house with her, Carlotta's, admirers. She had no lack of them, had she? She relied upon them to hold themselves prepared for any eventuality and to silence the adversaries, if, as she feared, they created a disturbance.

M. Richard's private secretary called to ask after the diva's health and returned with the assurance that she was perfectly well and that, "were she dying," she would sing the part of Margarita that evening. The secretary urged her, in his chief's name, to commit no imprudence, to stay at home all day and to be careful of drafts; and Carlotta could not help, after he had gone, comparing this unusual and unexpected advice with the threats contained in the letter.

It was five o'clock when the post brought a second anonymous letter in the same hand as the first. It was short and said simply:

You have a bad cold. If you are wise, you will see that it is madness to try to sing tonight.

Carlotta sneered, shrugged her handsome shoulders and sang two or three notes to reassure herself.

Her friends were faithful to their promise. They were all at the Opera that night, but looked round in vain for the fierce conspirators whom they were instructed to suppress. The only unusual thing was the presence of M. Richard and M. Moncharmin in Box Five. Carlotta's friends thought that, perhaps, the managers had wind, on their side, of the proposed disturbance and that they had determined to be in the house, so as to stop it then and there; but this was unjustifiable supposition, as the reader knows. M. Richard and M. Moncharmin were thinking of nothing but their ghost.

"Vain! In vain do I call, through my vigil weary,

On creation and its Lord!

Never reply will break the silence dreary!

No sign! No single word!"

The famous baritone, Carolus Fonta, had hardly finished Doctor Faust's first appeal to the powers of darkness, when M. Firmin Richard, who was sitting in the ghost's own chair, the front chair on the right, leaned over to his partner and asked him chaffingly:

"Well, has the ghost whispered a word in your ear yet?"

"Wait, don't be in such a hurry," replied M. Armand Moncharmin, in the same gay tone. "The performance has only begun and you know that the ghost does not usually come until the middle of the first act."

The first act passed without incident, which did not surprise Carlotta's friends, because Margarita does not sing in this act. As for the managers, they looked at each other, when the curtain fell.

"That's one!" said Moncharmin.

"Yes, the ghost is late," said Firmin Richard.

"It's not a bad house," said Moncharmin, "for 'a house with a curse on it.'"

M. Richard smiled and pointed to a fat, rather vulgar woman, dressed in black, sitting in a stall in the middle of the auditorium with a man in a broadcloth frock-coat on either side of her.

"Who on earth are 'those?'" asked Moncharmin.

"'Those,' my dear fellow, are my concierge, her husband and her brother."

"Did you give them their tickets?"

"I did.... My concierge had never been to the Opera – this is the first time – and, as she is now going to come every night, I wanted her to have a good seat, before spending her time showing other people to theirs."

Moncharmin asked what he meant and

Richard answered that he had persuaded his concierge, in whom he had the greatest confidence, to come and take Mame Giry's place. Yes, he would like to see if, with that woman instead of the old lunatic, Box Five would continue to astonish the natives?

"By the way," said Moncharmin, "you know that Mother Giry is going to lodge a complaint against you."

"With whom? The ghost?"

The ghost! Moncharmin had almost forgotten him. However, that mysterious person did nothing to bring himself to the memory of the managers; and they were just saying so to each other for the second time, when the door of the box suddenly opened to admit the startled stage-manager.

"What's the matter?" they both asked, amazed at seeing him there at such a time.

"It seems there's a plot got up by Christine Daaé's friends against Carlotta. Carlotta's furious."

"What on earth... ?" said Richard, knitting

his brows.

But the curtain rose on the kermess scene and Richard made a sign to the stage-manager to go away. When the two were alone again, Moncharmin leaned over to Richard:

"Then Daaé has friends?" he asked.

"Yes, she has."

"Whom?"

Richard glanced across at a box on the grand tier containing no one but two men.

"The Comte de Chagny?"

"Yes, he spoke to me in her favor with such warmth that, if I had not known him to be Sorelli's friend..."

"Really? Really?" said Moncharmin. "And who is that pale young man beside him?"

"That's his brother, the viscount."

"He ought to be in his bed. He looks ill."

The stage rang with gay song:

"Red or white liquor,
Coarse or fine!
What can it matter,

So we have wine?"

Students, citizens, soldiers, girls and matrons whirled light-heartedly before the inn with the figure of Bacchus for a sign. Siebel made her entrance. Christine Daaé looked charming in her boy's clothes; and Carlotta's partisans expected to hear her greeted with an ovation which would have enlightened them as to the intentions of her friends. But nothing happened.

On the other hand, when Margarita crossed the stage and sang the only two lines allotted her in this second act:

"No, my lord, not a lady am I, nor yet a beauty,

And do not need an arm to help me on my way,"

Carlotta was received with enthusiastic applause. It was so unexpected and so uncalled for that those who knew nothing about the rumors looked at one another and asked what was happening. And this act also was finished without incident.

Then everybody said: "Of course, it will be during the next act."

Some, who seemed to be better informed than the rest, declared that the "row" would begin with the ballad of the King of Thule and rushed to the subscribers' entrance to warn Carlotta. The managers left the box during the entr'acte to find out more about the cabal of which the stage-manager had spoken; but they soon returned to their seats, shrugging their shoulders and treating the whole affair as silly.

The first thing they saw, on entering the box, was a box of English sweets on the little shelf of the ledge. Who had put it there? They asked the box-keepers, but none of them knew. Then they went back to the shelf and, next to the box of sweets, found an opera glass. They looked at each other. They had no inclination to laugh. All that Mme. Giry had told them returned to their memory… and then… and then… they seemed to feel a curious sort of draft around them.... They sat down in silence.

The scene represented Margarita's garden:

"Gentle flow'rs in the dew,
Be message from me..."

As she sang these first two lines, with her bunch of roses and lilacs in her hand, Christine, raising her head, saw the Vicomte de Chagny in his box; and, from that moment, her voice seemed less sure, less crystal-clear than usual. Something seemed to deaden and dull her singing....

"What a queer girl she is!" said one of Carlotta's friends in the stalls, almost aloud. "The other day she was divine; and tonight she's simply bleating. She has no experience, no training."

"Gentle flow'rs, lie ye there
And tell her from me..."

The viscount put his head under his hands and wept. The count, behind him, viciously gnawed his mustache, shrugged his shoulders and frowned. For him, usually so cold and correct, to betray his inner feelings like that, by outward signs, the count must be very angry. He was. He had seen his brother return from a rapid and mysterious journey in an alarming state of health. The explanation that followed was unsatisfactory and the count asked Christine Daaé for an appointment. She had the audacity to reply that she could not see either him or his brother....

"Would she but deign to hear me
And with one smile to cheer me..."

"The little baggage!" growled the count.

And he wondered what she wanted. What she was hoping for.... She was a virtuous girl, she was said to have no friend, no protector of any sort.... That angel from the North must be very artful!

Raoul, behind the curtain of his hands that veiled his boyish tears, thought only of the letter which he received on his return to Paris, where Christine, fleeing from Perros like a thief in the night, had arrived before him:

My Dear Little Playfellow:

You must have the courage not to see me again, not to speak of me again. If you love me just a little, do this for me, for me who will never forget you, my dear Raoul. My life depends upon it. Your life depends upon it.

Your Little Christine.

Thunders of applause. Carlotta made her entrance.

"I wish I could but know who was he

That addressed me,

If he was noble, or, at least, what his name is..."

When Margarita had finished singing the ballad of the King of Thule, she was loudly cheered and again when she came to the end of the jewel song:

"Ah, the joy of past compare

These jewels bright to wear!..."

Thenceforth, certain of herself, certain of her friends in the house, certain of her voice and her success, fearing nothing, Carlotta flung herself into her part without restraint of modesty.... She was no longer Margarita, she was Carmen. She was applauded all the more; and her début with Faust seemed about to bring her a new success, when suddenly... a terrible thing happened.

Faust had knelt on one knee:

"Let me gaze on the form below me,

While from yonder ether blue

Look how the star of eve, bright and tender, lingers o'er me,

To love thy beauty too!"

And Margarita replied:

"Oh, how strange!

Like a spell does the evening bind me!

And a deep languid charm

I feel without alarm

With its melody enwind me

And all my heart subdue."

At that moment, at that identical moment, the terrible thing happened.... Carlotta croaked like a toad:

"**Co-ack!**"

There was consternation on Carlotta's face and consternation on the faces of all the audience. The two managers in their box could not suppress an exclamation of horror. Everyone felt that the thing was not natural, that there was witchcraft behind it. That toad smelt of brimstone. Poor, wretched, despairing, crushed Carlotta!

The uproar in the house was indescribable. If the thing had happened to anyone but Carlotta, she would have been hooted. But everybody knew how perfect an instrument her voice was; and there was no display of anger, but only of horror and dismay, the sort of dismay which men would have felt if they had witnessed the catastrophe that broke the arms of the Venus de Milo.... And even then they would have seen... and understood...

But here that toad was incomprehensible! So much so that, after some seconds spent in asking herself if she had really heard that note, that sound, that infernal noise issue from her throat, she tried to persuade herself that it was not so, that she was the victim of an illusion, an illusion of the ear, and not of an act of treachery on the part of her voice....

Meanwhile, in Box Five, Moncharmin and Richard had turned very pale. This extraordinary and inexplicable incident filled them with a dread which was the more mysterious inasmuch as for some little while, they had fallen within the direct influence of the ghost. They had felt his breath. Moncharmin's hair stood on end. Richard wiped the perspiration from his forehead. Yes, the ghost was there, around them, behind them, beside them; they felt his presence without seeing him, they heard his breath, close, close, close to them!... They were sure that there were three people in the box.... They trembled.... They thought of running away.... They dared not.... They dared not make a movement or exchange a word that would have told the ghost that they knew that he was there!... What was going to happen?

This happened.

"**Co-ack!**"

Their joint exclamation of horror was heard all over the house. **They felt that they were smarting under the ghost's attacks.** Leaning over the ledge of their box, they stared at Carlotta as though they did not recognize her. That infernal girl must have given the signal for some catastrophe. Ah, they were waiting for the catastrophe! The ghost had told them it would come! The house had a curse upon it! The two managers gasped and panted under the weight of the catastrophe. Richard's stifled voice was heard calling to Carlotta:

"Well, go on!"

No, Carlotta did not go on.... Bravely, heroically, she started afresh on the fatal line at the end of which the toad had appeared.

An awful silence succeeded the uproar. Carlotta's voice alone once more filled the resounding house:

"I feel without alarm..."

The audience also felt, but not without alarm...

"I feel without alarm...

I feel without alarm – **co-ack!**

With its melody enwind me – **co-ack!**

And all my heart sub – **co-ack!**"

The toad also had started afresh!

The house broke into a wild tumult. The two managers collapsed in their chairs and dared not even turn round; they had not the strength; the ghost was chuckling behind their backs! And, at last, they distinctly heard his voice in their right ears, the impossible voice, the mouthless voice, saying:

"**She is singing tonight to bring the chandelier down!**"

With one accord, they raised their eyes to the ceiling and uttered a terrible cry. The chandelier, the immense mass of the chandelier was slipping down, coming toward them, at the call of that fiendish voice. Released from its hook, it plunged from the ceiling and came smashing into the middle of the stalls, amid a thousand shouts of terror. A wild rush for the doors followed.

The papers of the day state that there were numbers wounded and one killed. The chandelier had crashed down upon the head of the wretched woman who had come to the Opera for the first time in her life, the one whom M. Richard had appointed to succeed Mame Giry, the ghost's box-keeper, in her functions! She died on the spot and, the next morning, a newspaper appeared with this heading:

Two Hundred Kilos on the Head of a Concierge

That was her sole epitaph!

CHAPTER EIGHT

The Mysterious Brougham

THAT TRAGIC EVENING WAS bad for everybody. Carlotta fell ill. As for Christine Daaé, she disappeared after the performance. A fortnight elapsed during which she was seen neither at the Opera nor outside.

Raoul, of course, was the first to be astonished at the prima donna's absence. He wrote to her at Mme. Valérius' flat and received no reply. His grief increased and he ended by being seriously alarmed at never seeing her name on the program. **Faust** was played without her.

One afternoon he went to the managers' office to ask the reason of Christine's disappearance. He found them both looking extremely worried. Their own friends did not recognize them: they had lost all their gaiety and spirits. They were seen crossing the stage with hanging heads, careworn brows, pale cheeks, as though pursued by some abominable thought or a prey to some persistent sport of fate.

The fall of the chandelier had involved them in no little responsibility; but it was difficult to make them speak about it. The inquest had ended in a verdict of accidental death, caused by the wear and tear of the chains by which the chandelier was hung from the ceiling; but it was the duty of both the old and the new managers to have discovered this wear and tear and to have remedied it in time. And I feel bound to say that

MM. Richard and Moncharmin at this time appeared so changed, so absentminded, so mysterious, so incomprehensible that many of the subscribers thought that some event even more horrible than the fall of the chandelier must have affected their state of mind.

In their daily intercourse, they showed themselves very impatient, except with Mme. Giry, who had been reinstated in her functions. And their reception of the Vicomte de Chagny, when he came to ask about Christine, was anything but cordial. They merely told him that she was taking a holiday. He asked how long the holiday was for, and they replied curtly that it was for an unlimited period, as Mlle. Daaé had requested leave of absence for reasons of health.

“Then she is ill!” he cried. “What is the matter with her?”

“We don’t know.”

“Didn’t you send the doctor of the Opera to see her?”

"No, she did not ask for him; and, as we trust her, we took her word."

Raoul left the building a prey to the gloomiest thoughts. He resolved, come what might, to go and inquire of Mamma Valérius. He remembered the strong phrases in Christine's letter, forbidding him to make any attempt to see her. But what he had seen at Perros, what he had heard behind the dressing-room door, his conversation with Christine at the edge of the moor made him suspect some machination which, devilish though it might be, was none the less human. The girl's highly strung imagination, her affectionate and credulous mind, the primitive education which had surrounded her childhood with a circle of legends, the constant brooding over her dead father and, above all, the state of sublime ecstasy into which music threw her from the moment that this art was made manifest to her in certain exceptional conditions, as in the churchyard at Perros; all this seemed to him to constitute a moral ground only too favorable for the malevolent designs of some mysterious and unscrupulous person. Of whom was Christine Daaé the victim? This was the very reasonable question which Raoul put to himself as he hurried off to Mamma Valérius.

He trembled as he rang at a little flat in the Rue Notre-Dame-des-Victoires. The door was opened by the maid whom he had seen coming out of Christine's dressing-room one evening. He asked if he could speak to Mme. Valérius. He was told that she was ill in bed and was not receiving visitors.

"Take in my card, please," he said.

The maid soon returned and showed him into a small and scantily furnished drawing-room, in which portraits of Professor Valérius and old Daaé hung on opposite walls.

"Madame begs **monsieur le vicomte** to excuse her," said the servant. "She can only see him in her bedroom, because she can no longer stand on her poor legs."

Five minutes later, Raoul was ushered into

an ill-lit room where he at once recognized the good, kind face of Christine's benefactress in the semidarkness of an alcove. Mamma Valérius' hair was now quite white, but her eyes had grown no older; never, on the contrary, had their expression been so bright, so pure, so childlike.

"M. de Chagny!" she cried gaily, putting out both her hands to her visitor. "Ah, it's Heaven that sends you here!... We can talk of **her**."

This last sentence sounded very gloomily in the young man's ears. He at once asked:

"Madame... where is Christine?"

And the old lady replied calmly:

"She is with her good genius!"

"What good genius?" exclaimed poor Raoul.

"Why, the Angel of Music!"

The viscount dropped into a chair. Really? Christine was with the Angel of Music? And there lay Mamma Valérius in bed, smiling to him and putting her finger to her lips, to warn him to be silent! And she added:

"You must not tell anybody!"

"You can rely on me," said Raoul.

He hardly knew what he was saying, for his ideas about Christine, already greatly confused, were becoming more and more entangled; and it seemed as if everything was beginning to turn around him, around the room, around that extraordinary good lady with the white hair and forget-me-not eyes.

"I know! I know I can!" she said, with a happy laugh. "But why don't you come near me, as you used to do when you were a little boy? Give me your hands, as when you brought me the story of little Lotte, which Daddy Daaé had told you. I am very fond of you, M. Raoul, you know. And so is Christine too!"

"She is fond of me!" sighed the young man. He found a difficulty in collecting his thoughts and bringing them to bear on Mamma Valérius' "good genius," on the Angel of Music of whom Christine had spoken to him so strangely, on the death's head which he had seen in a sort of nightmare on the high altar at Perros and also on the Opera ghost, whose fame had come to his ears one evening when he was standing behind the scenes, within hearing of a group of scene-shifters who were repeating the ghastly description which the hanged man, Joseph Buquet, had given of the ghost before his mysterious death.

He asked in a low voice: "What makes you think that Christine is fond of me, madame?"

"She used to speak of you every day."

"Really?... And what did she tell you?"

"She told me that you had made her a proposal!"

And the good old lady began laughing wholeheartedly. Raoul sprang from his chair, flushing to the temples, suffering agonies.

"What's this? Where are you going?... Sit down again at once, will you?... Do you think I will let you go like that?... If you're angry with me for laughing, I beg your pardon.... After all, what has happened isn't your fault.... Didn't you know?... Did you think that Christine was free?..."

"Is Christine engaged to be married?" the wretched Raoul asked, in a choking voice.

"Why no! Why no!... You know as well as I do that Christine couldn't marry, even if she wanted to!..."

"But I don't know anything about it!... And why can't Christine marry?"

"Because of the Angel of Music, of course!..."

"I don't follow..."

"Yes, he forbids her to!..."

"He forbids her!... The Angel of Music forbids her to marry!..."

"Oh, he forbids her... without forbidding her. It's like this: he tells her that, if she got married, she would never hear him again. That's all!... And that he would go away forever!... So, you understand, she can't let the Angel of Music go. It's quite natural."

"Yes, yes," echoed Raoul submissively,

"it's quite natural."

"Besides, I thought Christine had told you all that, when she met you at Perros, where she went with her good genius."

"Oh, she went to Perros with her good genius, did she?"

"That is to say, he arranged to meet her down there, in Perros churchyard, at Daaé's grave. He promised to play her 'The Resurrection of Lazarus' on her father's violin!"

Raoul de Chagny rose and, with a very authoritative air, pronounced these peremptory words:

"Madame, you will have the goodness to tell me where that genius lives."

The old lady did not seem surprised at this indiscreet command. She raised her eyes and said:

"In Heaven!"

Such simplicity baffled him. He did not know what to say in the presence of this candid and perfect faith in a genius who came down nightly from Heaven to haunt the dressing-rooms at the Opera.

He now realized the possible state of mind of a girl brought up between a superstitious fiddler and a visionary old lady and he shuddered when he thought of the consequences of it all.

"Is Christine still a good girl?" he asked suddenly, in spite of himself.

"I swear it, as I hope to be saved!" exclaimed the old woman, who, this time, seemed to be incensed. "And, if you doubt it, sir, I don't know what you are here for!"

Raoul tore at his gloves.

"How long has she known this 'genius?'"

"About three months.... Yes, it's quite three months since he began to give her lessons."

The viscount threw up his arms with a gesture of despair.

"The genius gives her lessons!... And where, pray?"

"Now that she has gone away with him, I

can't say; but, up to a fortnight ago, it was in Christine's dressing-room. It would be impossible in this little flat. The whole house would hear them. Whereas, at the Opera, at eight o'clock in the morning, there is no one about, do you see!"

"Yes, I see! I see!" cried the viscount.

And he hurriedly took leave of Mme. Valérius, who asked herself if the young nobleman was not a little off his head.

He walked home to his brother's house in a pitiful state. He could have struck himself, banged his head against the walls! To think that he had believed in her innocence, in her purity! The Angel of Music! He knew him now! He saw him! It was beyond a doubt some unspeakable tenor, a good-looking jackanapes, who mouthed and simpered as he sang! He thought himself as absurd and as wretched as could be. Oh, what a miserable, little, insignificant, silly young man was M. le Vicomte de Chagny! thought Raoul furiously. And she, what a bold and damnable sly creature!

His brother was waiting for him and Raoul fell into his arms, like a child. The count consoled him, without asking for explanations; and Raoul would certainly have long hesitated before telling him the story of the Angel of Music. His brother suggested taking him out to dinner. Overcome as he was with despair, Raoul would probably have refused any invitation that evening, if the count had not, as an inducement, told him that the lady of his thoughts had been seen, the night before, in company of the other sex in the Bois. At first, the viscount refused to believe; but he received such exact details that he ceased protesting. She had been seen, it appeared, driving in a brougham, with the window down. She seemed to be slowly taking in the icy night air. There was a glorious moon shining. She was recognized beyond a doubt. As for her companion, only his shadowy outline was distinguished leaning back in the dark.

The carriage was going at a walking pace in a lonely drive behind the grand stand at Longchamp.

Raoul dressed in frantic haste, prepared to forget his distress by flinging himself, as people say, into "the vortex of pleasure." Alas, he was a very sorry guest and, leaving his brother early, found himself, by ten o'clock in the evening, in a cab, behind the Longchamp racecourse.

It was bitterly cold. The road seemed deserted and very bright under the moonlight. He told the driver to wait for him patiently at the corner of a near turning and, hiding himself as well as he could, stood stamping his feet to keep warm. He had been indulging in this healthy exercise for half an hour or so, when a carriage turned the corner of the road and came quietly in his direction, at a walking pace.

As it approached, he saw that a woman was leaning her head from the window. And, suddenly, the moon shed a pale gleam over her features.

"Christine!"

The sacred name of his love had sprung from his heart and his lips. He could not keep it back.... He would have given anything to withdraw it, for that name, proclaimed in the stillness of the night, had acted as though it were the preconcerted signal for a furious rush on the part of the whole turnout, which dashed past him before he could put into execution his plan of leaping at the horses' heads. The carriage window had been closed and the girl's face had disappeared. And the brougham, behind which he was now running, was no more than a black spot on the white road.

He called out again: "Christine!"

No reply. And he stopped in the midst of the silence.

With a lackluster eye, he stared down that cold, desolate road and into the pale, dead night. Nothing was colder than his heart, nothing half so dead: he had loved an angel and now he despised a woman!

Raoul, how that little fairy of the North has trifled with you! Was it really, was it really necessary to have so fresh and young a face, a forehead so shy and always ready to cover itself with the pink blush of modesty in order to pass in the lonely night, in a carriage and pair, accompanied by a mysterious lover? Surely there should be some limit to hypocrisy and lying!...

She had passed without answering his cry.... And he was thinking of dying; and he was twenty years old!...

His valet found him in the morning sitting on his bed. He had not undressed and the servant feared, at the sight of his face, that some disaster had occurred. Raoul snatched his letters from the man's hands. He had recognized Christine's paper and handwriting. She said:

Dear:

Go to the masked ball at the Opera on the night after tomorrow. At twelve o'clock, be

in the little room behind the chimney-place of the big crush-room. Stand near the door that leads to the Rotunda. Don't mention this appointment to anyone on earth. Wear a white domino and be carefully masked. As you love me, do not let yourself be recognized.
Christine.

CHAPTER NINE

At the Masked Ball

THE ENVELOPE WAS COVERED with mud and unstamped. It bore the words "To be handed to M. le Vicomte Raoul de Chagny," with the address in pencil. It must have been flung out in the hope that a passerby would pick up the note and deliver it, which was what happened. The note had been picked up on the pavement of the Place de l'Opera.

Raoul read it over again with fevered eyes.

No more was needed to revive his hope. The somber picture which he had for a moment imagined of a Christine forgetting her duty to herself made way for his original conception of an unfortunate, innocent child, the victim of imprudence and exaggerated sensibility. To what extent, at this time, was she really a victim? Whose prisoner was she? Into what whirlpool had she been dragged? He asked himself these questions with a cruel anguish; but even this pain seemed endurable beside the frenzy into which he was thrown at the thought of a lying and deceitful Christine. What had happened? What influence had she undergone? What monster had carried her off and by what means?…

By what means indeed but that of music? He knew Christine's story. After her father's death, she acquired a distaste of everything in life, including her art. She went through the **conservatoire** like a poor soulless singing-machine. And, suddenly, she awoke as though through the intervention of a god. The Angel of Music appeared upon the scene! She sang Margarita in **Faust** and triumphed!...

The Angel of Music!... For three months the Angel of Music had been giving Christine lessons.... Ah, he was a punctual singing-master!... And now he was taking her for drives in the Bois!...

Raoul's fingers clutched at his flesh, above his jealous heart. In his inexperience, he now asked himself with terror what game the girl was playing? Up to what point could an opera-singer make a fool of a good-natured young man, quite new to love? O misery!...

Thus did Raoul's thoughts fly from one extreme to the other. He no longer knew whether to pity Christine or to curse her; and he pitied and cursed her turn and turn about. At all events, he bought a white domino.

The hour of the appointment came at last. With his face in a mask trimmed with long, thick lace, looking like a pierrot in his white wrap, the viscount thought himself very ridiculous. Men of the world do not go to the Opera ball in fancy-dress! It was absurd. One thought, however, consoled the viscount: he would certainly never be recognized!

This ball was an exceptional affair, given some time before Shrovetide, in honor of the anniversary of the birth of a famous draftsman; and it was expected to be much gayer, noisier, more Bohemian than the ordinary masked ball. Numbers of artists had arranged to go, accompanied by a whole cohort of models and pupils, who, by midnight, began to create a tremendous din. Raoul climbed the grand staircase at five minutes to twelve, did not linger to look at the motley dresses displayed all the way up the marble steps, one of the richest settings in the world, allowed no facetious mask to draw him into a war of wits, replied to no jests and shook off the bold familiarity of a number of couples who had already become a trifle too gay. Crossing the big crush-room and escaping from a mad whirl of dancers in which he was caught for a moment, he at last entered the room mentioned in Christine's letter. He found it crammed; for this small space was the point where all those who were going to supper in the Rotunda crossed those who were returning from taking a glass of champagne. The fun, here, waxed fast and furious.

Raoul leaned against a doorpost and waited. He did not wait long. A black domino passed and gave a quick squeeze to the tips of his fingers. He understood that it was she and followed her:

"Is that you, Christine?" he asked, between his teeth.

The black domino turned round promptly and raised her finger to her lips, no doubt to warn him not to mention her name again. Raoul continued to follow her in silence.

He was afraid of losing her, after meeting

her again in such strange circumstances. His grudge against her was gone. He no longer doubted that she had "nothing to reproach herself with," however peculiar and inexplicable her conduct might seem. He was ready to make any display of clemency, forgiveness or cowardice. He was in love. And, no doubt, he would soon receive a very natural explanation of her curious absence.

The black domino turned back from time to time to see if the white domino was still following.

As Raoul once more passed through the great crush-room, this time in the wake of his guide, he could not help noticing a group crowding round a person whose disguise, eccentric air and gruesome appearance were causing a sensation. It was a man dressed all in scarlet, with a huge hat and feathers on the top of a wonderful death's head. From his shoulders hung an immense red-velvet cloak, which trailed along the floor like a king's train; and on this cloak was embroidered, in gold letters, which everyone read and repeated aloud, "Don't touch me! I am Red Death stalking abroad!"

Then one, greatly daring, did try to touch him... but a skeleton hand shot out of a crimson sleeve and violently seized the rash one's wrist; and he, feeling the clutch of the knucklebones, the furious grasp of Death, uttered a cry of pain and terror. When Red Death released him at last, he ran away like a very madman, pursued by the jeers of the bystanders.

It was at this moment that Raoul passed in front of the funereal masquerader, who had just happened to turn in his direction. And he nearly exclaimed:

"The death's head of Perros-Guirec!"

He had recognized him!... He wanted to dart forward, forgetting Christine; but the black domino, who also seemed a prey to some strange excitement, caught him by the arm and dragged him from the crush-room, far from the mad crowd through which Red Death was stalking....

The black domino kept on turning back and, apparently, on two occasions saw something that startled her, for she hurried her pace and Raoul's as though they were being pursued.

They went up two floors. Here, the stairs and corridors were almost deserted. The black domino opened the door of a private box and beckoned to the white domino to follow her. Then Christine, whom he recognized by the sound of her voice, closed the door behind them and warned him, in a whisper, to remain at the back of the box and on no account to show himself. Raoul took off his mask. Christine kept hers on. And, when Raoul was about to ask her to remove it, he was surprised to see her put her ear to the partition and listen eagerly for a sound outside. Then she opened the door ajar, looked out into the corridor and, in a low voice, said:

"He must have gone up higher." Suddenly

she exclaimed: “He is coming down again!”

She tried to close the door, but Raoul prevented her; for he had seen, on the top step of the staircase that led to the floor above, **a red foot**, followed by another… and slowly, majestically, the whole scarlet dress of Red Death met his eyes. And he once more saw the death’s head of Perros-Guirec.

“It’s he!” he exclaimed. “This time, he shall not escape me!…”

But Christine had slammed the door at the moment when Raoul was on the point of rushing out. He tried to push her aside.

“Whom do you mean by ‘he’?” she asked, in a changed voice. “Who shall not escape you?”

Raoul tried to overcome the girl’s resistance by force, but she repelled him with a strength which he would not have suspected in her. He understood, or thought he understood, and at once lost his temper.

“Who?” he repeated angrily. “Why, he, the

man who hides behind that hideous mask of death!... The evil genius of the churchyard at Perros!... Red Death!... In a word, madam, your friend... your Angel of Music!... But I shall snatch off his mask, as I shall snatch off my own; and, this time, we shall look each other in the face, he and I, with no veil and no lies between us; and I shall know whom you love and who loves you!"

He burst into a mad laugh, while Christine gave a disconsolate moan behind her velvet mask. With a tragic gesture, she flung out her two arms, which fixed a barrier of white flesh against the door.

"In the name of our love, Raoul, you shall not pass!..."

He stopped. What had she said?... In the name of their love?... Never before had she confessed that she loved him. And yet she had had opportunities enough.... Pooh, her only object was to gain a few seconds!... She wished to give the Red Death time to escape.... And, in accents of childish hatred, he said:

"You lie, madam, for you do not love me and you have never loved me! What a poor fellow I must be to let you mock and flout me as you have done! Why did you give me every reason for hope, at Perros… for honest hope, madam, for I am an honest man and I believed you to be an honest woman, when your only intention was to deceive me! Alas, you have deceived us all! You have taken a shameful advantage of the candid affection of your benefactress herself, who continues to believe in your sincerity while you go about the Opera ball with Red Death!… I despise you!…"

And he burst into tears. She allowed him to insult her. She thought of but one thing, to keep him from leaving the box.

"You will beg my pardon, one day, for all those ugly words, Raoul, and when you do I shall forgive you!"

He shook his head. "No, no, you have driven me mad! When I think that I had only one object in life: to give my name to an opera wench!"

"Raoul!... How can you?"

"I shall die of shame!"

"No, dear, live!" said Christine's grave and changed voice. "And... goodbye. Goodbye, Raoul..."

The boy stepped forward, staggering as he went. He risked one more sarcasm:

"Oh, you must let me come and applaud you from time to time!"

"I shall never sing again, Raoul!..."

"Really?" he replied, still more satirically. "So he is taking you off the stage: I congratulate you!... But we shall meet in the Bois, one of these evenings!"

"Not in the Bois nor anywhere, Raoul: you shall not see me again..."

"May one ask at least to what darkness you are returning?... For what hell are you leaving, mysterious lady... or for what paradise?"

"I came to tell you, dear, but I can't tell you

now… you would not believe me! You have lost faith in me, Raoul; it is finished!"

She spoke in such a despairing voice that the lad began to feel remorse for his cruelty.

"But look here!" he cried. "Can't you tell me what all this means!… You are free, there is no one to interfere with you…. You go about Paris…. You put on a domino to come to the ball…. Why do you not go home?… What have you been doing this past fortnight?… What is this tale about the Angel of Music, which you have been telling Mamma Valérius? Someone may have taken you in, played upon your innocence. I was a witness of it myself, at Perros… but you know what to believe now! You seem to me quite sensible, Christine. You know what you are doing…. And meanwhile Mamma Valérius lies waiting for you at home and appealing to your 'good genius!'… Explain yourself, Christine, I beg of you! Anyone might have been deceived as I was. What is this farce?"

Christine simply took off her mask and said:

"Dear, it is a tragedy!"

Raoul now saw her face and could not restrain an exclamation of surprise and terror. The fresh complexion of former days was gone. A mortal pallor covered those features, which he had known so charming and so gentle, and sorrow had furrowed them with pitiless lines and traced dark and unspeakably sad shadows under her eyes.

"My dearest! My dearest!" he moaned, holding out his arms. "You promised to forgive me…"

"Perhaps!… Some day, perhaps!" she said, resuming her mask; and she went away, forbidding him, with a gesture, to follow her.

He tried to disobey her; but she turned round and repeated her gesture of farewell with such authority that he dared not move a step.

He watched her till she was out of sight. Then he also went down among the crowd, hardly knowing what he was doing, with throbbing temples and an aching heart;

and, as he crossed the dancing-floor, he asked if anybody had seen Red Death. Yes, everyone had seen Red Death; but Raoul could not find him; and, at two o'clock in the morning, he turned down the passage, behind the scenes, that led to Christine Daaé's dressing-room.

His footsteps took him to that room where he had first known suffering. He tapped at the door. There was no answer. He entered, as he had entered when he looked everywhere for "the man's voice." The room was empty. A gas-jet was burning, turned down low. He saw some writing-paper on a little desk. He thought of writing to Christine, but he heard steps in the passage. He had only time to hide in the inner room, which was separated from the dressing-room by a curtain.

Christine entered, took off her mask with a weary movement and flung it on the table. She sighed and let her pretty head fall into her two hands. What was she thinking of? Of Raoul? No, for Raoul heard her murmur:

"Poor Erik!"

At first, he thought he must be mistaken. To begin with, he was persuaded that, if anyone was to be pitied, it was he, Raoul. It would have been quite natural if she had said, "Poor Raoul," after what had happened between them. But, shaking her head, she repeated: "Poor Erik!"

What had this Erik to do with Christine's sighs and why was she pitying Erik when Raoul was so unhappy?

Christine began to write, deliberately, calmly and so placidly that Raoul, who was still trembling from the effects of the tragedy that separated them, was painfully impressed.

"What coolness!" he said to himself.

She wrote on, filling two, three, four sheets. Suddenly, she raised her head and hid the sheets in her bodice.... She seemed to be listening.... Raoul also listened.... Whence came that strange sound, that distant rhythm?... A faint singing seemed to issue from the walls… yes, it was as though the walls themselves were singing!… The song became plainer… the words were now distinguishable… he heard a voice, a very beautiful, very soft, very captivating voice… but, for all its softness, it remained a male voice…. The voice came nearer and nearer… it came through the wall… it approached… and now the voice was **in the room**, in front of Christine. Christine rose and addressed the voice, as though speaking to someone:

"Here I am, Erik," she said. "I am ready. But you are late."

Raoul, peeping from behind the curtain, could not believe his eyes, which showed him nothing. Christine's face lit up. A smile of happiness appeared upon her bloodless lips, a smile like that of sick people when they receive the first hope of recovery.

The voice without a body went on singing; and certainly Raoul had never in his life heard anything more absolutely and heroically sweet, more gloriously insidious, more delicate, more powerful, in short, more irresistibly triumphant. He listened to it in a fever and he now began to understand how Christine Daaé was able to appear one evening, before the stupefied audience, with accents of a beauty hitherto unknown, of a superhuman exaltation, while doubtless still under the influence of the mysterious and invisible master.

The voice was singing the Wedding-night Song from **Romeo and Juliet**. Raoul saw Christine stretch out her arms to the voice as she had done, in Perros churchyard, to the invisible violin playing "The Resurrection of Lazarus." And nothing could describe the passion with which the voice sang:

"Fate links thee to me forever and a day!"

The strains went through Raoul's heart. Struggling against the charm that seemed to deprive him of all his will and all his energy and of almost all his lucidity at the moment when he needed them most, he succeeded in drawing back the curtain that hid him and he walked to where Christine stood. She herself was moving to the back of the room, the whole wall of which was occupied by a great mirror that reflected her image, but not his, for he was just behind her and entirely covered by her.

"Fate links thee to me forever and a day!"

Christine walked toward her image in the glass and the image came toward her. The two Christines – the real one and the reflection – ended by touching; and Raoul put out his arms to clasp the two in one embrace. But, by a sort of dazzling miracle that sent him staggering, Raoul was suddenly flung back, while an icy blast swept over his face; he saw, not two, but four, eight, twenty Christines spinning round him, laughing at him and fleeing so swiftly that he could not touch one of them. At last, everything stood still again; and he saw himself in the glass. But Christine had disappeared.

He rushed up to the glass. He struck at the

walls. Nobody! And meanwhile the room still echoed with a distant passionate singing:

"Fate links thee to me forever and a day!"

Which way, which way had Christine gone?… Which way would she return?…

Would she return? Alas, had she not declared to him that everything was finished? And was the voice not repeating:

"Fate links thee to me forever and a day!"

To me? To whom?

Then, worn out, beaten, empty-brained, he sat down on the chair which Christine had just left. Like her, he let his head fall into his hands. When he raised it, the tears were streaming down his young cheeks, real, heavy tears like those which jealous children shed, tears that wept for a sorrow which was in no way fanciful, but which is common to all the lovers on earth and which he expressed aloud:

"Who is this Erik?" he said.

CHAPTER TEN

Forget the Name of the Man's Voice

THE DAY AFTER CHRISTINE had vanished before his eyes in a sort of dazzlement that still made him doubt the evidence of his senses, M. le Vicomte de Chagny called to inquire at Mamma Valérius'. He came upon a charming picture. Christine herself was seated by the bedside of the old lady, who was sitting up against the pillows, knitting. The pink and white had returned to the young girl's cheeks. The dark rings round her eyes had disappeared. Raoul no longer recognized the tragic face of the day before. If the veil of melancholy over those adorable features had not still appeared to the young man as the last trace of the weird drama in whose toils that mysterious child was struggling, he could have believed that Christine was not its heroine at all.

She rose, without showing any emotion, and offered him her hand. But Raoul's stupefaction was so great that he stood there dumbfounded, without a gesture, without a word.

"Well, M. de Chagny," exclaimed Mamma Valérius, "don't you know our Christine? Her good genius has sent her back to us!"

"Mamma!" the girl broke in promptly, while a deep blush mantled to her eyes. "I thought, mamma, that there was to be no more question of that!… You know there is no such thing as the Angel of Music!"

"But, child, he gave you lessons for three months!"

"Mamma, I have promised to explain everything to you one of these days; and I hope to do so… but you have promised me, until that day, to be silent and to ask me no more questions whatever!"

"Provided that you promised never to leave me again! But have you promised that, Christine?"

"Mamma, all this can not interest M. de Chagny."

"On the contrary, mademoiselle," said the young man, in a voice which he tried to make firm and brave, but which still trembled, "anything that concerns you interests me to an extent which perhaps you will one day understand. I do not deny that my surprise equals my pleasure at finding you with your adopted mother and that, after what happened between us yesterday, after what you said and what I was able to guess, I hardly expected to see you here so soon. I should be the first to delight at your return, if you were not so bent on preserving a secrecy that may be fatal to you… and I have been your friend too long not to be alarmed, with Mme. Valérius, at a disastrous adventure which will remain dangerous so long as we have not unraveled its threads and of which you will certainly end by being the victim, Christine."

At these words, Mamma Valérius tossed about in her bed.

"What does this mean?" she cried. "Is Christine in danger?"

"Yes, madame," said Raoul courageously, notwithstanding the signs which Christine made to him.

"My God!" exclaimed the good, simple old woman, gasping for breath. "You must tell me everything, Christine! Why did you try to reassure me? And what danger is it, M. de Chagny?"

"An impostor is abusing her good faith."

"Is the Angel of Music an impostor?"

"She told you herself that there is no Angel of Music."

"But then what is it, in Heaven's name? You will be the death of me!"

"There is a terrible mystery around us, madame, around you, around Christine, a mystery much more to be feared than any number of ghosts or genii!"

Mamma Valérius turned a terrified face to Christine, who had already run to her adopted mother and was holding her in her arms.

"Don't believe him, mummy, don't believe him," she repeated.

"Then tell me that you will never leave me again," implored the widow.

Christine was silent and Raoul resumed.

"That is what you must promise, Christine. It is the only thing that can reassure your mother and me. We will undertake not to ask you a single question about the past, if you promise us to remain under our protection in future."

"That is an undertaking which I have not asked of you and a promise which I refuse to make you!" said the young girl haughtily. "I am mistress of my own actions, M. de Chagny: you have no right to control them, and I will beg you to desist henceforth. As to what I have done during the last fortnight, there is only one man in the world who has the right to demand an account of me: my husband! Well, I have no husband and I never mean to marry!"

She threw out her hands to emphasize her words and Raoul turned pale, not only because of the words which he had heard, but because he had caught sight of a plain gold ring on Christine's finger.

"You have no husband and yet you wear a wedding-ring."

He tried to seize her hand, but she swiftly drew it back.

"That's a present!" she said, blushing

once more and vainly striving to hide her embarrassment.

"Christine! As you have no husband, that ring can only have been given by one who hopes to make you his wife! Why deceive us further? Why torture me still more? That ring is a promise; and that promise has been accepted!"

"That's what I said!" exclaimed the old lady.

"And what did she answer, madame?"

"What I chose," said Christine, driven to exasperation. "Don't you think, monsieur, that this cross-examination has lasted long enough? As far as I am concerned…"

Raoul was afraid to let her finish her speech. He interrupted her:

"I beg your pardon for speaking as I did, mademoiselle. You know the good intentions that make me meddle, just now, in matters which, you no doubt think, have nothing to do with me. But allow me to tell you what I have seen – and I have seen more than you suspect, Christine – or what I thought I saw, for, to tell you the truth, I have sometimes been inclined to doubt the evidence of my eyes."

"Well, what did you see, sir, or think you saw?"

"I saw your ecstasy **at the sound of the voice**, Christine: the voice that came from the wall or the next room to yours... yes, **your ecstasy**! And that is what makes me alarmed on your behalf. You are under a very dangerous spell. And yet it seems that you are aware of the imposture, because you say today **that there is no Angel of Music**! In that case, Christine, why did you follow him that time? Why did you stand up, with radiant features, as though you were really hearing angels?... Ah, it is a very dangerous voice, Christine, for I myself, when I heard it, was so much fascinated by it that you vanished before my eyes without my seeing which way you passed! Christine, Christine, in the name of Heaven, in the name of your father who is in Heaven now and who loved you so dearly and who loved me too, Christine, tell us, tell your benefactress and me, to whom does that voice belong? If you do, we will save you in spite of yourself. Come, Christine, the name of the man! The name of the man who had the audacity to put a ring on your finger!"

"M. de Chagny," the girl declared coldly, "you shall never know!"

Thereupon, seeing the hostility with which her ward had addressed the viscount, Mamma Valérius suddenly took Christine's part.

"And, if she does love that man, **monsieur le vicomte**, even then it is no business of yours!"

"Alas, madame," Raoul humbly replied, unable to restrain his tears, "alas, I believe that Christine really does love him!... But it is not only that which drives me to despair; for what I am not certain of, madame, is that the man whom Christine loves is worthy of her love!"

"It is for me to be the judge of that, monsieur!" said Christine, looking Raoul angrily in the face.

"When a man," continued Raoul, "adopts such romantic methods to entice a young girl's affections…"

"The man must be either a villain, or the girl a fool: is that it?"

"Christine!"

"Raoul, why do you condemn a man whom you have never seen, whom no one knows and about whom you yourself know nothing?"

"Yes, Christine…. Yes…. I at least know the name that you thought to keep from me forever…. The name of your Angel of Music, mademoiselle, is Erik!"

Christine at once betrayed herself. She turned as white as a sheet and stammered:

"Who told you?"

"You yourself!"

"How do you mean?"

"By pitying him the other night, the night of the masked ball. When you went to your dressing-room, did you not say, ‘Poor Erik?’ Well, Christine, there was a poor Raoul who overheard you.”

“This is the second time that you have listened behind the door, M. de Chagny!”

“I was not behind the door… I was in the dressing-room, in the inner room, mademoiselle.”

“Oh, unhappy man!” moaned the girl, showing every sign of unspeakable terror. “Unhappy man! Do you want to be killed?”

“Perhaps.”

Raoul uttered this “perhaps” with so much love and despair in his voice that Christine could not keep back a sob. She took his hands and looked at him with all the pure affection of which she was capable:

“Raoul,” she said, “forget **the man’s voice** and do not even remember its name…. You must never try to fathom the mystery of **the man’s voice**.”

“Is the mystery so very terrible?”

“There is no more awful mystery on this

earth. Swear to me that you will make no attempt to find out," she insisted. "Swear to me that you will never come to my dressing-room, unless I send for you."

"Then you promise to send for me sometimes, Christine?"

"I promise."

"When?"

"Tomorrow."

"Then I swear to do as you ask."

He kissed her hands and went away, cursing Erik and resolving to be patient.

CHAPTER ELEVEN

Above the Trap-Doors

THE NEXT DAY, he saw her at the Opera. She was still wearing the plain gold ring. She was gentle and kind to him. She talked to him of the plans which he was forming, of his future, of his career.

He told her that the date of the Polar expedition had been put forward and that he would leave France in three weeks, or a month at latest. She suggested, almost gaily, that he must look upon the voyage with delight, as a stage toward his coming fame. And when he replied that fame without love was no attraction in his eyes, she treated him as a child whose sorrows were only short-lived.

"How can you speak so lightly of such serious things?" he asked. "Perhaps we shall never see each other again! I may die during that expedition."

"Or I," she said simply.

She no longer smiled or jested. She seemed to be thinking of some new thing that had entered her mind for the first time. Her eyes were all aglow with it.

"What are you thinking of, Christine?"

"I am thinking that we shall not see each other again..."

"And does that make you so radiant?"

"And that, in a month, we shall have to say goodbye forever!"

"Unless, Christine, we pledge our faith and wait for each other forever."

She put her hand on his mouth.

"Hush, Raoul!... You know there is no question of that... And we shall never be married: that is understood!"

She seemed suddenly almost unable to contain an overpowering gaiety. She clapped her hands with childish glee. Raoul stared at her in amazement.

"But... but," she continued, holding out her two hands to Raoul, or rather giving them to him, as though she had suddenly resolved to make him a present of them, "but if we can not be married, we can... we can be engaged! Nobody will know but ourselves, Raoul. There have been plenty of secret marriages: why not a secret engagement?... We are engaged, dear, for a month! In a month, you will go away, and I can be happy at the thought of that month all my life long!"

She was enchanted with her inspiration. Then she became serious again.

"This," she said, "**is a happiness that will harm no one**."

Raoul jumped at the idea. He bowed to Christine and said:

"Mademoiselle, I have the honor to ask for your hand."

"Why, you have both of them already, my dear betrothed!... Oh, Raoul, how happy we shall be!... We must play at being engaged all day long."

It was the prettiest game in the world and they enjoyed it like the children that they were. Oh, the wonderful speeches they made to each other and the eternal vows they exchanged! They played at hearts as other children might play at ball; only, as it was really their two hearts that they flung to and fro, they had to be very, very handy to catch them, each time, without hurting them.

One day, about a week after the game began, Raoul's heart was badly hurt and he stopped playing and uttered these wild words:

"I shan't go to the North Pole!"

Christine, who, in her innocence, had not dreamed of such a possibility, suddenly discovered the danger of the game and reproached herself bitterly. She did not say a word in reply to Raoul's remark and went straight home.

This happened in the afternoon, in the singer's dressing-room, where they met every day and where they amused themselves by dining on three biscuits, two glasses of port and a bunch of violets. In the evening, she did not sing; and he did not receive his usual letter, though they had arranged to write to each other daily during that month. The next morning, he ran off to Mamma Valérius, who told him that Christine had gone away for two days. She had left at five o'clock the day before.

Raoul was distracted. He hated Mamma Valérius for giving him such news as that with such stupefying calmness. He tried to sound her, but the old lady obviously knew nothing.

Christine returned on the following day. She returned in triumph. She renewed her extraordinary success of the gala performance. Since the adventure of the "toad," Carlotta had not been able to appear on the stage. The terror of a fresh "**co-ack**" filled her heart and deprived her of all her power of singing; and the theater that had witnessed her incomprehensible disgrace had become odious to her. She contrived to cancel her contract. Daaé was offered the vacant place for the time. She received thunders of applause in the **Juive**.

The viscount, who, of course, was present, was the only one to suffer on hearing the thousand echoes of this fresh triumph; for Christine still wore her plain gold ring. A distant voice whispered in the young man's ear:

"She is wearing the ring again tonight; and you did not give it to her. She gave her soul again tonight and did not give it to you.... If she will not tell you what she has been doing the past two days… you must go and ask Erik!"

He ran behind the scenes and placed himself in her way. She saw him for her eyes were looking for him. She said:

"Quick! Quick!… Come!"

And she dragged him to her dressing-room.

Raoul at once threw himself on his knees before her. He swore to her that he would go and he entreated her never again to withhold a single hour of the ideal happiness which she had promised him. She let her tears flow. They kissed like a despairing brother and sister who have been smitten with a common loss and who meet to mourn a dead parent.

Suddenly, she snatched herself from the young man's soft and timid embrace, seemed to listen to something, and, with a quick gesture, pointed to the door. When he was on the threshold, she said, in so low a voice that the viscount guessed rather than heard her words:

"Tomorrow, my dear betrothed! And be happy, Raoul: I sang for you tonight!"

He returned the next day. But those two days of absence had broken the charm of their delightful make-believe. They looked at each other, in the dressing-room, with their sad eyes, without exchanging a word. Raoul had to restrain himself not to cry out:

"I am jealous! I am jealous! I am jealous!"

But she heard him all the same. Then she said:

"Come for a walk, dear. The air will do you good."

Raoul thought that she would propose a stroll in the country, far from that building which he detested as a prison whose jailer he could feel walking within the walls... the jailer Erik.... But she took him to the stage and made him sit on the wooden curb of a well, in the doubtful peace and coolness of a first scene set for the evening's performance.

On another day, she wandered with him,

hand in hand, along the deserted paths of a garden whose creepers had been cut out by a decorator's skilful hands. It was as though the real sky, the real flowers, the real earth were forbidden her for all time and she condemned to breathe no other air than that of the theater. An occasional fireman passed, watching over their melancholy idyll from afar. And she would drag him up above the clouds, in the magnificent disorder of the grid, where she loved to make him giddy by running in front of him along the frail bridges, among the thousands of ropes fastened to the pulleys, the windlasses, the rollers, in the midst of a regular forest of yards and masts. If he hesitated, she said, with an adorable pout of her lips:

"You, a sailor!"

And then they returned to **terra firma**, that is to say, to some passage that led them to the little girls' dancing-school, where brats between six and ten were practising their steps, in the hope of becoming great dancers one day, "covered with diamonds...." Meanwhile, Christine gave them sweets instead.

She took him to the wardrobe and property-rooms, took him all over her empire, which was artificial, but immense, covering seventeen stories from the ground-floor to the roof and inhabited by an army of subjects. She moved among them like a popular queen, encouraging them in their labors, sitting down in the workshops, giving words of advice to the workmen whose hands hesitated to cut into the rich stuffs that were to clothe heroes. There were inhabitants of that country who practised every trade. There were cobblers, there were goldsmiths. All had learned to know her and to love her, for she always interested herself in all their troubles and all their little hobbies.

She knew unsuspected corners that were secretly occupied by little old couples. She knocked at their door and introduced Raoul to them as a Prince Charming who had asked for her hand; and the two of them, sitting on some worm-eaten "property," would listen to the legends of the Opera, even as, in their childhood, they had listened to the old Breton tales. Those old people remembered nothing outside the Opera. They had lived there for years without number. Past managements had forgotten them; palace revolutions had taken no notice of them; the history of France had run its course unknown to them; and nobody recollected their existence.

The precious days sped in this way; and Raoul and Christine, by affecting excessive interest in outside matters, strove awkwardly to hide from each other the one thought of their hearts. One fact was certain, that Christine, who until then had shown herself the stronger of the two, became suddenly inexpressibly nervous. When on their expeditions, she would start running without reason or else suddenly stop; and her hand, turning ice-cold in a moment, would hold the young man back. Sometimes her eyes seemed to pursue imaginary shadows. She cried, "This way," and "This way," and "This way," laughing a breathless laugh that often ended in tears. Then Raoul tried to speak, to question her, in spite of his promises. But, even before he had worded his question, she answered feverishly:

"Nothing… I swear it is nothing."

Once, when they were passing before an open trapdoor on the stage, Raoul stopped over the dark cavity.

"You have shown me over the upper part of your empire, Christine, but there are strange stories told of the lower part. Shall we go down?"

She caught him in her arms, as though she feared to see him disappear down the black hole, and, in a trembling voice, whispered:

"Never!… I will not have you go there!… Besides, it's not mine… **everything that is underground belongs to him!**"

Raoul looked her in the eyes and said

roughly:

"So he lives down there, does he?"

"I never said so.... Who told you a thing like that? Come away! I sometimes wonder if you are quite sane, Raoul.... You always take things in such an impossible way.... Come along! Come!"

And she literally dragged him away, for he was obstinate and wanted to remain by the trap-door; that hole attracted him.

Suddenly, the trap-door was closed and so quickly that they did not even see the hand that worked it; and they remained quite dazed.

"Perhaps **he** was there," Raoul said, at last.

She shrugged her shoulders, but did not seem easy.

"No, no, it was the 'trap-door-shutters.' They must do something, you know.... They open and shut the trap-doors without any particular reason.... It's like the 'door-shutters:' they must spend their time somehow."

"But suppose it were **he**, Christine?"

"No, no! He has shut himself up, he is working."

"Oh, really! He's working, is he?"

"Yes, he can't open and shut the trap-doors and work at the same time." She shivered.

"What is he working at?"

"Oh, something terrible!... But it's all the better for us.... When he's working at that, he sees nothing; he does not eat, drink, or breathe for days and nights at a time... he becomes a living dead man and has no time to amuse himself with the trap-doors."

She shivered again. She was still holding him in her arms. Then she sighed and said, in her turn:

"Suppose it were **he**!"

"Are you afraid of him?"

"No, no, of course not," she said.

For all that, on the next day and the following days, Christine was careful to avoid the trap-doors. Her agitation only increased as the hours passed. At last, one afternoon, she arrived very late, with her face so desperately pale and her eyes so desperately red, that Raoul resolved to go to all lengths, including that which he foreshadowed when he blurted out that he would not go on the North Pole expedition unless she first told him the secret of the man's voice.

"Hush! Hush, in Heaven's name! Suppose **he** heard you, you unfortunate Raoul!"

And Christine's eyes stared wildly at everything around her.

"I will remove you from his power, Christine, I swear it. And you shall not think of him any more."

"Is it possible?"

She allowed herself this doubt, which was an encouragement, while dragging the young man up to the topmost floor of the theater, far, very far from the trap-doors.

"I shall hide you in some unknown corner of the world, where **he** can not come to look for you. You will be safe; and then I shall go away... as you have sworn never to marry."

Christine seized Raoul's hands and squeezed them with incredible rapture. But, suddenly becoming alarmed again, she turned away her head.

"Higher!" was all she said. "Higher still!"

And she dragged him up toward the summit.

He had a difficulty in following her. They were soon under the very roof, in the maze of timber-work. They slipped through the buttresses, the rafters, the joists; they ran from beam to beam as they might have run from tree to tree in a forest.

And, despite the care which she took to look behind her at every moment, she failed to see a shadow which followed her like her own shadow, which stopped when she stopped, which started again when she did and which made no more noise than a well-conducted shadow should. As for Raoul, he saw nothing either; for, when he had Christine in front of him, nothing interested him that happened behind.

CHAPTER TWELVE

Apollo's Lyre

IN THIS WAY, they reached the roof. Christine tripped over it as lightly as a swallow. Their eyes swept the empty space between the three domes and the triangular pediment. She breathed freely over Paris, the whole valley of which was seen at work below. She called Raoul to come quite close to her and they walked side by side along the zinc streets, in the leaden avenues;

they looked at their twin shapes in the huge tanks, full of stagnant water, where, in the hot weather, the little boys of the ballet, a score or so, learn to swim and dive.

The shadow had followed behind them, clinging to their steps; and the two children little suspected its presence when they at last sat down, trustingly, under the mighty protection of Apollo, who, with a great bronze gesture, lifted his huge lyre to the heart of a crimson sky.

It was a gorgeous spring evening. Clouds, which had just received their gossamer robe of gold and purple from the setting sun, drifted slowly by; and Christine said to Raoul:

"Soon we shall go farther and faster than the clouds, to the end of the world, and then you will leave me, Raoul. But, if, when the moment comes for you to take me away, I refuse to go with you – well you must carry me off by force!"

"Are you afraid that you will change your

mind, Christine?"

"I don't know," she said, shaking her head in an odd fashion. "He is a demon!" And she shivered and nestled in his arms with a moan. "I am afraid now of going back to live with him… in the ground!"

"What compels you to go back, Christine?"

"If I do not go back to him, terrible misfortunes may happen!… But I can't do it, I can't do it!… I know one ought to be sorry for people who live underground.… But he is too horrible! And yet the time is at hand; I have only a day left; and, if I do not go, he will come and fetch me with his voice. And he will drag me with him, underground, and go on his knees before me, with his death's head. And he will tell me that he loves me! And he will cry! Oh, those tears, Raoul, those tears in the two black eye-sockets of the death's head! I can not see those tears flow again!"

She wrung her hands in anguish, while Raoul pressed her to his heart.

"No, no, you shall never again hear him tell you that he loves you! You shall not see his tears! Let us fly, Christine, let us fly at once!"

And he tried to drag her away, then and there. But she stopped him.

"No, no," she said, shaking her head sadly. "Not now!... It would be too cruel... let him hear me sing tomorrow evening... and then we will go away. You must come and fetch me in my dressing-room at midnight exactly. He will then be waiting for me in the dining-room by the lake... we shall be free and you shall take me away.... You must promise me that, Raoul, even if I refuse; for I feel that, if I go back this time, I shall perhaps never return."

And she gave a sigh to which it seemed to her that another sigh, behind her, replied.

"Didn't you hear?"

Her teeth chattered.

"No," said Raoul, "I heard nothing."

"It is too terrible," she confessed, "to be always trembling like this!... And yet we run no danger here; we are at home, in the sky, in the open air, in the light. The sun is flaming; and night-birds can not bear to look at the sun. I have never seen **him** by daylight... it must be awful!... Oh, the first time I saw him!... I thought that he was going to die."

"Why?" asked Raoul, really frightened at the aspect which this strange confidence was taking.

"**Because I had seen him!**"

This time, Raoul and Christine turned round at the same time:

"There is someone in pain," said Raoul. "Perhaps someone has been hurt. Did you hear?"

"I can't say," Christine confessed. "Even when he is not there, my ears are full of his sighs. Still, if you heard..."

They stood up and looked around them. They were quite alone on the immense lead roof. They sat down again and Raoul said:

"Tell me how you saw him first."

"I had heard him for three months without

seeing him. The first time I heard it, I thought, as you did, that that adorable voice was singing in another room. I went out and looked everywhere; but, as you know, Raoul, my dressing-room is very much by itself; and I could not find the voice outside my room, whereas it went on steadily inside. And it not only sang, but it spoke to me and answered my questions, like a real man's voice, with this difference, that it was as beautiful as the voice of an angel. I had never got the Angel of Music whom my poor father had promised to send me as soon as he was dead. I really think that Mamma Valérius was a little bit to blame. I told her about it; and she at once said, 'It must be the Angel; at any rate, you can do no harm by asking him.' I did so; and the man's voice replied that, yes, it was the Angel's voice, the voice which I was expecting and which my father had promised me. From that time onward, the voice and I became great friends. It asked leave to give me lessons every day. I agreed and never failed to keep the appointment which it gave me in my dressing-room. You have no idea, though you have heard the voice, of what those lessons were like."

"No, I have no idea," said Raoul. "What was your accompaniment?"

"We were accompanied by a music which I do not know: it was behind the wall and wonderfully accurate. The voice seemed to understand mine exactly, to know precisely where my father had left off teaching me. In a few weeks' time, I hardly knew myself when I sang. I was even frightened. I seemed to dread a sort of witchcraft behind it; but Mamma Valérius reassured me. She said that she knew I was much too simple a girl to give the devil a hold on me.... My progress, by the voice's own order, was kept a secret between the voice, Mamma Valérius and myself. It was a curious thing, but, outside the dressing-room, I sang with my ordinary, everyday voice and nobody noticed anything.

I did all that the voice asked. It said, 'Wait and see: we shall astonish Paris!' And I waited and lived on in a sort of ecstatic dream. It was then that I saw you for the first time one evening, in the house. I was so glad that I never thought of concealing my delight when I reached my dressing-room. Unfortunately, the voice was there before me and soon noticed, by my air, that something had happened. It asked what was the matter and I saw no reason for keeping our story secret or concealing the place which you filled in my heart. Then the voice was silent. I called to it, but it did not reply; I begged and entreated, but in vain. I was terrified lest it had gone for good. I wish to Heaven it had, dear!... That night, I went home in a desperate condition. I told Mamma Valérius, who said, 'Why, of course, the voice is jealous!' And that, dear, first revealed to me that I loved you."

Christine stopped and laid her head on Raoul's shoulder. They sat like that for a moment, in silence, and they did not see, did not perceive the movement, at a few steps from them, of the creeping shadow of two great black wings, a shadow that came along the roof so near, so near them that it could have stifled them by closing over them.

"The next day," Christine continued, with a sigh, "I went back to my dressing-room in a very pensive frame of mind. The voice was there, spoke to me with great sadness and told me plainly that, if I must bestow my heart on earth, there was nothing for the voice to do but to go back to Heaven. And it said this with such an accent of **human** sorrow that I ought then and there to have suspected and begun to believe that I was the victim of my deluded senses. But my faith in the voice, with which the memory of my father was so closely intermingled, remained undisturbed. I feared nothing so much as that I might never hear it again; I had thought about my love for you and realized all the useless danger of it; and I did not even know if you remembered me. Whatever happened, your position in society forbade me to contemplate the possibility of ever marrying you; and I swore to the voice that you were no more than a brother to me nor ever would be and that my heart was incapable of any earthly love. And that, dear, was why I refused to recognize or see you when I met you on the stage or in the passages. Meanwhile, the hours during which the voice taught me were spent in a divine frenzy, until, at last, the voice said to me, 'You can now, Christine Daaé, give to men a little of the music of Heaven.' I don't know how it was that Carlotta did not come to the theater that night nor why I was called upon to sing in her stead; but I sang with a rapture I had never known before and I felt for a moment as if my soul were leaving my body!"

"Oh, Christine," said Raoul, "my heart quivered that night at every accent of your voice. I saw the tears stream down your cheeks and I wept with you. How could you sing, sing like that while crying?"

"I felt myself fainting," said Christine, "I closed my eyes. When I opened them, you were by my side. But the voice was there also, Raoul! I was afraid for your sake and again I would not recognize you and began to laugh when you reminded me that you had picked up my scarf in the sea!... Alas, there is no deceiving the voice!... The voice recognized you and the voice was jealous!... It said that, if I did not love you, I would not avoid you, but treat you like any other old friend. It made me scene upon scene. At last, I said to the voice, 'That will do! I am going to Perros tomorrow, to pray on my father's grave, and I shall ask M. Raoul de Chagny to go with me.' 'Do as you please,' replied the voice, 'but I shall be at Perros too, for I am wherever you are, Christine; and, if you are still worthy of me, if you have not lied to me, I will play you "The Resurrection of Lazarus," on the stroke of midnight, on your father's tomb and on your father's violin.' That, dear, was how I came to write you the letter that brought you to Perros. How could I have been so beguiled? How was it, when I saw the personal, the selfish point of view of the voice, that I did not suspect some impostor? Alas, I was no longer mistress of myself: I had become his thing!"

"But, after all," cried Raoul, "you soon came to know the truth! Why did you not at once rid yourself of that abominable nightmare?"

"Know the truth, Raoul? Rid myself of that nightmare? But, my poor boy, I was not caught in the nightmare until the day when I learned the truth!... Pity me, Raoul, pity me!... You remember the terrible evening when Carlotta thought that she had been turned into a toad on the stage and when the house was suddenly plunged in darkness through the chandelier crashing to the floor? There were killed and wounded that night and the whole theater rang with terrified screams. My first thought was for you and the voice. I was at once easy, where you were concerned, for I had seen you in your brother's box and I knew that you were not in danger. But the voice had told me that it would be at the performance and I was really afraid for it, just as if it had been an ordinary person who was capable of dying. I thought to myself, 'The chandelier may have come down upon the voice.' I was then on the stage and was nearly running into the house, to look for the voice among the killed and wounded, when I thought that, if the voice was safe, it would be sure to be in my dressing-room and I rushed to my room. The voice was not there. I locked my door and, with tears in my eyes, besought it, if it were still alive, to manifest itself to me. The voice did not reply, but suddenly I heard a long, beautiful wail which I knew well. It is the plaint of Lazarus when, at the sound of the Redeemer's voice, he begins to open his eyes and see the light of day. It was the music which you and I, Raoul, heard at Perros. And then the voice began to sing the leading phrase, 'Come! And believe in me! Whoso believes in me shall live! Walk! Whoso hath believed in me shall never die!...' I can not tell you the effect which that music had upon me. It seemed to command me, personally, to come, to stand up and come to it. It retreated and I followed. 'Come! And believe in me!' I believed in it, I came.... I came and – this was the extraordinary thing – my dressing-room, as I moved, seemed to lengthen out... to lengthen out.... Evidently, it must have been an effect of mirrors... for I had the mirror in front of me... And, suddenly, I was outside the room without knowing how!"

"What! Without knowing how? Christine, Christine, you must really stop dreaming!"

"I was not dreaming, dear, I was outside my room without knowing how. You, who saw me disappear from my room one evening, may be able to explain it; but I can not. I can only tell you that, suddenly, there was no mirror before me and no dressing-room. I was in a dark passage, I was frightened and I cried out. It was quite dark, but for a faint red glimmer at a distant corner of the wall. I cried out. My voice was the only sound, for the singing and the violin had stopped. And, suddenly, a hand was laid on mine… or rather a stone-cold, bony thing that seized my wrist and did not let go. I cried out again. An arm took me round the waist and supported me. I struggled for a little while and then gave up the attempt. I was dragged toward the little red light and then I saw that I was in the hands of a man wrapped in a large cloak and wearing a mask that hid his whole face. I made one last effort; my limbs stiffened, my mouth opened to scream, but a hand closed it, a hand which I felt on my lips, on my skin… a hand that smelt of death. Then I fainted away.

"When I opened my eyes, we were still surrounded by darkness. A lantern, standing on the ground, showed a bubbling well. The water splashing from the well disappeared, almost at once, under the floor on which I was lying, with my head on the knee of the man in the black cloak and the black mask. He was bathing my temples and his hands smelt of death. I tried to push them away and asked, 'Who are you? Where is the voice?' His only answer was a sigh. Suddenly, a hot breath passed over my face and I perceived a white shape, beside the man's black shape, in the darkness. The black shape lifted me on to the white shape, a glad neighing greeted my astounded ears and I murmured, 'César!' The animal quivered. Raoul, I was lying half back on a saddle and I had recognized the white horse out of the **Profeta**, which I had so often fed with sugar and sweets. I remembered that, one evening, there was a rumor in the theater that the horse had disappeared and that it had been stolen by the Opera ghost. I believed in the voice, but had never believed in the ghost. Now, however, I began to wonder, with a shiver, whether I was the ghost's prisoner. I called upon the voice to help me, for I should never have imagined that the voice and the ghost were one. You have heard about the Opera ghost, have you not, Raoul?"

"Yes, but tell me what happened when you were on the white horse of the **Profeta**?"

"I made no movement and let myself go. The black shape held me up, and I made no effort to escape. A curious feeling of peacefulness came over me and I thought that I must be under the influence of some cordial. I had the full command of my senses; and my eyes became used to the darkness, which was lit, here and there, by fitful gleams. I calculated that we were in a narrow circular gallery, probably running all round the Opera, which is immense, underground. I had once been down into those cellars, but had stopped at the third floor, though there were two lower still, large enough to hold a town. But the figures of which I caught sight had made me run away. There are demons down there, quite black, standing in front of boilers, and they wield shovels and pitchforks and poke up fires and stir up flames and, if you come too near them, they frighten you by suddenly opening the red mouths of their furnaces.... Well, while César was quietly carrying me on his back, I saw those black demons in the distance, looking quite small, in front of the red fires of their furnaces: they came into sight, disappeared and came into sight again, as we went on our winding way. At last, they disappeared altogether. The shape was still holding me up and César walked on, unled and surefooted. I could not tell you, even approximately, how long this ride lasted; I only know that we seemed to turn and turn and often went down a spiral stair into the very heart of the earth. Even then, it may be that my head was turning, but I don't think so: no, my mind was quite clear. At last, César raised his nostrils, sniffed the air and quickened his pace a little. I felt a moistness in the air and César stopped. The darkness had lifted. A sort of bluey light surrounded us. We were on the edge of a lake, whose leaden waters stretched into the distance, into the darkness; but the blue light lit up the bank and I saw a little boat fastened to an iron ring on the wharf!"

"A boat!"

"Yes, but I knew that all that existed and that there was nothing supernatural about that underground lake and boat. But think of the exceptional conditions in which I arrived upon that shore! I don't know whether the effects of the cordial had worn off when the man's shape lifted me into the boat, but my terror began all over again. My gruesome escort must have noticed it, for he sent César back and I heard his hoofs trampling up a staircase while the man jumped into the boat, untied the rope that held it and seized the oars. He rowed with a quick, powerful stroke; and his eyes, under the mask, never left me. We slipped across the noiseless water in the bluey light which I told you of; then we were in the dark again and we touched shore. And I was once more taken up in the man's arms. I cried aloud. And then, suddenly, I was silent, dazed by the light.... Yes, a dazzling light in the midst of which I had been put down. I sprang to my feet. I was in the middle of a drawing-room that seemed to me to be decorated, adorned and furnished with nothing but flowers, flowers both magnificent and stupid, because of the silk ribbons that tied them to baskets, like those which they sell in the shops on the boulevards. They were much too civilized flowers, like those which I used to find in my dressing-room after a first night. And, in the midst of all these flowers, stood the black shape of the man in the mask, with arms crossed, and he said, 'Don't be afraid, Christine; you are in no danger.' **It was the voice!**

"My anger equaled my amazement. I rushed at the mask and tried to snatch it away, so as to see the face of the voice. The man said, 'You are in no danger, so long as you do not touch the mask.' And, taking me gently by the wrists, he forced me into a chair and then went down on his knees before me and said nothing more! His humility gave me back some of my courage; and the light restored me to the realities of life. However extraordinary the adventure might be, I was now surrounded by mortal, visible, tangible things. The furniture, the hangings, the candles, the vases and the very flowers in their baskets, of which I could almost have told whence they came and what they cost, were bound to confine my imagination to the limits of a drawing-room quite as commonplace as any that, at least, had the excuse of not being in the cellars of the Opera. I had, no doubt, to do with a terrible, eccentric person, who, in some mysterious fashion, had succeeded in taking up his abode there, under the Opera house, five stories below the level of the ground. And the voice, the voice which I had recognized under the mask, was on its knees before me, **was a man**! And I began to cry.... The man, still kneeling, must have understood the cause of my tears, for he said, 'It is true, Christine!... I am not an Angel, nor a genius, nor a ghost... I am Erik!'"

Christine's narrative was again interrupted. An echo behind them seemed to repeat the word after her.

"Erik!"

What echo?... They both turned round and saw that night had fallen. Raoul made a movement as though to rise, but Christine kept him beside her.

"Don't go," she said. "I want you to know everything **here**!"

"But why here, Christine? I am afraid of your catching cold."

"We have nothing to fear except the trap-doors, dear, and here we are miles away from the trap-doors... and I am not allowed to see you outside the theater. This is not the time to annoy him. We must not arouse his suspicion."

"Christine! Christine! Something tells

me that we are wrong to wait till tomorrow evening and that we ought to fly at once."

"I tell you that, if he does not hear me sing tomorrow, it will cause him infinite pain."

"It is difficult not to cause him pain and yet to escape from him for good."

"You are right in that, Raoul, for certainly he will die of my flight." And she added in a dull voice, "But then it counts both ways… for we risk his killing us."

"Does he love you so much?"

"He would commit murder for me."

"But one can find out where he lives. One can go in search of him. Now that we know that Erik is not a ghost, one can speak to him and force him to answer!"

Christine shook her head.

"No, no! There is nothing to be done with Erik… except to run away!"

"Then why, when you were able to run away, did you go back to him?"

"Because I had to. And you will understand that when I tell you how I left him."

"Oh, I hate him!" cried Raoul. "And you, Christine, tell me, do you hate him too?"

"No," said Christine simply.

"No, of course not.... Why, you love him! Your fear, your terror, all of that is just love and love of the most exquisite kind, the kind which people do not admit even to themselves," said Raoul bitterly. "The kind that gives you a thrill, when you think of it.... Picture it: a man who lives in a palace underground!" And he gave a leer.

"Then you want me to go back there?" said the young girl cruelly. "Take care, Raoul; I have told you: I should never return!"

There was an appalling silence between the three of them: the two who spoke and the shadow that listened, behind them.

"Before answering that," said Raoul, at last, speaking very slowly, "I should like to know with what feeling he inspires you, since you do not hate him."

"With horror!" she said. "That is the terrible thing about it. He fills me with horror and

I do not hate him. How can I hate him, Raoul? Think of Erik at my feet, in the house on the lake, underground. He accuses himself, he curses himself, he implores my forgiveness!… He confesses his cheat. He loves me! He lays at my feet an immense and tragic love.… He has carried me off for love!… He has imprisoned me with him, underground, for love!… But he respects me: he crawls, he moans, he weeps!… And, when I stood up, Raoul, and told him that I could only despise him if he did not, then and there, give me my liberty… he offered it… he offered to show me the mysterious road… Only… only he rose too… and I was made to remember that, though he was not an angel, nor a ghost, nor a genius, he remained the voice… for he sang. And I listened… and stayed!… That night, we did not exchange another word. He sang me to sleep.

"When I woke up, I was alone, lying on a sofa in a simply furnished little bedroom, with an ordinary mahogany bedstead, lit by a lamp standing on the marble top of an old Louis-Philippe chest of drawers. I soon discovered that I was a prisoner and that the only outlet from my room led to a very comfortable bathroom. On returning to the bedroom, I saw on the chest of drawers a note, in red ink, which said, 'My dear Christine, you need have no concern as to your fate. You have no better nor more respectful friend in the world than myself. You are alone, at present, in this home which is yours. I am going out shopping to fetch you all the things that you can need.' I felt sure that I had fallen into the hands of a madman. I ran round my little apartment, looking for a way of escape which I could not find. I upbraided myself for my absurd superstition, which had caused me to fall into the trap. I felt inclined to laugh and to cry at the same time.

"This was the state of mind in which Erik found me. After giving three taps on the wall, he walked in quietly through a door which I had not noticed and which he left open. He had his arms full of boxes and parcels and arranged them on the bed, in a leisurely fashion, while I overwhelmed him with abuse and called upon him to take off his mask, if it covered the face of an honest man. He replied serenely, 'You shall never see Erik's face.' And he reproached me with not having finished dressing at that time of day: he was good enough to tell me that it was two o'clock in the afternoon. He said he would give me half an hour and, while he spoke, wound up my watch and set it for me. After which, he asked me to come to the dining-room, where a nice lunch was waiting for us.

"I was very angry, slammed the door in his face and went to the bathroom.... When I came out again, feeling greatly refreshed, Erik said that he loved me, but that he would never tell me so except when I allowed him and that the rest of the time would be devoted to music. 'What do you mean by the rest of the time?' I asked. 'Five days,' he said, with decision. I asked him if I should then be free and he said, 'You will be free, Christine, for, when those five days are past, you will have learned not to see me; and then, from time to time, you will come to see your poor Erik!' He pointed to a chair opposite him, at a small table, and I sat down, feeling greatly perturbed. However, I ate a few prawns and the wing of a chicken and drank half a glass of tokay, which he had himself, he told me, brought from the Königsberg cellars. Erik did not eat or drink. I asked him what his nationality was and if that name of Erik did not point to his Scandinavian origin. He said that he had no name and no country and that he had taken the name of Erik by accident.

"After lunch, he rose and gave me the tips of his fingers, saying he would like to show me over his flat; but I snatched away my hand and gave a cry. What I had touched was cold and, at the same time, bony; and I remembered that his hands smelt of death. ‘Oh, forgive me!’ he moaned. And he opened a door before me. ‘This is my bedroom, if you care to see it. It is rather curious.’ His manners, his words, his attitude gave me confidence and I went in without hesitation. I felt as if I were entering the room of a dead person. The walls were all hung with black, but, instead of the white trimmings that usually set off that funereal upholstery, there was an enormous stave of music with the notes of the **Dies Irae**, many times repeated. In the middle of the room was a canopy, from which hung curtains of red brocaded stuff, and, under the canopy, an open coffin. ‘That is where I sleep,’ said Erik. ‘One has to get used to everything in life, even to eternity.’ The sight upset me so much that I turned away my head.

“Then I saw the keyboard of an organ which filled one whole side of the walls. On the desk was a music-book covered with red notes. I asked leave to look at it and read, '**Don Juan Triumphant**.' 'Yes,' he said, 'I compose sometimes. I began that work twenty years ago. When I have finished, I shall take it away with me in that coffin and never wake up again.' 'You must work at it as seldom as you can,' I said. He replied, 'I sometimes work at it for fourteen days and nights together, during which I live on music only, and then I rest for years at a time.' 'Will you play me something out of your **Don Juan Triumphant**?' I asked, thinking to please him. 'You must never ask me that,' he said, in a gloomy voice. 'I will play you Mozart, if you like, which will only make you weep; but my **Don Juan**, Christine, burns; and yet he is not struck by fire from Heaven.' Thereupon we returned to the drawing-room. I noticed that there was no mirror in the whole apartment. I was going to remark upon this, but Erik had already sat down to the piano. He said, 'You see, Christine, there is some music that is so terrible that it consumes all those who approach it. Fortunately, you have not come to that music yet, for you would lose all your pretty coloring and nobody would know you when you returned to Paris. Let us sing something from the Opera, Christine Daaé.' He spoke these last words as though he were flinging an insult at me."

"What did you do?"

"I had no time to think about the meaning he put into his words. We at once began the duet in **Othello** and already the catastrophe was upon us. I sang Desdemona with a despair, a terror which I had never displayed before. As for him, his voice thundered forth his revengeful soul at every note. Love, jealousy, hatred, burst out around us in harrowing cries. Erik's black mask made me think of the natural mask of the Moor of Venice. He was Othello himself. Suddenly, I felt a need to see beneath the mask. I wanted to know the **face** of the voice, and, with a movement which I was utterly unable to control, swiftly my fingers tore away the mask. Oh, horror, horror, horror!"

Christine stopped, at the thought of the vision that had scared her, while the echoes of the night, which had repeated the name of Erik, now thrice moaned the cry:

"Horror!... Horror!... Horror!"

Raoul and Christine, clasping each other closely, raised their eyes to the stars that shone in a clear and peaceful sky. Raoul said:

"Strange, Christine, that this calm, soft night should be so full of plaintive sounds. One would think that it was sorrowing with us."

"When you know the secret, Raoul, your ears, like mine, will be full of lamentations."

She took Raoul's protecting hands in hers and, with a long shiver, continued:

"Yes, if I lived to be a hundred, I should always hear the superhuman cry of grief and rage which he uttered when the terrible sight appeared before my eyes.... Raoul, you have seen death's heads, when they have been dried and withered by the centuries, and, perhaps, if you were not the victim of a nightmare, you saw **his** death's head at Perros. And then you saw Red Death stalking about at the last masked ball. But all those death's heads were motionless and their dumb horror was not alive. But imagine, if you can, Red Death's mask suddenly coming to life in order to express, with the four black holes of its eyes, its nose, and its mouth, the extreme anger, the mighty fury of a demon; **and not a ray of light from the sockets**, for, as I learned later, you can not see his blazing eyes except in the dark.

"I fell back against the wall and he came up to me, grinding his teeth, and, as I fell upon my knees, he hissed mad, incoherent words and curses at me. Leaning over me, he cried, 'Look! You want to see! See! Feast your eyes, glut your soul on my cursed ugliness! Look at Erik's face! Now you know the face of the voice! You were not content to hear me, eh? You wanted to know what I looked like! Oh, you women are so inquisitive! Well, are you satisfied? I'm a very good-looking fellow, eh?... When a woman has seen me, as you have, she belongs to me. She loves me forever. I am a kind of Don Juan, you know!' And, drawing himself up to his full height, with his hand on his hip, wagging the hideous thing that was his head on his shoulders, he roared, 'Look at me! **I am Don Juan triumphant!**' And, when I turned away my head and begged for mercy, he drew it to him, brutally, twisting his dead fingers into my hair."

"Enough! Enough!" cried Raoul. "I will kill him. In Heaven's name, Christine, tell me where the dining-room on the lake is! I must kill him!"

"Oh, be quiet, Raoul, if you want to know!"

"Yes, I want to know how and why you went back; I must know!... But, in any case,

I will kill him!"

"Oh, Raoul, listen, listen!... He dragged me by my hair and then... and then... Oh, it is too horrible!"

"Well, what? Out with it!" exclaimed Raoul fiercely. "Out with it, quick!"

"Then he hissed at me. 'Ah, I frighten you, do I?... I dare say!... Perhaps you think that I have another mask, eh, and that this... this... my head is a mask? Well,' he roared, 'tear it off as you did the other! Come! Come along! I insist! Your hands! Your hands! Give me your hands!' And he seized my hands and dug them into his awful face. He tore his flesh with my nails, tore his terrible dead flesh with my nails!... 'Know,' he shouted, while his throat throbbed and panted like a furnace, 'know that I am built up of death from head to foot and that it is a corpse that loves you and adores you and will never, never leave you!... Look, I am not laughing now, I am crying, crying for you, Christine, who have torn off my mask and who therefore can never leave me again!... As long as you thought me handsome, you could have come back, I know you would have come back... but, now that you know my hideousness, you would run away for good.... So I shall keep you here!... Why did you want to see me? Oh, mad Christine, who wanted to see me!... When my own father never saw me and when my mother, so as not to see me, made me a present of my first mask!'

"He had let go of me at last and was dragging himself about on the floor, uttering terrible sobs. And then he crawled away like a snake, went into his room, closed the door and left me alone to my reflections. Presently I heard the sound of the organ; and then I began to understand Erik's contemptuous phrase when he spoke about Opera music. What I now heard was utterly different from what I had heard up to then. His **Don Juan Triumphant** (for I had not a doubt but that he had rushed to his masterpiece to forget the horror of the moment) seemed to me at first one long, awful, magnificent sob. But, little by little, it expressed every emotion, every suffering of which mankind is capable. It intoxicated me; and I opened the door that separated us. Erik rose, as I entered, **but dared not turn in my direction**. 'Erik,' I cried, 'show me your face without fear! I swear that you are the most unhappy and sublime of men; and, if ever again I shiver when I look at you, it will be because I am thinking of the splendor of your genius!' Then Erik turned round, for he believed me, and I also had faith in myself. He fell at my feet, with words of love… with words of love in his dead mouth… and the music had ceased… He kissed the hem of my dress and did not see that I closed my eyes.

"What more can I tell you, dear? You now know the tragedy. It went on for a fortnight – a fortnight during which I lied to him. My lies were as hideous as the monster who inspired them; but they were the price of my liberty. I burned his mask; and I managed so well that, even when he was not singing, he tried to catch my eye, like a dog sitting by its master. He was my faithful slave and paid me endless little attentions. Gradually, I gave him such confidence that he ventured to take me walking on the banks of the lake and to row me in the boat on its leaden waters; toward the end of my captivity he let me out through the gates that closed the underground passages in the Rue Scribe. Here a carriage awaited us and took us to the Bois. The night when we met you was nearly fatal to me, for he is terribly jealous of you and I had to tell him that you were soon going away.... Then, at last, after a fortnight of that horrible captivity, during which I was filled with pity, enthusiasm, despair and horror by turns, he believed me when I said, '**I will come back!**'"

"And you went back, Christine," groaned

Raoul.

"Yes, dear, and I must tell you that it was not his frightful threats when setting me free that helped me to keep my word, but the harrowing sob which he gave on the threshold of the tomb.... That sob attached me to the unfortunate man more than I myself suspected when saying goodbye to him. Poor Erik! Poor Erik!"

"Christine," said Raoul, rising, "you tell me that you love me; but you had recovered your liberty hardly a few hours before you returned to Erik! Remember the masked ball!"

"Yes; and do you remember those hours which I passed with you, Raoul... to the great danger of both of us?"

"I doubted your love for me, during those hours."

"Do you doubt it still, Raoul?... Then know that each of my visits to Erik increased my horror of him; for each of those visits, instead of calming him, as I hoped, made him mad with love!... And I am so frightened, so frightened!..."

"You are frightened... but do you love me? If Erik were good-looking, would you love me, Christine?"

She rose in her turn, put her two trembling arms round the young man's neck and said:

"Oh, my betrothed of a day, if I did not love you, I would not give you my lips! Take them, for the first time and the last."

He kissed her lips; but the night that surrounded them was rent asunder, they fled as at the approach of a storm and their eyes, filled with dread of Erik, showed them, before they disappeared, high up above them, an immense night-bird that stared at them with its blazing eyes and seemed to cling to the string of Apollo's lyre.

CHAPTER THIRTEEN

A Masterstroke of the Trap-Door Lover

RAOUL AND CHRISTINE RAN, eager to escape from the roof and the blazing eyes that showed only in the dark; and they did not stop before they came to the eighth floor on the way down.

There was no performance at the Opera that night and the passages were empty.

Suddenly, a queer-looking form stood before them and blocked the road:

"No, not this way!"

And the form pointed to another passage by which they were to reach the wings. Raoul wanted to stop and ask for an explanation. But the form, which wore a sort of long frock-coat and a pointed cap, said:

"Quick! Go away quickly!"

Christine was already dragging Raoul, compelling him to start running again.

"But who is he? Who is that man?" he asked.

Christine replied: "It's the Persian."

"What's he doing here?"

"Nobody knows. He is always in the Opera."

"You are making me run away, for the first time in my life. If we really saw Erik, what I ought to have done was to nail him to Apollo's lyre, just as we nail the owls to the walls of our Breton farms; and there would have been no more question of him."

"My dear Raoul, you would first have had to climb up to Apollo's lyre: that is no easy matter."

"The blazing eyes were there!"

"Oh, you are getting like me now, seeing him everywhere! What I took for blazing eyes was probably a couple of stars shining through the strings of the lyre."

And Christine went down another floor, with Raoul following her.

"As you have quite made up your mind to go, Christine, I assure you it would be better to go at once. Why wait for tomorrow? He may have heard us tonight."

"No, no, he is working, I tell you, at his **Don Juan Triumphant** and not thinking of us."

"You're so sure of that you keep on looking behind you!"

"Come to my dressing-room."

"Hadn't we better meet outside the Opera?"

"Never, till we go away for good! It would

bring us bad luck, if I did not keep my word. I promised him to see you only here."

"It's a good thing for me that he allowed you even that. Do you know," said Raoul bitterly, "that it was very plucky of you to let us play at being engaged?"

"Why, my dear, he knows all about it! He said, 'I trust you, Christine. M. de Chagny is in love with you and is going abroad. Before he goes, I want him to be as happy as I am.' Are people so unhappy when they love?"

"Yes, Christine, when they love and are not sure of being loved."

They came to Christine's dressing-room.

"Why do you think that you are safer in this room than on the stage?" asked Raoul. "You heard him through the walls here, therefore he can certainly hear us."

"No. He gave me his word not to be behind the walls of my dressing-room again and I believe Erik's word. This room and my bedroom on the lake are for me, exclusively, and not to be approached by him."

"How can you have gone from this room into that dark passage, Christine? Suppose we try to repeat your movements; shall we?"

"It is dangerous, dear, for the glass might carry me off again; and, instead of running away, I should be obliged to go to the end of the secret passage to the lake and there call Erik."

"Would he hear you?"

"Erik will hear me wherever I call him. He told me so. He is a very curious genius. You must not think, Raoul, that he is simply a man who amuses himself by living underground. He does things that no other man could do; he knows things which nobody in the world knows."

"Take care, Christine, you are making a ghost of him again!"

"No, he is not a ghost; he is a man of Heaven and earth, that is all."

"A man of Heaven and earth… that is all!

A nice way to speak of him!... And are you still resolved to run away from him?"

"Yes, tomorrow."

"Tomorrow, you will have no resolve left!"

"Then, Raoul, you must run away with me in spite of myself; is that understood?"

"I shall be here at twelve tomorrow night; I shall keep my promise, whatever happens. You say that, after listening to the performance, he is to wait for you in the dining-room on the lake?"

"Yes."

"And how are you to reach him, if you don't know how to go out by the glass?"

"Why, by going straight to the edge of the lake."

Christine opened a box, took out an enormous key and showed it to Raoul.

"What's that?" he asked.

"The key of the gate to the underground passage in the Rue Scribe."

"I understand, Christine. It leads straight to the lake. Give it to me, Christine, will you?"

"Never!" she said. "That would be treacherous!"

Suddenly Christine changed color. A mortal pallor overspread her features.

"Oh heavens!" she cried. "Erik! Erik! Have pity on me!"

"Hold your tongue!" said Raoul. "You told me he could hear you!"

But the singer's attitude became more and more inexplicable. She wrung her fingers, repeating, with a distraught air:

"Oh, Heaven! Oh, Heaven!"

"But what is it? What is it?" Raoul implored.

"The ring… the gold ring he gave me."

"Oh, so Erik gave you that ring!"

"You know he did, Raoul! But what you don't know is that, when he gave it to me, he said, 'I give you back your liberty, Christine, on condition that this ring is always on your finger. As long as you keep it, you will be protected against all danger and Erik will remain your friend. But woe to you if you ever part with it, for Erik will have his revenge!'…

My dear, my dear, the ring is gone!... Woe to us both!"

They both looked for the ring, but could not find it. Christine refused to be pacified.

"It was while I gave you that kiss, up above, under Apollo's lyre," she said. "The ring must have slipped from my finger and dropped into the street! We can never find it. And what misfortunes are in store for us now! Oh, to run away!"

"Let us run away at once," Raoul insisted, once more.

She hesitated. He thought that she was going to say yes.... Then her bright pupils became dimmed and she said:

"No! Tomorrow!"

And she left him hurriedly, still wringing and rubbing her fingers, as though she hoped to bring the ring back like that.

Raoul went home, greatly perturbed at all that he had heard.

"If I don't save her from the hands of that humbug," he said, aloud, as he went to bed, "she is lost. But I shall save her."

He put out his lamp and felt a need to insult Erik in the dark. Thrice over, he shouted:

"Humbug!... Humbug!... Humbug!"

But, suddenly, he raised himself on his elbow. A cold sweat poured from his temples. Two eyes, like blazing coals, had appeared at the foot of his bed. They stared at him fixedly, terribly, in the darkness of the night.

Raoul was no coward; and yet he trembled. He put out a groping, hesitating hand toward the table by his bedside. He found the matches and lit his candle. The eyes disappeared.

Still uneasy in his mind, he thought to himself:

"She told me that **his** eyes only showed in the dark. His eyes have disappeared in the light, but **he** may be there still."

And he rose, hunted about, went round the room. He looked under his bed, like a child. Then he thought himself absurd, got into bed again and blew out the candle. The eyes reappeared.

He sat up and stared back at them with all the courage he possessed. Then he cried:

"Is that you, Erik? Man, genius, or ghost, is it you?"

He reflected: "If it's he, he's on the balcony!"

Then he ran to the chest of drawers and groped for his revolver. He opened the balcony window, looked out, saw nothing and closed the window again. He went back to bed, shivering, for the night was cold, and put the revolver on the table within his reach.

The eyes were still there, at the foot of the bed. Were they between the bed and the windowpane or behind the pane, that is to say, on the balcony? That was what Raoul wanted to know. He also wanted to know if those eyes belonged to a human being.... He wanted to know everything.

Then, patiently, calmly, he seized his revolver and took aim. He aimed a little above the two eyes. Surely, if they were eyes and if above those two eyes there was a forehead and if Raoul was not too clumsy...

The shot made a terrible din amid the silence of the slumbering house. And, while footsteps came hurrying along the passages, Raoul sat up with outstretched arm, ready to fire again, if need be.

This time, the two eyes had disappeared.

Servants appeared, carrying lights; Count Philippe, terribly anxious:

"What is it?"

"I think I have been dreaming," replied the young man. "I fired at two stars that kept me from sleeping."

"You're raving! Are you ill? For God's sake, tell me, Raoul: what happened?"

And the count seized hold of the revolver.

"No, no, I'm not raving.... Besides, we shall soon see..."

He got out of bed, put on a dressing-gown and slippers, took a light from the hands of a servant and, opening the window, stepped out on the balcony.

The count saw that the window had been pierced by a bullet at a man's height. Raoul was leaning over the balcony with his candle:

"Aha!" he said. "Blood!... Blood!... Here, there, more blood!... That's a good thing! A ghost who bleeds is less dangerous!" he grinned.

"Raoul! Raoul! Raoul!"

The count was shaking him as though he were trying to waken a sleepwalker.

"But, my dear brother, I'm not asleep!" Raoul protested impatiently. "You can see the blood for yourself. I thought I had been dreaming and firing at two stars. It was Erik's eyes... and here is his blood!... After all, perhaps I was wrong to shoot; and Christine is quite capable of never forgiving me.... All this would not have happened if I had drawn the curtains before going to bed."

"Raoul, have you suddenly gone mad? Wake up!"

"What, still? You would do better to help

me find Erik... for, after all, a ghost who bleeds can always be found."

The count's valet said:

"That is so, sir; there is blood on the balcony."

The other manservant brought a lamp, by the light of which they examined the balcony carefully. The marks of blood followed the rail till they reached a gutter-spout; then they went up the gutter-spout.

"My dear fellow," said Count Philippe, "you have fired at a cat."

"The misfortune is," said Raoul, with a grin, "that it's quite possible. With Erik, you never know. Is it Erik? Is it the cat? Is it the ghost? No, with Erik, you can't tell!"

Raoul went on making this strange sort of remarks which corresponded so intimately and logically with the preoccupation of his brain and which, at the same time, tended to persuade many people that his mind was unhinged. The count himself was seized with this idea; and, later, the examining magistrate, on receiving the report of the commissary of police, came to the same conclusion.

"Who is Erik?" asked the count, pressing his brother's hand.

"He is my rival. And, if he's not dead, it's a pity."

He dismissed the servants with a wave of the hand and the two Chagnys were left alone. But the men were not out of earshot before the count's valet heard Raoul say, distinctly and emphatically:

"I shall carry off Christine Daaé tonight."

This phrase was afterward repeated to M. Faure, the examining-magistrate. But no one ever knew exactly what passed between the two brothers at this interview. The servants declared that this was not their first quarrel. Their voices penetrated the wall; and it was always an actress called Christine Daaé that was in question.

At breakfast – the early morning breakfast, which the count took in his study – Philippe sent for his brother. Raoul arrived silent and gloomy. The scene was a very short one. Philippe handed his brother a copy of the **Epoque** and said:

"Read that!"

The viscount read:

The latest news in the Faubourg is that there is a promise of marriage between Mlle. Christine Daaé, the opera-singer, and M. le Vicomte Raoul de Chagny. If the gossips are to be credited, Count Philippe has sworn that, for the first time on record, the Chagnys shall not keep their promise. But, as love is all-powerful, at the Opera as – and even more than – elsewhere, we wonder how Count Philippe intends to prevent the viscount, his brother, from leading the new Margarita to the altar. The two brothers are said to adore each other; but the count is curiously mistaken if he imagines that brotherly love will triumph over love pure and simple.

"You see, Raoul," said the count, "you

are making us ridiculous! That little girl has turned your head with her ghost-stories."

The viscount had evidently repeated Christine's narrative to his brother, during the night. All that he now said was:

"Goodbye, Philippe."

"Have you quite made up your mind? You are going tonight? With her?"

No reply.

"Surely you will not do anything so foolish? I **shall** know how to prevent you!"

"Goodbye, Philippe," said the viscount again and left the room.

This scene was described to the examining-magistrate by the count himself, who did not see Raoul again until that evening, at the Opera, a few minutes before Christine's disappearance.

Raoul, in fact, devoted the whole day to his preparations for the flight. The horses, the carriage, the coachman, the provisions, the luggage, the money required for the journey, the road to be taken (he had resolved not to go by train, so as to throw the ghost off the scent): all this had to be settled and provided for; and it occupied him until nine o'clock at night.

At nine o'clock, a sort of traveling-barouche with the curtains of its windows close-down, took its place in the rank on the Rotunda side. It was drawn by two powerful horses driven by a coachman whose face was almost concealed in the long folds of a muffler. In front of this traveling-carriage were three broughams, belonging respectively to Carlotta, who had suddenly returned to Paris, to Sorelli and, at the head of the rank, to Comte Philippe de Chagny. No one left the barouche. The coachman remained on his box, and the three other coachmen remained on theirs.

A shadow in a long black cloak and a soft black felt hat passed along the pavement between the Rotunda and the carriages, examined the barouche carefully, went up to the horses and the coachman and then moved away without saying a word. The magistrate afterward believed that this shadow was that of the Vicomte Raoul de Chagny; but I do not agree, seeing that that evening, as every evening, the Vicomte de Chagny was wearing a tall hat, which hat, besides, was subsequently found. I am more inclined to think that the shadow was that of the ghost, who knew all about the whole affair, as the reader will soon perceive.

They were giving **Faust**, as it happened, before a splendid house. The Faubourg was magnificently represented; and the paragraph in that morning's **Epoque** had already produced its effect, for all eyes were turned to the box in which Count Philippe sat alone, apparently in a very indifferent and careless frame of mind. The feminine element in the brilliant audience seemed curiously puzzled; and the viscount's absence gave rise to any amount of whispering behind the fans. Christine Daaé met with a rather cold reception. That special audience could not forgive her for aiming so high.

The singer noticed this unfavorable attitude of a portion of the house and was confused by it.

The regular frequenters of the Opera, who pretended to know the truth about the viscount's love-story, exchanged significant smiles at certain passages in Margarita's part; and they made a show of turning and looking at Philippe de Chagny's box when Christine sang:

"I wish I could but know who was he
That addressed me,
If he was noble, or, at least, what his name is."

The count sat with his chin on his hand and seemed to pay no attention to these manifestations. He kept his eyes fixed on the stage; but his thoughts appeared to be far away.

Christine lost her self-assurance more and more. She trembled. She felt on the verge of a breakdown.... Carolus Fonta wondered if she was ill, if she could keep the stage until the end of the Garden Act. In the front of the house, people remembered the catastrophe that had befallen Carlotta at the end of that act and the historic "**co-ack**" which had momentarily interrupted her career in Paris.

Just then, Carlotta made her entrance in a box facing the stage, a sensational entrance. Poor Christine raised her eyes upon this fresh subject of excitement. She recognized her rival. She thought she saw a sneer on her lips. That saved her. She forgot everything, in order to triumph once more.

From that moment the prima donna sang with all her heart and soul. She tried to surpass all that she had done till then; and she succeeded. In the last act when she began the invocation to the angels, she made all the members of the audience feel as though they too had wings.

In the center of the amphitheater a man stood up and remained standing, facing the singer. It was Raoul.

"Holy angel, in Heaven blessed…"

And Christine, her arms outstretched, her throat filled with music, the glory of her hair falling over her bare shoulders, uttered the divine cry:

"My spirit longs with thee to rest!"

It was at that moment that the stage was suddenly plunged in darkness. It happened so quickly that the spectators hardly had time to utter a sound of stupefaction, for the gas at once lit up the stage again. But Christine Daaé was no longer there!

What had become of her? What was that miracle? All exchanged glances without understanding, and the excitement at once reached its height. Nor was the tension any less great on the stage itself. Men rushed from the wings to the spot where Christine had been singing that very instant. The performance was interrupted amid the greatest disorder.

Where had Christine gone? What witchcraft had snatched her away before the eyes of thousands of enthusiastic onlookers and from the arms of Carolus Fonta himself? It was as though the angels had really carried her up "to rest."

Raoul, still standing up in the amphitheater, had uttered a cry. Count Philippe had sprung to his feet in his box. People looked at the stage, at the count, at Raoul, and wondered if this curious event was connected in any way with the paragraph in that morning's paper. But Raoul hurriedly left his seat, the count disappeared from his box and, while the curtain was lowered, the subscribers rushed to the door that led behind the scenes. The rest of the audience waited amid an indescribable hubbub. Everyone spoke at once. Everyone tried to suggest an explanation of the extraordinary incident.

At last, the curtain rose slowly and Carolus Fonta stepped to the conductor's desk and, in a sad and serious voice, said:

"Ladies and gentlemen, an unprecedented event has taken place and thrown us into a state of the greatest alarm. Our sister-artist, Christine Daaé, has disappeared before our eyes and nobody can tell us how!"

CHAPTER FOURTEEN

The Singular Attitude of a Safety-Pin

BEHIND THE CURTAIN, there was an indescribable crowd. Artists, scene-shifters, dancers, supers, choristers, subscribers were all asking questions, shouting and hustling one another.

"What became of her?"

"She's run away."

"With the Vicomte de Chagny, of course!"

"No, with the count!"

"Ah, here's Carlotta! Carlotta did the trick!"

"No, it was the ghost!"

And a few laughed, especially as a careful examination of the trap-doors and boards had put the idea of an accident out of the question.

Amid this noisy throng, three men stood talking in a low voice and with despairing gestures. They were Gabriel, the chorus-master; Mercier, the acting-manager; and Rémy, the secretary. They retired to a corner of the lobby by which the stage communicates with the wide passage leading to the foyer of the ballet. Here they stood and argued behind some enormous "properties."

"I knocked at the door," said Rémy. "They did not answer. Perhaps they are not in the office. In any case, it's impossible to find out, for they took the keys with them."

"They" were obviously the managers, who

had given orders, during the last entr'acte, that they were not to be disturbed on any pretext whatever. They were not in to anybody.

"All the same," exclaimed Gabriel, "a singer isn't run away with, from the middle of the stage, every day!"

"Did you shout that to them?" asked Mercier, impatiently.

"I'll go back again," said Rémy, and disappeared at a run.

Thereupon the stage-manager arrived.

"Well, M. Mercier, are you coming? What are you two doing here? You're wanted, Mr. Acting-Manager."

"I refuse to know or to do anything before the commissary arrives," declared Mercier. "I have sent for Mifroid. We shall see when he comes!"

"And I tell you that you ought to go down to the organ at once."

"Not before the commissary comes."

"I've been down to the organ myself

already."

"Ah! And what did you see?"

"Well, I saw nobody! Do you hear – nobody!"

"What do you want me to go down there for?"

"You're right!" said the stage-manager, frantically pushing his hands through his rebellious hair. "You're right! But there might be someone at the organ who could tell us how the stage came to be suddenly darkened. Now Mauclair is nowhere to be found. Do you understand that?"

Mauclair was the gasman, who dispensed day and night at will on the stage of the Opera.

"Mauclair is not to be found!" repeated Mercier, taken aback. "Well, what about his assistants?"

"There's no Mauclair and no assistants! No one at the lights, I tell you! You can imagine," roared the stage-manager, "that that little girl must have been carried off by somebody else: she didn't run away by herself! It was a calculated stroke and we have to find out about it.... And what are the managers doing all this time?... I gave orders that no one was to go down to the lights and I posted a fireman in front of the gasman's box beside the organ. Wasn't that right?"

"Yes, yes, quite right, quite right. And now let's wait for the commissary."

The stage-manager walked away, shrugging his shoulders, fuming, muttering insults at those milksops who remained quietly squatting in a corner while the whole theater was topsy-turvy.

Gabriel and Mercier were not so quiet as all that. Only they had received an order that paralyzed them. The managers were not to be disturbed on any account. Rémy had violated that order and met with no success.

At that moment he returned from his new expedition, wearing a curiously startled air.

"Well, have you seen them?" asked

Mercier.

"Moncharmin opened the door at last. His eyes were starting out of his head. I thought he meant to strike me. I could not get a word in; and what do you think he shouted at me? 'Have you a safety-pin?' 'No!' 'Well, then, clear out!' I tried to tell him that an unheard-of thing had happened on the stage, but he roared, 'A safety-pin! Give me a safety-pin at once!' A boy heard him – he was bellowing like a bull – ran up with a safety-pin and gave it to him; whereupon Moncharmin slammed the door in my face, and there you are!"

"And couldn't you have said, 'Christine Daaé.'"

"I should like to have seen you in my place. He was foaming at the mouth. He thought of nothing but his safety-pin. I believe, if they hadn't brought him one on the spot, he would have fallen down in a fit!... Oh, all this isn't natural; and our managers are going mad!... Besides, it can't go on like this! I'm not used to being treated in that fashion!"

Suddenly Gabriel whispered:

"It's another trick of O. G.'s."

Rémy gave a grin, Mercier a sigh and seemed about to speak... but, meeting Gabriel's eye, said nothing.

However, Mercier felt his responsibility increased as the minutes passed without the managers' appearing; and, at last, he could stand it no longer.

"Look here, I'll go and hunt them out myself!"

Gabriel, turning very gloomy and serious, stopped him.

"Be careful what you're doing, Mercier! If they're staying in their office, it's probably because they have to! O. G. has more than one trick in his bag!"

But Mercier shook his head.

"That's their lookout! I'm going! If people had listened to me, the police would have known everything long ago!"

And he went.

"What's everything?" asked Rémy. "What

was there to tell the police? Why don't you answer, Gabriel?... Ah, so you know something! Well, you would do better to tell me, too, if you don't want me to shout out that you are all going mad!... Yes, that's what you are: mad!"

Gabriel put on a stupid look and pretended not to understand the private secretary's unseemly outburst.

"What 'something' am I supposed to know?" he said. "I don't know what you mean."

Rémy began to lose his temper.

"This evening, Richard and Moncharmin were behaving like lunatics, here, between the acts."

"I never noticed it," growled Gabriel, very much annoyed.

"Then you're the only one!... Do you think that I didn't see them?... And that M. Parabise, the manager of the Crédit Central, noticed nothing?... And that M. de La Borderie, the ambassador, has no eyes to see with?...

Why, all the subscribers were pointing at our managers!"

"But what were our managers doing?" asked Gabriel, putting on his most innocent air.

"What were they doing? You know better than anyone what they were doing!... You were there!... And you were watching them, you and Mercier!... And you were the only two who didn't laugh...."

"I don't understand!"

Gabriel raised his arms and dropped them to his sides again, which gesture was meant to convey that the question did not interest him in the least. Rémy continued:

"What is the sense of this new mania of theirs? **Why won't they have anyone come near them now?**"

"What? **Won't they have anyone come near them?**"

"**And they won't let anyone touch them!**"

"Really? Have you noticed **that they won't let anyone touch them**? That is certainly odd!"

"Oh, so you admit it! And high time, too! And **then, they walk backward**!"

"**Backward!** You have seen our managers **walk backward**? Why, I thought that only crabs walked backward!"

"Don't laugh, Gabriel; don't laugh!"

"I'm not laughing," protested Gabriel, looking as solemn as a judge.

"Perhaps you can tell me this, Gabriel, as you're an intimate friend of the management: When I went up to M. Richard, outside the foyer, during the Garden interval, with my hand out before me, why did M. Moncharmin hurriedly whisper to me, 'Go away! Go away! Whatever you do, don't touch **M. le directeur**!' Am I supposed to have an infectious disease?"

"It's incredible!"

"And, a little later, when M. de La Borderie went up to M. Richard, didn't you see M. Moncharmin fling himself between them and hear him exclaim, '**M. l'ambassadeur**,

I entreat you not to touch **M. le directeur**'?"

"It's terrible!... And what was Richard doing meanwhile?"

"What was he doing? Why, you saw him! He turned about, **bowed in front of him, though there was nobody in front of him**, and withdrew **backward**."

"**Backward?**"

"And Moncharmin, behind Richard, also turned about; that is, he described a semicircle behind Richard and also **walked backward**!... And they went **like that** to the staircase leading to the managers' office: **backward, backward, backward!**... Well, if they are not mad, will you explain what it means?"

"Perhaps they were practising a figure in the ballet," suggested Gabriel, without much conviction in his voice.

The secretary was furious at this wretched joke, made at so dramatic a moment. He knit his brows and contracted his lips. Then he put his mouth to Gabriel's ear:

"Don't be so sly, Gabriel. There are things going on for which you and Mercier are partly responsible."

"What do you mean?" asked Gabriel.

"Christine Daaé is not the only one who suddenly disappeared tonight."

"Oh, nonsense!"

"There's no nonsense about it. Perhaps you can tell me why, when Mother Giry came down to the foyer just now, Mercier took her by the hand and hurried her away with him?"

"Really?" said Gabriel, "I never saw it."

"You did see it, Gabriel, for you went with Mercier and Mother Giry to Mercier's office. Since then, you and Mercier have been seen, but no one has seen Mother Giry."

"Do you think we've eaten her?"

"No, but you've locked her up in the office; and anyone passing the office can hear her yelling, 'Oh, the scoundrels! Oh, the scoundrels!'"

At this point of this singular conversation,

Mercier arrived, all out of breath.

"There!" he said, in a gloomy voice. "It's worse than ever!... I shouted, 'It's a serious matter! Open the door! It's I, Mercier.' I heard footsteps. The door opened and Moncharmin appeared. He was very pale. He said, 'What do you want?' I answered, 'Someone has run away with Christine Daaé.' What do you think he said? 'And a good job, too!' And he shut the door, after putting this in my hand."

Mercier opened his hand; Rémy and Gabriel looked.

"The safety-pin!" cried Rémy.

"Strange! Strange!" muttered Gabriel, who could not help shivering.

Suddenly a voice made them all three turn round.

"I beg your pardon, gentlemen. Could you tell me where Christine Daaé is?"

In spite of the seriousness of the circumstances, the absurdity of the question would have made them roar with laughter, if they had not caught sight of a face so sorrow-stricken that they were at once seized with pity. It was the Vicomte Raoul de Chagny.

CHAPTER FIFTEEN

Christine! Christine!

RAOUL'S FIRST THOUGHT, after Christine Daaé's fantastic disappearance, was to accuse Erik. He no longer doubted the almost supernatural powers of the Angel of Music, in this domain of the Opera in which he had set up his empire. And Raoul rushed on the stage, in a mad fit of love and despair.

"Christine! Christine!" he moaned, calling

to her as he felt that she must be calling to him from the depths of that dark pit to which the monster had carried her. "Christine! Christine!"

And he seemed to hear the girl's screams through the frail boards that separated him from her. He bent forward, he listened,… he wandered over the stage like a madman. Ah, to descend, to descend into that pit of darkness every entrance to which was closed to him,… for the stairs that led below the stage were forbidden to one and all that night!

"Christine! Christine!…"

People pushed him aside, laughing. They made fun of him. They thought the poor lover's brain was gone!

By what mad road, through what passages of mystery and darkness known to him alone had Erik dragged that pure-souled child to the awful haunt, with the Louis-Philippe room, opening out on the lake?

"Christine! Christine!… Why don't you

answer?... Are you alive?..."

Hideous thoughts flashed through Raoul's congested brain. Of course, Erik must have discovered their secret, must have known that Christine had played him false. What a vengeance would be his!

And Raoul thought again of the yellow stars that had come, the night before, and roamed over his balcony. Why had he not put them out for good? There were some men's eyes that dilated in the darkness and shone like stars or like cats' eyes. Certainly Albinos, who seemed to have rabbits' eyes by day, had cats' eyes at night: everybody knew that!... Yes, yes, he had undoubtedly fired at Erik. Why had he not killed him? The monster had fled up the gutter-spout like a cat or a convict who – everybody knew that also – would scale the very skies, with the help of a gutter-spout.... No doubt Erik was at that time contemplating some decisive step against Raoul, but he had been wounded and had escaped to turn against poor Christine instead.

Such were the cruel thoughts that haunted Raoul as he ran to the singer's dressing-room.

"Christine! Christine!"

Bitter tears scorched the boy's eyelids as he saw scattered over the furniture the clothes which his beautiful bride was to have worn at the hour of their flight. Oh, why had she refused to leave earlier?

Why had she toyed with the threatening catastrophe? Why toyed with the monster's heart? Why, in a final access of pity, had she insisted on flinging, as a last sop to that demon's soul, her divine song:

"Holy angel, in Heaven blessed,
My spirit longs with thee to rest!"

Raoul, his throat filled with sobs, oaths and insults, fumbled awkwardly at the great mirror that had opened one night, before his eyes, to let Christine pass to the murky dwelling below. He pushed, pressed, groped about, but the glass apparently obeyed no one but Erik.... Perhaps actions were not enough with a glass of the kind? Perhaps he was expected to utter certain words? When he was a little boy, he had heard that there were things that obeyed the spoken word!

Suddenly, Raoul remembered something about a gate opening into the Rue Scribe, an underground passage running straight to the Rue Scribe from the lake.... Yes, Christine had told him about that.... And, when he found that the key was no longer in the box, he nevertheless ran to the Rue Scribe.

Outside, in the street, he passed his trembling hands over the huge stones, felt for outlets... met with iron bars... were those they?... Or these?... Or could it be that air-hole?... He plunged his useless eyes through the bars.... How dark it was in there!... He listened.... All was silence!... He went round the building... and came to bigger bars, immense gates!... It was the entrance to the Cour de l'Administration.

Raoul rushed into the doorkeeper's lodge.

"I beg your pardon, madame, could you tell me where to find a gate or door, made of bars, iron bars, opening into the Rue Scribe... and leading to the lake?... You know the lake I mean?... Yes, the underground lake... under the Opera."

"Yes, sir, I know there is a lake under the Opera, but I don't know which door leads to it. I have never been there!"

"And the Rue Scribe, madame, the Rue Scribe? Have you never been to the Rue Scribe?"

The woman laughed, screamed with laughter! Raoul darted away, roaring with anger, ran upstairs, four stairs at a time, downstairs, rushed through the whole of the business side of the opera-house, found himself once more in the light of the stage.

He stopped, with his heart thumping in his chest: suppose Christine Daaé had been found? He saw a group of men and asked:

"I beg your pardon, gentlemen. Could you

tell me where Christine Daaé is?"

And somebody laughed.

At the same moment the stage buzzed with a new sound and, amid a crowd of men in evening-dress, all talking and gesticulating together, appeared a man who seemed very calm and displayed a pleasant face, all pink and chubby-cheeked, crowned with curly hair and lit up by a pair of wonderfully serene blue eyes. Mercier, the acting-manager, called the Vicomte de Chagny's attention to him and said:

"This is the gentleman to whom you should put your question, monsieur. Let me introduce M. Mifroid, the commissary of police."

"Ah, M. le Vicomte de Chagny! Delighted to meet you, monsieur," said the commissary. "Would you mind coming with me?... And now where are the managers?... Where are the managers?..."

Mercier did not answer, and Rémy, the secretary, volunteered the information that the managers were locked up in their office and that they knew nothing as yet of what had happened.

"You don't mean to say so! Let us go up to the office!"

And M. Mifroid, followed by an ever-increasing crowd, turned toward the business side of the building. Mercier took advantage of the confusion to slip a key into Gabriel's hand:

"This is all going very badly," he whispered. "You had better let Mother Giry out."

And Gabriel moved away.

They soon came to the managers' door. Mercier stormed in vain: the door remained closed.

"Open in the name of the law!" commanded M. Mifroid, in a loud and rather anxious voice.

At last the door was opened. All rushed in to the office, on the commissary's heels.

Raoul was the last to enter. As he was about to follow the rest into the room, a hand was laid on his shoulder and he heard these words spoken in his ear:

"**Erik's secrets concern no one but himself!**"

He turned around, with a stifled exclamation. The hand that was laid on his shoulder was now placed on the lips of a person with an ebony skin, with eyes of jade and with an astrakhan cap on his head: the Persian!

The stranger kept up the gesture that recommended discretion and then, at the moment when the astonished viscount was about to ask the reason of his mysterious intervention, bowed and disappeared.

CHAPTER SIXTEEN

Mme. Giry's Astounding Revelations as to Her Personal Relations with the Opera Ghost

BEFORE FOLLOWING the commissary into the manager's office I must describe certain extraordinary occurrences that took place in that office which Rémy and Mercier had vainly tried to enter and into which

MM. Richard and Moncharmin had locked themselves with an object which the reader does not yet know, but which it is my duty, as an historian, to reveal without further postponement.

I have had occasion to say that the managers' mood had undergone a disagreeable change for some time past and to convey the fact that this change was due not only to the fall of the chandelier on the famous night of the gala performance.

The reader must know that the ghost had calmly been paid his first twenty thousand francs. Oh, there had been wailing and gnashing of teeth, indeed! And yet the thing had happened as simply as could be.

One morning, the managers found on their table an envelope addressed to "Monsieur O. G. (private)" and accompanied by a note from O. G. himself:

The time has come to carry out the clause in the memorandum-book. Please put twenty notes of a thousand francs each into this envelope, seal it with your own seal and hand it to Mme. Giry, who will do what is necessary.

The managers did not hesitate; without wasting time in asking how these confounded communications came to be delivered in an office which they were careful to keep locked, they seized this opportunity of laying hands on the mysterious blackmailer. And, after telling the whole story, under the promise of secrecy, to Gabriel and Mercier, they put the twenty thousand francs into the envelope and without asking for explanations, handed it to Mme. Giry, who had been reinstated in her functions. The box-keeper displayed no astonishment. I need hardly say that she was well watched. She went straight to the ghost's box and placed the precious envelope on the little shelf attached to the ledge. The two managers, as well as Gabriel and

Mercier, were hidden in such a way that they did not lose sight of the envelope for a second during the performance and even afterward, for, as the envelope had not moved, those who watched it did not move either; and Mme. Giry went away while the managers, Gabriel and Mercier were still there. At last, they became tired of waiting and opened the envelope, after ascertaining that the seals had not been broken.

At first sight, Richard and Moncharmin thought that the notes were still there; but soon they perceived that they were not the same. The twenty real notes were gone and had been replaced by twenty notes of the "Bank of St. Farce!"[2]

The managers' rage and fright were unmistakable. Moncharmin wanted to send

---

[2] Flash notes drawn on the "Bank of St. Farce" in France correspond with those drawn on the "Bank of Engraving" in England. — Translator's note

for the commissary of police, but Richard objected. He no doubt had a plan, for he said:

"Don't let us make ourselves ridiculous! All Paris would laugh at us. O. G. has won the first game: we will win the second."

He was thinking of the next month's allowance.

Nevertheless, they had been so absolutely tricked that they were bound to suffer a certain dejection. And, upon my word, it was not difficult to understand. We must not forget that the managers had an idea at the back of their minds, all the time, that this strange incident might be an unpleasant practical joke on the part of their predecessors and that it would not do to divulge it prematurely. On the other hand, Moncharmin was sometimes troubled with a suspicion of Richard himself, who occasionally took fanciful whims into his head. And so they were content to await events, while keeping an eye on Mother

Giry. Richard would not have her spoken to.

"If she is a confederate," he said, "the notes are gone long ago. But, in my opinion, she is merely an idiot."

"She's not the only idiot in this business," said Moncharmin pensively.

"Well, who could have thought it?" moaned Richard. "But don't be afraid… next time, I shall have taken my precautions."

The next time fell on the same day that beheld the disappearance of Christine Daaé. In the morning, a note from the ghost reminded them that the money was due. It read:

Do just as you did last time. It went very well. Put the twenty thousand in the envelope and hand it to our excellent Mme. Giry.

And the note was accompanied by the usual envelope. They had only to insert the notes.

This was done about half an hour before the curtain rose on the first act of **Faust**. Richard showed the envelope to Moncharmin. Then he counted the twenty thousand-franc notes in front of him and put the notes into the envelope, but without closing it.

"And now," he said, "let's have Mother Giry in."

The old woman was sent for. She entered with a sweeping courtesy. She still wore her black taffeta dress, the color of which was rapidly turning to rust and lilac, to say nothing of the dingy bonnet. She seemed in a good temper. She at once said:

"Good evening, gentlemen! It's for the envelope, I suppose?"

"Yes, Mme. Giry," said Richard, most amiably. "For the envelope… and something else besides."

"At your service, M. Richard, at your service. And what is the something else, please?"

"First of all, Mme. Giry, I have a little question to put to you."

"By all means, M. Richard: Mme. Giry is here to answer you."

"Are you still on good terms with the ghost?"

"Couldn't be better, sir; couldn't be better."

"Ah, we are delighted.... Look here, Mme. Giry," said Richard, in the tone of making an important confidence. "We may just as well tell you, among ourselves... you're no fool!"

"Why, sir," exclaimed the box-keeper, stopping the pleasant nodding of the black feathers in her dingy bonnet, "I assure you no one has ever doubted that!"

"We are quite agreed and we shall soon understand one another. The story of the ghost is all humbug, isn't it?... Well, still between ourselves,... it has lasted long enough."

Mme. Giry looked at the managers as though they were talking Chinese. She walked up to Richard's table and asked, rather anxiously:

"What do you mean? I don't understand."

"Oh, you understand quite well. In any case, you've got to understand.... And, first of all, tell us his name."

"Whose name?"

"The name of the man whose accomplice you are, Mme. Giry!"

"I am the ghost's accomplice? I?... His accomplice in what, pray?"

"You do all he wants."

"Oh! He's not very troublesome, you know."

"And does he still tip you?"

"I mustn't complain."

"How much does he give you for bringing him that envelope?"

"Ten francs."

"You poor thing! That's not much, is it?"

"Why?"

"I'll tell you that presently, Mme. Giry. Just now we should like to know for what extraordinary reason you have given yourself body and soul, to this ghost... Mme. Giry's friendship and devotion are not to be bought for five francs or ten francs."

"That's true enough.... And I can tell you the reason, sir. There's no disgrace about it... on the contrary."

"We're quite sure of that, Mme. Giry!"

"Well, it's like this... only the ghost doesn't like me to talk about his business."

"Indeed?" sneered Richard.

"But this is a matter that concerns myself alone.... Well, it was in Box Five one evening, I found a letter addressed to myself, a sort of note written in red ink. I needn't read the letter to you, sir; I know it by heart, and I shall never forget it if I live to be a hundred!"

And Mme. Giry, drawing herself up, recited the letter with touching eloquence:

Madam:

1825. Mlle. Ménétrier, leader of the ballet, became Marquise de Cussy.

1832. Mlle. Marie Taglioni, a dancer, became Comtesse Gilbert des Voisins.

1846. La Sota, a dancer, married a brother of the King of Spain.

1847. Lola Montes, a dancer, became the morganatic wife of King Louis of Bavaria and was created Countess of Landsfeld.

1848. Mlle. Maria, a dancer, became

Baronne d'Herneville.

1870. Thérèsa Hessier, a dancer, married Dom Fernando, brother to the King of Portugal.

Richard and Moncharmin listened to the old woman, who, as she proceeded with the enumeration of these glorious nuptials, swelled out, took courage and, at last, in a voice bursting with pride, flung out the last sentence of the prophetic letter:

1885. Meg Giry, Empress!

Exhausted by this supreme effort, the box-keeper fell into a chair, saying:

"Gentlemen, the letter was signed, 'Opera Ghost.' I had heard much of the ghost, but only half believed in him. From the day when he declared that my little Meg, the flesh of my flesh, the fruit of my womb, would be empress, I believed in him altogether."

And really it was not necessary to make a long study of Mme. Giry's excited features to understand what could be got out of that fine intellect with the two words "ghost" and "empress."

But who pulled the strings of that extraordinary puppet? That was the question.

"You have never seen him; he speaks to you and you believe all he says?" asked Moncharmin.

"Yes. To begin with, I owe it to him that my little Meg was promoted to be the leader of a row. I said to the ghost, 'If she is to be empress in 1885, there is no time to lose; she must become a leader at once.' He said, 'Look upon it as done.' And he had only a word to say to M. Poligny and the thing was done."

"So you say that M. Poligny saw him!"

"No, not any more than I did; but he heard him. The ghost said a word in his ear, you know, on the evening when he left Box Five, looking so dreadfully pale."

Moncharmin heaved a sigh. "What a business!" he groaned.

"Ah!" said Mme. Giry. "I always thought

there were secrets between the ghost and M. Poligny. Anything that the ghost asked M. Poligny to do M. Poligny did. M. Poligny could refuse the ghost nothing."

"You hear, Richard: Poligny could refuse the ghost nothing."

"Yes, yes, I hear!" said Richard. "M. Poligny is a friend of the ghost; and, as Mme. Giry is a friend of M. Poligny, there we are!... But I don't care a hang about M. Poligny," he added roughly. "The only person whose fate really interests me is Mme. Giry.... Mme. Giry, do you know what is in this envelope?"

"Why, of course not," she said.

"Well, look."

Mme. Giry looked into the envelope with a lackluster eye, which soon recovered its brilliancy.

"Thousand-franc notes!" she cried.

"Yes, Mme. Giry, thousand-franc notes! And you knew it!"

"I, sir? I?... I swear..."

"Don't swear, Mme. Giry!... And now I will

tell you the second reason why I sent for you. Mme. Giry, I am going to have you arrested."

The two black feathers on the dingy bonnet, which usually affected the attitude of two notes of interrogation, changed into two notes of exclamation; as for the bonnet itself, it swayed in menace on the old lady's tempestuous chignon. Surprise, indignation, protest and dismay were furthermore displayed by little Meg's mother in a sort of extravagant movement of offended virtue, half bound, half slide, that brought her right under the nose of M. Richard, who could not help pushing back his chair.

"**Have me arrested!**"

The mouth that spoke those words seemed to spit the three teeth that were left to it into Richard's face.

M. Richard behaved like a hero. He retreated no farther. His threatening forefinger seemed already to be pointing out the keeper of Box Five to the absent magistrates.

"I am going to have you arrested, Mme. Giry, as a thief!"

"Say that again!"

And Mme. Giry caught Mr. Manager Richard a mighty box on the ear, before Mr. Manager Moncharmin had time to intervene. But it was not the withered hand of the angry old beldame that fell on the managerial ear, but the envelope itself, the cause of all the trouble, the magic envelope that opened with the blow, scattering the banknotes, which escaped in a fantastic whirl of giant butterflies.

The two managers gave a shout, and the same thought made them both go on their knees, feverishly picking up and hurriedly examining the precious scraps of paper.

"Are they still genuine, Moncharmin?"

"Are they still genuine, Richard?"

"Yes, they are still genuine!"

Above their heads, Mame Giry's three teeth were clashing in a noisy contest, full of hideous interjections. But all that could be clearly distinguished was this leitmotif:

"I, a thief!… I, a thief, I?"

She choked with rage. She shouted:

"I never heard of such a thing!"

And, suddenly, she darted up to Richard again.

"In any case," she yelped, "you, M. Richard, ought to know better than I where the twenty thousand francs went to!"

"I?" asked Richard, astounded. "And how should I know?"

Moncharmin, looking severe and dissatisfied, at once insisted that the good lady should explain herself.

"What does this mean, Mme. Giry?" he asked. "And why do you say that M. Richard ought to know better than you where the twenty-thousand francs went to?"

As for Richard, who felt himself turning red under Moncharmin's eyes, he took Mme. Giry by the wrist and shook it violently. In a voice growling and rolling like thunder, he roared:

"Why should I know better than you where the twenty-thousand francs went to? Why? Answer me!"

"Because they went into your pocket!" gasped the old woman, looking at him as if he were the devil incarnate.

Richard would have rushed upon Mme. Giry, if Moncharmin had not stayed his avenging hand and hastened to ask her, more gently:

"How can you suspect my partner, M. Richard, of putting twenty-thousand francs in his pocket?"

"I never said that," declared Mame Giry, "seeing that it was myself who put the twenty-thousand francs into M. Richard's pocket." And she added, under her voice, "There! It's out!... And may the ghost forgive me!"

Richard began bellowing anew, but Moncharmin authoritatively ordered him to be silent.

"Allow me! Allow me! Let the woman explain herself. Let me question her." And he added: "It is really astonishing that you should take up such a tone!… We are on the verge of clearing up the whole mystery. And you're in a rage!… You're wrong to behave like that…. I'm enjoying myself immensely."

Mame Giry, like the martyr that she was, raised her head, her face beaming with faith in her own innocence.

"You tell me there were twenty-thousand francs in the envelope which I put into M. Richard's pocket; but I tell you again that I knew nothing about it…. Nor M. Richard either, for that matter!"

"Aha!" said Richard, suddenly assuming a swaggering air which Moncharmin did not like. "I knew nothing either! You put twenty-thousand francs in my pocket and I knew nothing either! I am very glad to hear it, Mme. Giry!"

"Yes," the terrible dame agreed, "yes, it's true. We neither of us knew anything. But you, you must have ended by finding out!"

Richard would certainly have swallowed Mame Giry alive, if Moncharmin had not been there! But Moncharmin protected her. He resumed his questions:

"What sort of envelope did you put in M. Richard's pocket? It was not the one which we gave you, the one which you took to Box Five before our eyes; and yet that was the one which contained the twenty-thousand francs."

"I beg your pardon. The envelope which **M. le directeur** gave me was the one which I slipped into **M. le directeur's** pocket," explained Mame Giry. "The one which I took to the ghost's box was another envelope, just like it, which the ghost gave me beforehand and which I hid up my sleeve."

So saying, Mame Giry took from her sleeve an envelope ready prepared and similarly addressed to that containing the twenty-thousand francs. The managers took it from her. They examined it and saw that it was fastened with seals stamped with their own managerial seal. They opened it. It contained twenty Bank of St. Farce notes like those which had so much astounded them the month before.

"How simple!" said Richard.

"How simple!" repeated Moncharmin. And he continued with his eyes fixed upon Mame Giry, as though trying to hypnotize her.

"So it was the ghost who gave you this envelope and told you to substitute it for the one which we gave you? And it was the ghost who told you to put the other into M. Richard's pocket?"

"Yes, it was the ghost."

"Then would you mind giving us a specimen of your little talents? Here is the envelope. Act as though we knew nothing."

"As you please, gentlemen."

Mame Giry took the envelope with the twenty notes inside it and made for the door. She was on the point of going out when the two managers rushed at her:

"Oh, no! Oh, no! We're not going to be 'done' a second time! Once bitten, twice shy!"

"I beg your pardon, gentlemen," said the old woman, in self-excuse, "you told me to act as though you knew nothing.... Well, if you knew nothing, I should go away with your envelope!"

"And then how would you slip it into my pocket?" argued Richard, whom Moncharmin fixed with his left eye, while keeping his right on Mame Giry: a proceeding likely to strain his sight, but Moncharmin was prepared to go to any length to discover the truth.

"I am to slip it into your pocket when you least expect it, sir. You know that I always take a little turn behind the scenes, in the course of the evening, and I often go with my daughter to the ballet-foyer, which I am entitled to do, as her mother; I bring her her shoes, when the ballet is about to begin... in fact, I come and go as I please.... The subscribers come and go too.... So do you, sir.... There are lots of people about.... I go behind you and slip the envelope into the tail-pocket of your dress-coat.... There's no witchcraft about that!"

"No witchcraft!" growled Richard, rolling his eyes like Jupiter Tonans. "No witchcraft! Why, I've just caught you in a lie, you old witch!"

Mame Giry bristled, with her three teeth sticking out of her mouth.

"And why, may I ask?"

"Because I spent that evening watching Box Five and the sham envelope which you put there. I did not go to the ballet-foyer for a second."

"No, sir, and I did not give you the envelope that evening, but at the next performance... on the evening when the undersecretary of state for fine arts..."

At these words, M. Richard suddenly interrupted Mame Giry:

"Yes, that's true, I remember now! The undersecretary went behind the scenes. He asked for me. I went down to the ballet-foyer for a moment. I was on the foyer steps.... The undersecretary and his chief clerk were in the foyer itself.... I suddenly turned around... you had passed behind me, Mme. Giry.... You seemed to push against me.... Oh, I can see you still, I can see you still!"

"Yes, that's it, sir, that's it. I had just finished my little business. That pocket of yours, sir, is very handy!"

And Mame Giry once more suited the action to the word. She passed behind M. Richard and, so nimbly that Moncharmin himself was impressed by it, slipped the envelope into the pocket of one of the tails of M. Richard's dress-coat.

"Of course!" exclaimed Richard, looking a little pale. "It's very clever of O. G. The problem which he had to solve was this: how to do away with any dangerous intermediary between the man who gives the twenty-thousand francs and the man who receives it. And by far the best thing he could hit upon was to come and take the money from my pocket without my noticing it, as I myself did not know that it was there. It's wonderful!"

"Oh, wonderful, no doubt!" Moncharmin agreed. "Only, you forget, Richard, that I provided ten-thousand francs of the twenty and that nobody put anything in my pocket!"

CHAPTER SEVENTEEN

The Safety-Pin Again

MONCHARMIN'S LAST PHRASE so clearly expressed the suspicion in which he now held his partner that it was bound to cause a stormy explanation, at the end of which it was agreed that Richard should yield to all Moncharmin's wishes, with the object of helping him to discover the miscreant who was victimizing them.

This brings us to the interval after the Garden

Act, with the strange conduct observed by M. Rémy and those curious lapses from the dignity that might be expected of the managers. It was arranged between Richard and Moncharmin, first, that Richard should repeat the exact movements which he had made on the night of the disappearance of the first twenty-thousand francs; and, second, that Moncharmin should not for an instant lose sight of Richard's coattail pocket, into which Mame Giry was to slip the twenty-thousand francs.

M. Richard went and placed himself at the identical spot where he had stood when he bowed to the undersecretary for fine arts. M. Moncharmin took up his position a few steps behind him.

Mame Giry passed, rubbed up against M. Richard, got rid of her twenty-thousand francs in the manager's coattail pocket and disappeared.... Or rather she was conjured away. In accordance with the instructions received from Moncharmin a few minutes earlier, Mercier took the good lady to the acting-manager's office and turned the key on her, thus making it impossible for her to communicate with her ghost.

Meanwhile, M. Richard was bending and bowing and scraping and walking backward, just as if he had that high and mighty minister, the undersecretary for fine arts, before him. Only, though these marks of politeness would have created no astonishment if the undersecretary of state had really been in front of M. Richard, they caused an easily comprehensible amazement to the spectators of this very natural but quite inexplicable scene when M. Richard had nobody in front of him.

M. Richard bowed... to nobody; bent his back... before nobody; and walked backward... before nobody.... And, a few steps behind him, M. Moncharmin did the same thing that he was doing, in addition to pushing away M. Rémy and begging M. de La Borderie, the ambassador, and the manager of the Crédit Central "not to touch **M. le directeur**."

Moncharmin, who had his own ideas, did not want Richard to come to him presently, when the twenty-thousand francs were gone, and say:

"Perhaps it was the ambassador… or the manager of the Crédit Central… or Rémy."

The more so as, at the time of the first scene, as Richard himself admitted, Richard had met nobody in that part of the theater after Mame Giry had brushed up against him….

Having begun by walking backward in order to bow, Richard continued to do so from prudence, until he reached the passage leading to the offices of the management. In this way, he was constantly watched by Moncharmin from behind and himself kept an eye on anyone approaching from the front. Once more, this novel method of walking behind the scenes, adopted by the managers of our National Academy of Music, attracted attention; but the managers themselves thought of nothing but their twenty-thousand francs.

On reaching the half-dark passage, Richard said to Moncharmin, in a low voice:

"I am sure that nobody has touched me.... You had now better keep at some distance from me and watch me till I come to door of the office: it is better not to arouse suspicion and we can see anything that happens."

But Moncharmin replied. "No, Richard, no! You walk ahead and I'll walk immediately behind you! I won't leave you by a step!"

"But, in that case," exclaimed Richard, "they will never steal our twenty-thousand francs!"

"I should hope not, indeed!" declared Moncharmin.

"Then what we are doing is absurd!"

"We are doing exactly what we did last time.... Last time, I joined you as you were leaving the stage and followed close behind you down this passage."

"That's true!" sighed Richard, shaking his head and passively obeying Moncharmin.

Two minutes later, the joint managers locked themselves into their office. Moncharmin himself put the key in his pocket:

"We remained locked up like this, last time," he said, "until you left the Opera to go home."

"That's so. No one came and disturbed us, I suppose?"

"No one."

"Then," said Richard, who was trying to collect his memory, "then I must certainly have been robbed on my way home from the Opera."

"No," said Moncharmin in a drier tone than ever, "no, that's impossible. For I dropped you in my cab. The twenty-thousand francs disappeared at your place: there's not a shadow of a doubt about that."

"It's incredible!" protested Richard. "I am sure of my servants… and if one of them had done it, he would have disappeared since."

Moncharmin shrugged his shoulders, as though to say that he did not wish to enter into details, and Richard began to think that Moncharmin was treating him in a very insupportable fashion.

"Moncharmin, I've had enough of this!"

"Richard, I've had too much of it!"

"Do you dare to suspect me?"

"Yes, of a silly joke."

"One doesn't joke with twenty-thousand francs."

"That's what I think," declared Moncharmin, unfolding a newspaper and ostentatiously studying its contents.

"What are you doing?" asked Richard. "Are you going to read the paper next?"

"Yes, Richard, until I take you home."

"Like last time?"

"Yes, like last time."

Richard snatched the paper from Moncharmin's hands. Moncharmin stood up, more irritated than ever, and found himself faced by an exasperated Richard, who, crossing his arms on his chest, said:

"Look here, I'm thinking of this, **I'm thinking of what I might think** if, like last time, after my spending the evening alone with you, you brought me home and if, at the moment of parting, I perceived that twenty-thousand francs had disappeared from my coat-pocket… like last time."

"And what might you think?" asked Moncharmin, crimson with rage.

"I might think that, as you hadn't left me by a foot's breadth and as, by your own wish, you were the only one to approach me, like last time, I might think that, if that twenty-thousand francs was no longer in my pocket, it stood a very good chance of being in yours!"

Moncharmin leaped up at the suggestion.

"Oh!" he shouted. "A safety-pin!"

"What do you want a safety-pin for?"

"To fasten you up with!… A safety-pin!… A safety-pin!"

"You want to fasten me with a safety-pin?"

"Yes, to fasten you to the twenty-thousand francs! Then, whether it's here, or on the drive from here to your place, or at your place, you will feel the hand that pulls at your pocket and you will see if it's mine! Oh, so you're suspecting me now, are you? A safety-pin!"

And that was the moment when Moncharmin opened the door on the passage and shouted:

"A safety-pin!... Somebody give me a safety-pin!"

And we also know how, at the same moment, Rémy, who had no safety-pin, was received by Moncharmin, while a boy procured the pin so eagerly longed for. And what happened was this: Moncharmin first locked the door again. Then he knelt down behind Richard's back.

"I hope," he said, "that the notes are still there?"

"So do I," said Richard.

"The real ones?" asked Moncharmin, resolved not to be "had" this time.

"Look for yourself," said Richard. "I refuse to touch them."

Moncharmin took the envelope from Richard's pocket and drew out the banknotes with a trembling hand, for, this time, in order frequently to make sure of the presence of the notes, he had not sealed the envelope nor even fastened it. He felt reassured on finding that they were all there and quite genuine. He put them back in the tail-pocket and pinned them with great care. Then he sat down behind Richard's coattails and kept his eyes fixed on them, while Richard, sitting at his writing-table, did not stir.

"A little patience, Richard," said Moncharmin. "We have only a few minutes to wait.... The clock will soon strike twelve. Last time, we left at the last stroke of twelve."

"Oh, I shall have all the patience necessary!"

The time passed, slow, heavy, mysterious, stifling. Richard tried to laugh.

"I shall end by believing in the omnipotence of the ghost," he said. "Just now, don't you find something uncomfortable, disquieting, alarming in the atmosphere of this room?"

"You're quite right," said Moncharmin, who was really impressed.

"The ghost!" continued Richard, in a low voice, as though fearing lest he should be overheard by invisible ears. "The ghost! Suppose, all the same, it were a ghost who puts the magic envelopes on the table... who talks in Box Five... who killed Joseph Buquet... who unhooked the chandelier... and who robs us! For, after all, after all, after all, there is no one here except you and me, and, if the notes disappear and neither you nor I have anything to do with it, well, we shall have to believe in the ghost... in the ghost."

At that moment, the clock on the mantelpiece gave its warning click and the first stroke of twelve struck.

The two managers shuddered. The

perspiration streamed from their foreheads. The twelfth stroke sounded strangely in their ears.

When the clock stopped, they gave a sigh and rose from their chairs.

"I think we can go now," said Moncharmin.

"I think so," Richard agreed.

"Before we go, do you mind if I look in your pocket?"

"But, of course, Moncharmin, **you must**!… Well?" he asked, as Moncharmin was feeling at the pocket.

"Well, I can feel the pin."

"Of course, as you said, we can't be robbed without noticing it."

But Moncharmin, whose hands were still fumbling, bellowed:

"I can feel the pin, but I can't feel the notes!"

"Come, no joking, Moncharmin!… This isn't the time for it."

"Well, feel for yourself."

Richard tore off his coat. The two managers turned the pocket inside out. **The pocket**

was empty. And the curious thing was that the pin remained, stuck in the same place.

Richard and Moncharmin turned pale. There was no longer any doubt about the witchcraft.

"The ghost!" muttered Moncharmin.

But Richard suddenly sprang upon his partner.

"No one but you has touched my pocket! Give me back my twenty-thousand francs!... Give me back my twenty-thousand francs!..."

"On my soul," sighed Moncharmin, who was ready to swoon, "on my soul, I swear that I haven't got it!"

Then somebody knocked at the door. Moncharmin opened it automatically, seemed hardly to recognize Mercier, his business-manager, exchanged a few words with him, without knowing what he was saying and, with an unconscious movement, put the safety-pin, for which he had no further use, into the hands of his bewildered subordinate....

CHAPTER EIGHTEEN

The Commissary, the Viscount and the Persian

THE FIRST WORDS of the commissary of police, on entering the managers' office, were to ask after the missing prima donna.

"Is Christine Daaé here?"

"Christine Daaé here?" echoed Richard. "No. Why?"

As for Moncharmin, he had not the strength

left to utter a word.

Richard repeated, for the commissary and the compact crowd which had followed him into the office observed an impressive silence.

“Why do you ask if Christine Daaé is here, **M. le commissaire**?”

“Because she has to be found,” declared the commissary of police solemnly.

“What do you mean, she has to be found? Has she disappeared?”

“In the middle of the performance!”

“In the middle of the performance? This is extraordinary!”

“Isn’t it? And what is quite as extraordinary is that you should first learn it from me!”

“Yes,” said Richard, taking his head in his hands and muttering. “What is this new business? Oh, it’s enough to make a man send in his resignation!”

And he pulled a few hairs out of his mustache without even knowing what he was doing.

"So she... so she disappeared in the middle of the performance?" he repeated.

"Yes, she was carried off in the Prison Act, at the moment when she was invoking the aid of the angels; but I doubt if she was carried off by an angel."

"And I am sure that she was!"

Everybody looked round. A young man, pale and trembling with excitement, repeated:

"I am sure of it!"

"Sure of what?" asked Mifroid.

"That Christine Daaé was carried off by an angel, **M. le commissaire**, and I can tell you his name."

"Aha, M. le Vicomte de Chagny! So you maintain that Christine Daaé was carried off by an angel: an angel of the Opera, no doubt?"

"Yes, monsieur, by an angel of the Opera; and I will tell you where he lives... when we are alone."

"You are right, monsieur."

And the commissary of police, inviting Raoul to take a chair, cleared the room of all the rest, excepting the managers.

Then Raoul spoke:

"**M. le commissaire**, the angel is called Erik, he lives in the Opera and he is the Angel of Music!"

"The Angel of Music! Really! That is very curious!... The Angel of Music!" And, turning to the managers, M. Mifroid asked, "Have you an Angel of Music on the premises, gentlemen?"

Richard and Moncharmin shook their heads, without even speaking.

"Oh," said the viscount, "those gentlemen have heard of the Opera ghost. Well, I am in a position to state that the Opera ghost and the Angel of Music are one and the same person; and his real name is Erik."

M. Mifroid rose and looked at Raoul attentively.

"I beg your pardon, monsieur, but is it your intention to make fun of the law? And, if not, what is all this about the Opera ghost?"

"I say that these gentlemen have heard of him."

"Gentlemen, it appears that you know the Opera ghost?"

Richard rose, with the remaining hairs of his mustache in his hand.

"No, M. Commissary, no, we do not know him, but we wish that we did, for this very evening he has robbed us of twenty-thousand francs!"

And Richard turned a terrible look on Moncharmin, which seemed to say:

"Give me back the twenty-thousand francs, or I'll tell the whole story."

Moncharmin understood what he meant, for, with a distracted gesture, he said:

"Oh, tell everything and have done with it!"

As for Mifroid, he looked at the managers and at Raoul by turns and wondered whether he had strayed into a lunatic asylum. He passed his hand through his hair.

"A ghost," he said, "who, on the same

evening, carries off an opera-singer and steals twenty-thousand francs is a ghost who must have his hands very full! If you don't mind, we will take the questions in order. The singer first, the twenty-thousand francs after. Come, M. de Chagny, let us try to talk seriously. You believe that Mlle. Christine Daaé has been carried off by an individual called Erik. Do you know this person? Have you seen him?"

"Yes."

"Where?"

"In a churchyard."

M. Mifroid gave a start, began to scrutinize Raoul again and said:

"Of course!... That's where ghosts usually hang out!... And what were you doing in that churchyard?"

"Monsieur," said Raoul, "I can quite understand how absurd my replies must seem to you. But I beg you to believe that I am in full possession of my faculties. The safety of the person dearest to me in the world is at stake. I should like to convince you in a few words, for time is pressing and every minute is valuable. Unfortunately, if I do not tell you the strangest story that ever was from the beginning, you will not believe me. I will tell you all I know about the Opera ghost, M. Commissary. Alas, I do not know much!..."

"Never mind, go on, go on!" exclaimed Richard and Moncharmin, suddenly greatly interested.

Unfortunately for their hopes of learning some detail that could put them on the track of their hoaxer, they were soon compelled to accept the fact that M. Raoul de Chagny had completely lost his head. All that story about Perros-Guirec, death's heads and enchanted violins, could only have taken birth in the disordered brain of a youth mad with love. It was evident, also, that Mr. Commissary Mifroid shared their view; and the magistrate would certainly have cut short the incoherent narrative if circumstances had not taken it upon themselves to interrupt it.

The door opened and a man entered, curiously dressed in an enormous frock-coat and a tall hat, at once shabby and shiny, that came down to his ears. He went up to the commissary and spoke to him in a whisper. It was doubtless a detective come to deliver an important communication.

During this conversation, M. Mifroid did not take his eyes off Raoul. At last, addressing him, he said:

"Monsieur, we have talked enough about the ghost. We will now talk about yourself a little, if you have no objection: you were to carry off Mlle. Christine Daaé tonight?"

"Yes, **M. le commissaire**."

"After the performance?"

"Yes, **M. le commissaire**."

"All your arrangements were made?"

"Yes, **M. le commissaire**."

"The carriage that brought you was to take you both away.... There were fresh horses in readiness at every stage...."

"That is true, **M. le commissaire**."

"And nevertheless your carriage is still outside the Rotunda awaiting your orders, is it not?"

"Yes, **M. le commissaire**."

"Did you know that there were three other carriages there, in addition to yours?"

"I did not pay the least attention."

"They were the carriages of Mlle. Sorelli, which could not find room in the Cour de l'Administration; of Carlotta; and of your brother, M. le Comte de Chagny...."

"Very likely...."

"What is certain is that, though your carriage and Sorelli's and Carlotta's are still there, by the Rotunda pavement, M. le Comte de Chagny's carriage is gone."

"This has nothing to say to..."

"I beg your pardon. Was not M. le Comte opposed to your marriage with Mlle. Daaé?"

"That is a matter that only concerns the family."

"You have answered my question: he was

opposed to it… and that was why you were carrying Christine Daaé out of your brother's reach.… Well, M. de Chagny, allow me to inform you that your brother has been smarter than you! It is he who has carried off Christine Daaé!"

"Oh, impossible!" moaned Raoul, pressing his hand to his heart. "Are you sure?"

"Immediately after the artist's disappearance, which was procured by means which we have still to ascertain, he flung into his carriage, which drove right across Paris at a furious pace."

"Across Paris?" asked poor Raoul, in a hoarse voice. "What do you mean by across Paris?"

"Across Paris and out of Paris… by the Brussels road."

"Oh," cried the young man, "I shall catch them!"

And he rushed out of the office.

"And bring her back to us!" cried the commissary gaily.… "Ah, that's a trick worth two of the Angel of Music's!"

And, turning to his audience, M. Mifroid delivered a little lecture on police methods.

"I don't know for a moment whether M. le Comte de Chagny has really carried Christine Daaé off or not... but I want to know and I believe that, at this moment, no one is more anxious to inform us than his brother.... And now he is flying in pursuit of him! He is my chief auxiliary! This, gentlemen, is the art of the police, which is believed to be so complicated and which, nevertheless, appears so simple as soon as you see that it consists in getting your work done by people who have nothing to do with the police."

But M. le Commissaire de Police Mifroid would not have been quite so satisfied with himself if he had known that the rush of his rapid emissary was stopped at the entrance to the very first corridor. A tall figure blocked Raoul's way.

"Where are you going so fast, M. de

Chagny?" asked a voice.

Raoul impatiently raised his eyes and recognized the astrakhan cap of an hour ago. He stopped:

"It's you!" he cried, in a feverish voice. "You, who know Erik's secrets and don't want me to speak of them. Who are you?"

"You know who I am!... I am the Persian!"

CHAPTER NINETEEN

The Viscount and the Persian

RAOUL NOW REMEMBERED that his brother had once shown him that mysterious person, of whom nothing was known except that he was a Persian and that he lived in a little old-fashioned flat in the Rue de Rivoli.

The man with the ebony skin, the eyes of jade and the astrakhan cap bent over Raoul.

"I hope, M. de Chagny," he said, "that you

have not betrayed Erik's secret?"

"And why should I hesitate to betray that monster, sir?" Raoul rejoined haughtily, trying to shake off the intruder. "Is he your friend, by any chance?"

"I hope that you said nothing about Erik, sir, because Erik's secret is also Christine Daaé's and to talk about one is to talk about the other!"

"Oh, sir," said Raoul, becoming more and more impatient, "you seem to know about many things that interest me; and yet I have no time to listen to you!"

"Once more, M. de Chagny, where are you going so fast?"

"Can not you guess? To Christine Daaé's assistance...."

"Then, sir, stay here, for Christine Daaé is here!"

"With Erik?"

"With Erik."

"How do you know?"

"I was at the performance and no one in the

world but Erik could contrive an abduction like that!... Oh," he said, with a deep sigh, "I recognized the monster's touch!..."

"You know him then?"

The Persian did not reply, but heaved a fresh sigh.

"Sir," said Raoul, "I do not know what your intentions are, but can you do anything to help me? I mean, to help Christine Daaé?"

"I think so, M. de Chagny, and that is why I spoke to you."

"What can you do?"

"Try to take you to her... and to him."

"If you can do me that service, sir, my life is yours!... One word more: the commissary of police tells me that Christine Daaé has been carried off by my brother, Count Philippe."

"Oh, M. de Chagny, I don't believe a word of it."

"It's not possible, is it?"

"I don't know if it is possible or not; but there are ways and ways of carrying people off; and M. le Comte Philippe has never, as far as I know, had anything to do with witchcraft."

"Your arguments are convincing, sir, and I am a fool!... Oh, let us make haste! I place myself entirely in your hands!... How should I not believe you, when you are the only one to believe me... when you are the only one not to smile when Erik's name is mentioned?"

And the young man impetuously seized the Persian's hands. They were ice-cold.

"Silence!" said the Persian, stopping and listening to the distant sounds of the theater. "We must not mention that name here. Let us say 'he' and 'him;' then there will be less danger of attracting his attention."

"Do you think he is near us?"

"It is quite possible, sir, if he is not, at this moment, with his victim, **in the house on the lake**."

"Ah, so you know that house too?"

"If he is not there, he may be here, in this wall, in this floor, in this ceiling!... Come!"

And the Persian, asking Raoul to deaden

the sound of his footsteps, led him down passages which Raoul had never seen before, even at the time when Christine used to take him for walks through that labyrinth.

"If only Darius has come!" said the Persian.

"Who is Darius?"

"Darius? My servant."

They were now in the center of a real deserted square, an immense apartment ill-lit by a small lamp. The Persian stopped Raoul and, in the softest of whispers, asked:

"What did you say to the commissary?"

"I said that Christine Daaé's abductor was the Angel of Music, **alias** the Opera ghost, and that the real name was..."

"Hush!... And did he believe you?"

"No."

"He attached no importance to what you said?"

"No."

"He took you for a bit of a madman?"

"Yes."

"So much the better!" sighed the Persian.

And they continued their road. After going up and down several staircases which Raoul had never seen before, the two men found themselves in front of a door which the Persian opened with a master-key. The Persian and Raoul were both, of course, in dress-clothes; but, whereas Raoul had a tall hat, the Persian wore the astrakhan cap which I have already mentioned. It was an infringement of the rule which insists upon the tall hat behind the scenes; but in France foreigners are allowed every license: the Englishman his traveling-cap, the Persian his cap of astrakhan.

"Sir," said the Persian, "your tall hat will be in your way: you would do well to leave it in the dressing-room."

"What dressing-room?" asked Raoul.

"Christine Daaé's."

And the Persian, letting Raoul through the door which he had just opened, showed him the actress' room opposite.

They were at the end of the passage the whole length of which Raoul had been accustomed to traverse before knocking at Christine's door.

"How well you know the Opera, sir!"

"Not so well as 'he' does!" said the Persian modestly.

And he pushed the young man into Christine's dressing-room, which was as Raoul had left it a few minutes earlier.

Closing the door, the Persian went to a very thin partition that separated the dressing-room from a big lumber-room next to it. He listened and then coughed loudly.

There was a sound of someone stirring in the lumber-room; and, a few seconds later, a finger tapped at the door.

"Come in," said the Persian.

A man entered, also wearing an astrakhan cap and dressed in a long overcoat. He bowed and took a richly carved case from under his coat, put it on the dressing-table, bowed once again and went to the door.

"Did no one see you come in, Darius?"

"No, master."

"Let no one see you go out."

The servant glanced down the passage and swiftly disappeared.

The Persian opened the case. It contained a pair of long pistols.

"When Christine Daaé was carried off, sir, I sent word to my servant to bring me these pistols. I have had them a long time and they can be relied upon."

"Do you mean to fight a duel?" asked the young man.

"It will certainly be a duel which we shall have to fight," said the other, examining the priming of his pistols. "And what a duel!" Handing one of the pistols to Raoul, he added, "In this duel, we shall be two to one; but you must be prepared for everything, for we shall be fighting the most terrible adversary that you can imagine. But you love Christine Daaé, do you not?"

"I worship the ground she stands on! But you, sir, who do not love her, tell me why I find you ready to risk your life for her! You must certainly hate Erik!"

"No, sir," said the Persian sadly, "I do not hate him. If I hated him, he would long ago have ceased doing harm."

"Has he done you harm?"

"I have forgiven him the harm which he has done me."

"I do not understand you. You treat him as a monster, you speak of his crime, he has done you harm and I find in you the same inexplicable pity that drove me to despair when I saw it in Christine!"

The Persian did not reply. He fetched a stool and set it against the wall facing the great mirror that filled the whole of the wall-space opposite. Then he climbed on the stool and, with his nose to the wallpaper, seemed to be looking for something.

"Ah," he said, after a long search, "I have it!"

And, raising his finger above his head, he pressed against a corner in the pattern of the paper. Then he turned round and jumped off the stool:

"In half a minute," he said, "we shall be **on his road**!" and crossing the whole length of the dressing-room he felt the great mirror.

"No, it is not yielding yet," he muttered.

"Oh, are we going out by the mirror?" asked Raoul. "Like Christine Daaé."

"So you knew that Christine Daaé went out by that mirror?"

"She did so before my eyes, sir! I was hidden behind the curtain of the inner room and I saw her vanish not by the glass, but in the glass!"

"And what did you do?"

"I thought it was an aberration of my senses, a mad dream...."

"Or some new fancy of the ghost's!" chuckled the Persian. "Ah, M. de Chagny," he continued, still with his hand on the mirror, "would that we had to do with a ghost! We could then leave our pistols in their case.... Put down your hat, please... there... and now cover your shirtfront as much as you can with your coat... as I am doing.... Bring the lapels forward... turn up the collar.... We must make ourselves as invisible as possible...."

Bearing against the mirror, after a short silence, he said:

"It takes some time to release the counterbalance, when you press on the spring from the inside of the room. It is different when you are behind the wall and can act directly on the counterbalance. Then the mirror turns at once and is moved with incredible rapidity."

"What counterbalance?" asked Raoul.

"Why, the counterbalance that lifts the whole of this wall on to its pivot. You surely don't expect it to move of itself, by enchantment! If you watch, you will see the mirror first rise an inch or two and then shift an inch or two from left to right. It will then be on a pivot and will swing round."

"It's not turning!" said Raoul impatiently.

"Oh, wait! You have time enough to be impatient, sir! The mechanism has obviously become rusty, or else the spring isn't working.... Unless it is something else," added the Persian anxiously.

"What?"

"He may simply have cut the cord of the counterbalance and blocked the whole apparatus."

"Why should he? He does not know that we are coming this way!"

"I dare say he suspects it, for he knows that I understand the system."

"It's not turning!... And Christine, sir, Christine?"

The Persian said coldly:

"We shall do all that it is humanly possible to do!... But he may stop us at the first step!... He commands the walls, the doors and the trapdoors. In my country, he was known by a name which means the 'trap-door lover.'"

"But why do these walls obey him alone? He did not build them!"

"Yes, sir, that is just what he did!"

Raoul looked at him in amazement; but the Persian made a sign to him to be silent and pointed to the glass.... There was a sort of shivering reflection. Their image was troubled as in a rippling sheet of water and then all became stationary again.

"You see, sir, that it is not turning! Let us take another road!"

"Tonight, there is no other!" declared the Persian, in a singularly mournful voice. "And now, look out! And be ready to fire."

He himself raised his pistol opposite the glass. Raoul imitated his movement. With his free arm, the Persian drew the young man to his chest and, suddenly, the mirror turned, in a blinding daze of cross-lights: it turned like one of those revolving doors which have lately been fixed to the entrances of most restaurants, it turned, carrying Raoul and the Persian with it and suddenly hurling them from the full light into the deepest darkness.

CHAPTER TWENTY

In the Cellars of the Opera

"YOUR HAND HIGH, ready to fire!" repeated Raoul's companion quickly.

The wall, behind them, having completed the circle which it described upon itself, closed again; and the two men stood motionless for a moment, holding their breath.

At last, the Persian decided to make a movement; and Raoul heard him slip on his knees and feel for something in the dark with his groping hands. Suddenly, the darkness was made visible by a small dark lantern and Raoul instinctively stepped backward as though to escape the scrutiny of a secret enemy. But he soon perceived that the light belonged to the Persian, whose movements he was closely observing. The little red disk was turned in every direction and Raoul saw that the floor, the walls and the ceiling were all formed of planking. It must have been the ordinary road taken by Erik to reach Christine's dressing-room and impose upon her innocence. And Raoul, remembering the Persian's remark, thought that it had been mysteriously constructed by the ghost himself. Later, he learned that Erik had found, all prepared for him, a secret passage, long known to himself alone and contrived at the time of the Paris Commune to allow the jailers to convey their prisoners straight to the dungeons that had been constructed for them in the cellars; for the

Federates had occupied the opera-house immediately after the eighteenth of March and had made a starting-place right at the top for their Mongolfier balloons, which carried their incendiary proclamations to the departments, and a state prison right at the bottom.

The Persian went on his knees and put his lantern on the ground. He seemed to be working at the floor; and suddenly he turned off his light. Then Raoul heard a faint click and saw a very pale luminous square in the floor of the passage. It was as though a window had opened on the Opera cellars, which were still lit. Raoul no longer saw the Persian, but he suddenly felt him by his side and heard him whisper:

"Follow me and do all that I do."

Raoul turned to the luminous aperture. Then he saw the Persian, who was still on his knees, hang by his hands from the rim of the opening, with his pistol between his teeth, and slide into the cellar below.

Curiously enough, the viscount had absolute confidence in the Persian, though he knew nothing about him. His emotion when speaking of the “monster” struck him as sincere; and, if the Persian had cherished any sinister designs against him, he would not have armed him with his own hands. Besides, Raoul must reach Christine at all costs. He therefore went on his knees also and hung from the trap with both hands.

“Let go!” said a voice.

And he dropped into the arms of the Persian, who told him to lie down flat, closed the trap-door above him and crouched down beside him. Raoul tried to ask a question, but the Persian’s hand was on his mouth and he heard a voice which he recognized as that of the commissary of police.

Raoul and the Persian were completely hidden behind a wooden partition. Near them, a small staircase led to a little room in which the commissary appeared to be walking up and down, asking questions.

The faint light was just enough to enable Raoul to distinguish the shape of things around him. And he could not restrain a dull cry: there were three corpses there.

The first lay on the narrow landing of the little staircase; the two others had rolled to the bottom of the staircase. Raoul could have touched one of the two poor wretches by passing his fingers through the partition.

"Silence!" whispered the Persian.

He too had seen the bodies and he gave one word in explanation:

"**He!**"

The commissary's voice was now heard more distinctly. He was asking for information about the system of lighting, which the stage-manager supplied. The commissary therefore must be in the "organ" or its immediate neighborhood.

Contrary to what one might think, especially in connection with an opera-house, the "organ" is not a musical instrument. At that time, electricity was employed only for a very few scenic effects and for the bells. The immense building and the stage itself were still lit by gas; hydrogen was used to regulate and modify the lighting of a scene; and this was done by means of a special apparatus which, because of the multiplicity of its pipes, was known as the "organ." A box beside the prompter's box was reserved for the chief gasman, who from there gave his orders to his assistants and saw that they were executed. Mauclair stayed in this box during all the performances.

But now Mauclair was not in his box and his assistants not in their places.

"Mauclair! Mauclair!"

The stage-manager's voice echoed through the cellars. But Mauclair did not reply.

I have said that a door opened on a little staircase that led to the second cellar. The commissary pushed it, but it resisted.

"I say," he said to the stage-manager, "I can't open this door: is it always so difficult?"

The stage-manager forced it open with his shoulder. He saw that, at the same time, he was pushing a human body and he could not keep back an exclamation, for he recognized the body at once:

"Mauclair! Poor devil! He is dead!"

But Mr. Commissary Mifroid, whom nothing surprised, was stooping over that big body.

"No," he said, "he is dead-drunk, which is not quite the same thing."

"It's the first time, if so," said the stage-manager.

"Then someone has given him a narcotic. That is quite possible."

Mifroid went down a few steps and said:

"Look!"

By the light of a little red lantern, at the foot of the stairs, they saw two other bodies. The stage-manager recognized Mauclair's assistants. Mifroid went down and listened to their breathing.

"They are sound asleep," he said. "Very curious business! Some person unknown must have interfered with the gasman and his staff… and that person unknown was obviously working on behalf of the kidnapper…. But what a funny idea to kidnap a performer on the stage!… Send for the doctor of the theater, please." And Mifroid repeated, "Curious, decidedly curious business!"

Then he turned to the little room, addressing the people whom Raoul and the Persian were unable to see from where they lay.

"What do you say to all this, gentlemen? You are the only ones who have not given your views. And yet you must have an opinion of some sort."

Thereupon, Raoul and the Persian saw the startled faces of the joint managers appear above the landing – and they heard Moncharmin's excited voice:

"There are things happening here, Mr. Commissary, which we are unable to explain."

And the two faces disappeared.

“Thank you for the information, gentlemen,” said Mifroid, with a jeer.

But the stage-manager, holding his chin in the hollow of his right hand, which is the attitude of profound thought, said:

“It is not the first time that Mauclair has fallen asleep in the theater. I remember finding him, one evening, snoring in his little recess, with his snuffbox beside him.”

“Is that long ago?” asked M. Mifroid, carefully wiping his eyeglasses.

“No, not so very long ago.... Wait a bit!... It was the night... of course, yes... It was the night when Carlotta – you know, Mr. Commissary – gave her famous ‘**co-ack**’!”

“Really? The night when Carlotta gave her famous ‘**co-ack**’?”

And M. Mifroid, replacing his gleaming glasses on his nose, fixed the stage-manager with a contemplative stare.

“So Mauclair takes snuff, does he?” he asked carelessly.

“Yes, Mr. Commissary.... Look, there is

his snuffbox on that little shelf.... Oh, he's a great snuff-taker!"

"So am I," said Mifroid and put the snuffbox in his pocket.

Raoul and the Persian, themselves unobserved, watched the removal of the three bodies by a number of scene-shifters, who were followed by the commissary and all the people with him. Their steps were heard for a few minutes on the stage above. When they were alone the Persian made a sign to Raoul to stand up. Raoul did so; but, as he did not lift his hand in front of his eyes, ready to fire, the Persian told him to resume that attitude and to continue it, whatever happened.

"But it tires the hand unnecessarily," whispered Raoul. "If I do fire, I shan't be sure of my aim."

"Then shift your pistol to the other hand," said the Persian.

"I can't shoot with my left hand."

Thereupon, the Persian made this queer

reply, which was certainly not calculated to throw light into the young man's flurried brain:

"It's not a question of shooting with the right hand or the left; it's a question of holding one of your hands as though you were going to pull the trigger of a pistol with your arm bent. As for the pistol itself, when all is said, you can put that in your pocket!" And he added, "Let this be clearly understood, or I will answer for nothing. It is a matter of life and death. And now, silence and follow me!"

The cellars of the Opera are enormous and they are five in number. Raoul followed the Persian and wondered what he would have done without his companion in that extraordinary labyrinth. They went down to the third cellar; and their progress was still lit by some distant lamp.

The lower they went, the more precautions the Persian seemed to take. He kept on turning to Raoul to see if he was holding his arm properly, showing him how he himself carried his hand as if always ready to fire, though the pistol was in his pocket.

Suddenly, a loud voice made them stop. Someone above them shouted:

"All the door-shutters on the stage! The commissary of police wants them!"

Steps were heard and shadows glided through the darkness. The Persian drew Raoul behind a set piece. They saw passing before and above them old men bent by age and the past burden of opera-scenery. Some could hardly drag themselves along; others, from habit, with stooping bodies and outstretched hands, looked for doors to shut.

They were the door-shutters, the old, worn-out scene-shifters, on whom a charitable management had taken pity, giving them the job of shutting doors above and below the stage. They went about incessantly, from top to bottom of the building, shutting the doors; and they were also called "The draft-expellers," at least at that time, for I have little doubt that by now they are all dead.

Drafts are very bad for the voice, wherever they may come from.[3]

The Persian and Raoul welcomed this incident, which relieved them of inconvenient witnesses, for some of those door-shutters, having nothing else to do or nowhere to lay their heads, stayed at the Opera, from idleness or necessity, and spent the night there. The two men might have stumbled over them, waking them up and provoking a request for explanations. For the moment, M. Mifroid's inquiry saved them from any such unpleasant encounters.

But they were not left to enjoy their solitude for long. Other shades now came down by the same way by which the door-shutters had gone up. Each of these shades carried a little lantern and moved it about, above,

---

[3] M. Pedro Gailhard has himself told me that he created a few additional posts as door-shutters for old stage-carpenters whom he was unwilling to dismiss from the service of the Opera.

below and all around, as though looking for something or somebody.

"Hang it!" muttered the Persian. "I don't know what they are looking for, but they might easily find us.... Let us get away, quick!... Your hand up, sir, ready to fire!... Bend your arm... more... that's it!... Hand at the level of your eye, as though you were fighting a duel and waiting for the word to fire!... Oh, leave your pistol in your pocket. Quick, come along, downstairs. Level of your eye! Question of life or death!... Here, this way, these stairs!" They reached the fifth cellar. "Oh, what a duel, sir, what a duel!"

Once in the fifth cellar, the Persian drew breath. He seemed to enjoy a rather greater sense of security than he had displayed when they both stopped in the third; but he never altered the attitude of his hand. And Raoul, remembering the Persian's observation – "I know these pistols can be relied upon" – was more and more astonished, wondering why anyone should be so gratified at being able to rely upon a pistol which he did not intend to use!

But the Persian left him no time for reflection. Telling Raoul to stay where he was, he ran up a few steps of the staircase which they had just left and then returned.

"How stupid of us!" he whispered. "We shall soon have seen the end of those men with their lanterns. It is the firemen going their rounds."[4]

The two men waited five minutes longer. Then the Persian took Raoul up the stairs again; but suddenly he stopped him with a

---

[4] In those days, it was still part of the firemen's duty to watch over the safety of the Opera house outside the performances; but this service has since been suppressed. I asked M. Pedro Gailhard the reason, and he replied: "It was because the management was afraid that, in their utter inexperience of the cellars of the Opera, the firemen might set fire to the building!"

gesture. Something moved in the darkness before them.

"Flat on your stomach!" whispered the Persian.

The two men lay flat on the floor.

They were only just in time. A shade, this time carrying no light, just a shade in the shade, passed. It passed close to them, near enough to touch them.

They felt the warmth of its cloak upon them. For they could distinguish the shade sufficiently to see that it wore a cloak which shrouded it from head to foot. On its head it had a soft felt hat....

It moved away, drawing its feet against the walls and sometimes giving a kick into a corner.

"Whew!" said the Persian. "We've had a narrow escape; that shade knows me and has twice taken me to the managers' office."

"Is it someone belonging to the theater police?" asked Raoul.

"It's someone much worse than that!"

replied the Persian, without giving any further explanation.[5]

"It's not... **he**?"

"**He?**... If he does not come behind us, we shall always see his yellow eyes!... That is

---

5 Like the Persian, I can give no further explanation touching the apparition of this shade. Whereas, in this historic narrative, everything else will be normally explained, however abnormal the course of events may seem, I can not give the reader expressly to understand what the Persian meant by the words, "It is someone much worse than that!" The reader must try to guess for himself, for I promised M. Pedro Gailhard, the former manager of the Opera, to keep his secret regarding the extremely interesting and useful personality of the wandering, cloaked shade which, while condemning itself to live in the cellars of the Opera, rendered such immense services to those who, on gala evenings, for instance, venture to stray away from the stage. I am speaking of state services; and, upon my word of honor, I can say no more.

more or less our safeguard tonight.... But he may come from behind, stealing up; and we are dead men if we do not keep our hands as though about to fire, at the level of our eyes, in front!"

The Persian had hardly finished speaking, when a fantastic face came in sight... a whole fiery face, not only two yellow eyes!

Yes, a head of fire came toward them, at a man's height, but with no body attached to it. The face shed fire, looked in the darkness like a flame shaped as a man's face.

"Oh," said the Persian, between his teeth. "I have never seen this before!... Pampin was not mad, after all: he had seen it!... What can that flame be? It is not **he**, but he may have sent it!... Take care!... Take care!... Your hand at the level of your eyes, in Heaven's name, at the level of your eyes!... I know most of his tricks... but not this one.... Come, let us run... it is safer. Hand at the level of your eyes!"

And they fled down the long passage that

opened before them.

After a few seconds, that seemed to them like long minutes, they stopped.

"He doesn't often come this way," said the Persian. "This side has nothing to do with him. This side does not lead to the lake nor to the house on the lake.... But perhaps he knows that we are at his heels... although I promised him to leave him alone and never to meddle in his business again!"

So saying, he turned his head and Raoul also turned his head; and they again saw the head of fire behind their two heads. It had followed them. And it must have run also, and perhaps faster than they, for it seemed to be nearer to them.

At the same time, they began to perceive a certain noise of which they could not guess the nature. They simply noticed that the sound seemed to move and to approach with the fiery face. It was a noise as though thousands of nails had been scraped against a blackboard, the perfectly unendurable noise that is sometimes made by a little stone inside the chalk that grates on the blackboard.

They continued to retreat, but the fiery face came on, came on, gaining on them. They could see its features clearly now. The eyes were round and staring, the nose a little crooked and the mouth large, with a hanging lower lip, very like the eyes, nose and lip of the moon, when the moon is quite red, bright red.

How did that red moon manage to glide through the darkness, at a man's height, with nothing to support it, at least apparently? And how did it go so fast, so straight ahead, with such staring, staring eyes? And what was that scratching, scraping, grating sound which it brought with it?

The Persian and Raoul could retreat no farther and flattened themselves against the wall, not knowing what was going to happen because of that incomprehensible head of fire, and especially now, because of the more intense, swarming, living, "numerous" sound, for the sound was certainly made up of hundreds of little sounds that moved in the darkness, under the fiery face.

And the fiery face came on... with its noise... came level with them!...

And the two companions, flat against their wall, felt their hair stand on end with horror, for they now knew what the thousand noises meant. They came in a troop, hustled along in the shadow by innumerable little hurried waves, swifter than the waves that rush over the sands at high tide, little night-waves foaming under the moon, under the fiery head that was like a moon. And the little waves passed between their legs, climbing up their legs, irresistibly, and Raoul and the Persian could no longer restrain their cries of horror, dismay and pain. Nor could they continue to hold their hands at the level of their eyes: their hands went down to their legs to push back the waves, which were full of little legs and nails and claws and teeth.

Yes, Raoul and the Persian were ready to faint, like Pampin the fireman. But the head of fire turned round in answer to their cries, and spoke to them:

"Don't move! Don't move!… Whatever you do, don't come after me!… I am the rat-catcher!… Let me pass, with my rats!…"

And the head of fire disappeared, vanished in the darkness, while the passage in front of it lit up, as the result of the change which the rat-catcher had made in his dark lantern. Before, so as not to scare the rats in front of him, he had turned his dark lantern on himself, lighting up his own head; now, to hasten their flight, he lit the dark space in front of him. And he jumped along, dragging with him the waves of scratching rats, all the thousand sounds.

Raoul and the Persian breathed again, though still trembling.

"I ought to have remembered that Erik

talked to me about the rat-catcher," said the Persian. "But he never told me that he looked like that… and it's funny that I should never have met him before…. Of course, Erik never comes to this part!"

"Are we very far from the lake, sir?" asked Raoul. "When shall we get there?… Take me to the lake, oh, take me to the lake!… When we are at the lake, we will call out!… Christine will hear us!… And **he** will hear us, too!… And, as you know him, we shall talk to him!"

"Baby!" said the Persian. "We shall never enter the house on the lake by the lake!… I myself have never landed on the other bank… the bank on which the house stands…. You have to cross the lake first… and it is well guarded!… I fear that more than one of those men – old scene-shifters, old door-shutters – who have never been seen again were simply tempted to cross the lake…. It is terrible…. I myself would have been nearly killed there… if the monster had not recognized me in time!... One piece of advice, sir; never go near the lake.... And, above all, shut your ears if you hear the voice singing under the water, the siren's voice!"

"But then, what are we here for?" asked Raoul, in a transport of fever, impatience and rage. "If you can do nothing for Christine, at least let me die for her!"

The Persian tried to calm the young man.

"We have only one means of saving Christine Daaé, believe me, which is to enter the house unperceived by the monster."

"And is there any hope of that, sir?"

"Ah, if I had not that hope, I would not have come to fetch you!"

"And how can one enter the house on the lake without crossing the lake?"

"From the third cellar, from which we were so unluckily driven away. We will go back there now.... I will tell you," said the Persian, with a sudden change in his voice, "I will tell you the exact place, sir: it is between a set piece and a discarded scene from **Roi de Lahore**, exactly at the spot where Joseph Buquet died.... Come, sir, take courage and follow me! And hold your hand at the level of your eyes!... But where are we?"

The Persian lit his lamp again and flung its rays down two enormous corridors that crossed each other at right angles.

"We must be," he said, "in the part used more particularly for the waterworks. I see no fire coming from the furnaces."

He went in front of Raoul, seeking his road, stopping abruptly when he was afraid of meeting some waterman. Then they had to protect themselves against the glow of a sort of underground forge, which the men were extinguishing, and at which Raoul recognized the demons whom Christine had seen at the time of her first captivity.

In this way, they gradually arrived beneath the huge cellars below the stage. They must at this time have been at the very bottom of the "tub" and at an extremely great depth, when we remember that the earth was dug out at fifty feet below the water that lay under the whole of that part of Paris.[6]

The Persian touched a partition-wall and said:

"If I am not mistaken, this is a wall that might easily belong to the house on the lake."

He was striking a partition-wall of the "tub," and perhaps it would be as well for the reader to know how the bottom and the partition-walls of the tub were built. In order to prevent the water surrounding the building-operations from remaining in immediate contact with the

---

6 All the water had to be exhausted, in the building of the Opera. To give an idea of the amount of water that was pumped up, I can tell the reader that it represented the area of the courtyard of the Louvre and a height half as deep again as the towers of Notre Dame. And nevertheless the engineers had to leave a lake.

walls supporting the whole of the theatrical machinery, the architect was obliged to build a double case in every direction. The work of constructing this double case took a whole year. It was the wall of the first inner case that the Persian struck when speaking to Raoul of the house on the lake. To anyone understanding the architecture of the edifice, the Persian's action would seem to indicate that Erik's mysterious house had been built in the double case, formed of a thick wall constructed as an embankment or dam, then of a brick wall, a tremendous layer of cement and another wall several yards in thickness.

At the Persian's words, Raoul flung himself against the wall and listened eagerly. But he heard nothing... nothing... except distant steps sounding on the floor of the upper portions of the theater.

The Persian darkened his lantern again.

"Look out!" he said. "Keep your hand up! And silence! For we shall try another way of getting in."

And he led him to the little staircase by which they had come down lately.

They went up, stopping at each step, peering into the darkness and the silence, till they came to the third cellar. Here the Persian motioned to Raoul to go on his knees; and, in this way, crawling on both knees and one hand – for the other hand was held in the position indicated – they reached the end wall.

Against this wall stood a large discarded scene from the **Roi de Lahore**. Close to this scene was a set piece. Between the scene and the set piece there was just room for a body… for a body which one day was found hanging there. The body of Joseph Buquet.

The Persian, still kneeling, stopped and listened. For a moment, he seemed to hesitate and looked at Raoul; then he turned his eyes upward, toward the second cellar, which sent down the faint glimmer of a lantern, through a cranny between two boards. This glimmer seemed to trouble the

Persian.

At last, he tossed his head and made up his mind to act. He slipped between the set piece and the scene from the **Roi de Lahore**, with Raoul close upon his heels. With his free hand, the Persian felt the wall. Raoul saw him bear heavily upon the wall, just as he had pressed against the wall in Christine's dressing-room. Then a stone gave way, leaving a hole in the wall.

This time, the Persian took his pistol from his pocket and made a sign to Raoul to do as he did. He cocked the pistol.

And, resolutely, still on his knees, he wiggled through the hole in the wall. Raoul, who had wished to pass first, had to be content to follow him.

The hole was very narrow. The Persian stopped almost at once. Raoul heard him feeling the stones around him. Then the Persian took out his dark lantern again, stooped forward, examined something beneath him and immediately extinguished his lantern. Raoul heard him say, in a whisper:

"We shall have to drop a few yards, without making a noise; take off your boots."

The Persian handed his own shoes to Raoul.

"Put them outside the wall," he said. "We shall find them there when we leave."[7]

He crawled a little farther on his knees, then turned right round and said:

"I am going to hang by my hands from the edge of the stone and let myself drop **into his house**. You must do exactly the same. Do not be afraid. I will catch you in my arms."

Raoul soon heard a dull sound, evidently produced by the fall of the Persian, and then

---

[7] These two pairs of boots, which were placed, according to the Persian's papers, just between the set piece and the scene from the Roi de Lahore, on the spot where Joseph Buquet was found hanging, were never discovered. They must have been taken by some stage-carpenter or "door-shutter."

dropped down.

He felt himself clasped in the Persian's arms.

"Hush!" said the Persian.

And they stood motionless, listening.

The darkness was thick around them, the silence heavy and terrible.

Then the Persian began to make play with the dark lantern again, turning the rays over their heads, looking for the hole through which they had come, and failing to find it:

"Oh!" he said. "The stone has closed of itself!"

And the light of the lantern swept down the wall and over the floor.

The Persian stooped and picked up something, a sort of cord, which he examined for a second and flung away with horror.

"The Punjab lasso!" he muttered.

"What is it?" asked Raoul.

The Persian shivered. "It might very well be the rope by which the man was hanged, and which was looked for so long."

And, suddenly seized with fresh anxiety, he moved the little red disk of his lantern over the walls. In this way, he lit up a curious thing: the trunk of a tree, which seemed still quite alive, with its leaves; and the branches of that tree ran right up the walls and disappeared in the ceiling.

Because of the smallness of the luminous disk, it was difficult at first to make out the appearance of things: they saw a corner of a branch… and a leaf… and another leaf… and, next to it, nothing at all, nothing but the ray of light that seemed to reflect itself…. Raoul passed his hand over that nothing, over that reflection.

“Hullo!” he said. “The wall is a looking-glass!”

“Yes, a looking-glass!” said the Persian, in a tone of deep emotion. And, passing the hand that held the pistol over his moist forehead, he added, “We have dropped into the torture-chamber!”

What the Persian knew of this torture-chamber and what there befell him and his companion shall be told in his own words, as set down in a manuscript which he left behind him, and which I copy **verbatim**.

CHAPTER TWENTY ONE

Interesting and Instructive Vicissitudes of a Persian in the Cellars of the Opera

THE PERSIAN'S NARRATIVE

It was the first time that I entered the house on the lake. I had often begged the "trap-door lover," as we used to call Erik in my country, to open its mysterious doors to me. He always refused. I made very many attempts, but in vain, to obtain admittance. Watch him as I might, after I first learned that he had taken up his permanent abode at the Opera, the darkness was always too thick to enable me to see how he worked the door in the wall on the lake. One day, when I thought myself alone, I stepped into the boat and rowed toward that part of the wall through which I had seen Erik disappear. It was then that I came into contact with the siren who guarded the approach and whose charm was very nearly fatal to me.

I had no sooner put off from the bank than the silence amid which I floated on the water was disturbed by a sort of whispered singing that hovered all around me. It was half breath, half music; it rose softly from the waters of the lake; and I was surrounded by it through I knew not what artifice. It followed me, moved with me and was so soft that it did not alarm me. On the contrary, in my longing to approach the source of that sweet and enticing harmony, I leaned out of my little boat over the water, for there was no doubt in my mind that the singing came from the water itself. By this time, I was alone in the boat in the middle of the lake; the voice – for it was now distinctly a voice – was beside me, on the water. I leaned over, leaned still farther. The lake was perfectly calm, and a moonbeam that passed through the air hole in the Rue Scribe showed me absolutely nothing on its surface, which was smooth and black as ink. I shook my ears to get rid of a possible humming; but I soon had to accept the fact that there was no humming in the ears so harmonious as the singing whisper that followed and now attracted me.

Had I been inclined to superstition, I should have certainly thought that I had to do with some siren whose business it was to confound the traveler who should venture on the waters of the house on the lake. Fortunately, I come from a country where we are too fond of fantastic things not to know them through and through; and I had no doubt but that I was face to face with some new invention of Erik's. But this invention was so perfect that, as I leaned out of the boat, I was impelled less by a desire to discover its trick than to enjoy its charm; and I leaned out, leaned out until I almost overturned the boat.

Suddenly, two monstrous arms issued from the bosom of the waters and seized me by the neck, dragging me down to the depths with irresistible force. I should certainly have been lost, if I had not had time to give a cry by which Erik knew me. For it was he; and, instead of drowning me, as was certainly his first intention, he swam with me and laid me gently on the bank:

"How imprudent you are!" he said, as he stood before me, dripping with water. "Why try to enter my house? I never invited you! I don't want you there, nor anybody! Did you save my life only to make it unbearable to me? However great the service you rendered him, Erik may end by forgetting it; and you know that nothing can restrain Erik, not even Erik himself."

He spoke, but I had now no other wish than to know what I already called the trick of the siren. He satisfied my curiosity, for Erik, who is a real monster – I have seen him at work in Persia, alas – is also, in certain respects, a regular child, vain and self-conceited, and there is nothing he loves so much, after astonishing people, as to prove all the really miraculous ingenuity of his mind.

He laughed and showed me a long reed.

"It's the silliest trick you ever saw," he said, "but it's very useful for breathing and singing in the water. I learned it from the Tonkin pirates, who are able to remain hidden for hours in the beds of the rivers."[8]

---

8 An official report from Tonkin, received in Paris at the end of July, 1909, relates how the famous pirate chief De Tham was tracked,

I spoke to him severely.

"It's a trick that nearly killed me!" I said. "And it may have been fatal to others! You know what you promised me, Erik? No more murders!"

"Have I really committed murders?" he asked, putting on his most amiable air.

"Wretched man!" I cried. "Have you forgotten the rosy hours of Mazenderan?"

"Yes," he replied, in a sadder tone, "I prefer to forget them. I used to make the little sultana laugh, though!"

"All that belongs to the past," I declared; "but there is the present... and you are responsible to me for the present, because, if I had wished, there would have been none at all for you. Remember that, Erik: I saved your life!"

And I took advantage of the turn of conversation to speak to him of something

---

together with his men, by our soldiers; and how all of them succeeded in escaping, thanks to this trick of the reeds.

that had long been on my mind:

“Erik,” I asked, “Erik, swear that…”

“What?” he retorted. “You know I never keep my oaths. Oaths are made to catch gulls with.”

“Tell me… you can tell me, at any rate….”

“Well?”

“Well, the chandelier… the chandelier, Erik?…”

“What about the chandelier?”

“You know what I mean.”

“Oh,” he sniggered, “I don’t mind telling you about the chandelier!… **It wasn’t I!**… The chandelier was very old and worn.”

When Erik laughed, he was more terrible than ever. He jumped into the boat, chuckling so horribly that I could not help trembling.

“Very old and worn, my dear daroga![9] Very old and worn, the chandelier!… It fell of itself!… It came down with a smash!… And now, daroga, take my advice and go and dry

---

9 Daroga is Persian for chief of police.

yourself, or you'll catch a cold in the head!... And never get into my boat again.... And, whatever you do, don't try to enter my house: I'm not always there... daroga! And I should be sorry to have to dedicate my Requiem Mass to you!"

So saying, swinging to and fro, like a monkey, and still chuckling, he pushed off and soon disappeared in the darkness of the lake.

From that day, I gave up all thought of penetrating into his house by the lake. That entrance was obviously too well guarded, especially since he had learned that I knew about it. But I felt that there must be another entrance, for I had often seen Erik disappear in the third cellar, when I was watching him, though I could not imagine how.

Ever since I had discovered Erik installed in the Opera, I lived in a perpetual terror of his horrible fancies, not in so far as I was concerned, but I dreaded everything for others.[10] And whenever some accident, some fatal event happened, I always thought to myself, "I should not be surprised if that were Erik," even as others used to say, "It's the ghost!" How often have I not heard people utter that phrase with a smile! Poor devils! If they had known that the ghost existed in the flesh, I swear they would not have laughed!

Although Erik announced to me very solemnly that he had changed and that he had become the most virtuous of men **since he was loved for himself** – a sentence

---

[10] The Persian might easily have admitted that Erik's fate also interested himself, for he was well aware that, if the government of Teheran had learned that Erik was still alive, it would have been all up with the modest pension of the erstwhile daroga. It is only fair, however, to add that the Persian had a noble and generous heart; and I do not doubt for a moment that the catastrophes which he feared for others greatly occupied his mind. His conduct, throughout this business, proves it and is above all praise.

that, at first, perplexed me most terribly – I could not help shuddering when I thought of the monster. His horrible, unparalleled and repulsive ugliness put him without the pale of humanity; and it often seemed to me that, for this reason, he no longer believed that he had any duty toward the human race. The way in which he spoke of his love-affairs only increased my alarm, for I foresaw the cause of fresh and more hideous tragedies in this event to which he alluded so boastfully.

On the other hand, I soon discovered the curious moral traffic established between the monster and Christine Daaé. Hiding in the lumber-room next to the young prima donna's dressing-room, I listened to wonderful musical displays that evidently flung Christine into marvelous ecstasy; but, all the same, I would never have thought that Erik's voice – which was loud as thunder or soft as angels' voices, at will – could have made her forget his ugliness. I understood all when I learned that Christine had not yet seen him! I had occasion to go to the dressing-room and, remembering the lessons he had once given me, I had no difficulty in discovering the trick that made the wall with the mirror swing round and I ascertained the means – of hollow bricks and so on – by which he made his voice carry to Christine as though she heard it close beside her. In this way also I discovered the road that led to the well and the dungeon – the Communists' dungeon – and also the trap-door that enabled Erik to go straight to the cellars below the stage.

A few days later, what was not my amazement to learn by my own eyes and ears that Erik and Christine Daaé saw each other and to catch the monster stooping over the little well, in the Communists' road and sprinkling the forehead of Christine Daaé, who had fainted. A white horse, the horse out of the **Profeta**, which had disappeared from the stables under the Opera, was standing quietly beside them. I showed myself. It was terrible. I saw sparks fly from those yellow eyes and, before I had time to say a word, I received a blow on the head that stunned me.

When I came to myself, Erik, Christine and the white horse had disappeared. I felt sure that the poor girl was a prisoner in the house on the lake. Without hesitation, I resolved to return to the bank, notwithstanding the attendant danger. For twenty-four hours, I lay in wait for the monster to appear; for I felt that he must go out, driven by the need of obtaining provisions. And, in this connection, I may say, that, when he went out in the streets or ventured to show himself in public, he wore a pasteboard nose, with a mustache attached to it, instead of his own horrible hole of a nose. This did not quite take away his corpse-like air, but it made him almost, I say almost, endurable to look at.

I therefore watched on the bank of the lake and, weary of long waiting, was beginning to think that he had gone through the other door, the door in the third cellar, when I heard a slight splashing in the dark, I saw the two yellow eyes shining like candles and soon the boat touched shore. Erik jumped out and walked up to me:

"You've been here for twenty-four hours," he said, "and you're annoying me. I tell you, all this will end very badly. And you will have brought it upon yourself; for I have been extraordinarily patient with you. You think you are following me, you great booby, whereas it's I who am following you; and I know all that you know about me, here. I spared you yesterday, in **my Communists' road**; but I warn you, seriously, don't let me catch you there again! Upon my word, you don't seem able to take a hint!"

He was so furious that I did not think, for the moment, of interrupting him. After puffing and blowing like a walrus, he put his horrible thought into words:

"Yes, you must learn, once and for all – once and for all, I say – to take a hint! I tell you that, with your recklessness – for you have already been twice arrested by the shade in the felt hat, who did not know what you were doing in the cellars and took you to the managers, who looked upon you as an eccentric Persian interested in stage mechanism and life behind the scenes: I know all about it, I was there, in the office; you know I am everywhere – well, I tell you that, with your recklessness, they will end by wondering what you are after here… and they will end by knowing that you are after Erik… and then they will be after Erik themselves and they will discover the house on the lake…. If they do, it will be a bad lookout for you, old chap, a bad lookout!… I won't answer for anything."

Again he puffed and blew like a walrus.

"I won't answer for anything!… If Erik's secrets cease to be Erik's secrets, **it will be a bad lookout for a goodly number of the human race!** That's all I have to tell you, and unless you are a great booby, it ought to be enough for you… except that you don't know how to take a hint."

He had sat down on the stern of his boat and was kicking his heels against the planks, waiting to hear what I had to answer. I simply said:

"It's not Erik that I'm after here!"

"Who then?"

"You know as well as I do: it's Christine Daaé," I answered.

He retorted: "I have every right to see her in my own house. I am loved for my own sake."

"That's not true," I said. "You have carried her off and are keeping her locked up."

"Listen," he said. "Will you promise never to meddle with my affairs again, if I prove to you that I am loved for my own sake?"

"Yes, I promise you," I replied, without hesitation, for I felt convinced that for such a monster the proof was impossible.

"Well, then, it's quite simple.… Christine Daaé shall leave this as she pleases and come back again!… Yes, come back again, because she wishes… come back of herself, because she loves me for myself!…"

"Oh, I doubt if she will come back!… But it is your duty to let her go."

"My duty, you great booby!… It is my wish… my wish to let her go; and she will come back again… for she loves me!… All this will end in a marriage… a marriage at the Madeleine, you great booby! Do you believe me now? When I tell you that my nuptial mass is written… wait till you hear the 'Kyrie'…."

He beat time with his heels on the planks of the boat and sang:

"**Kyrie!… Kyrie!… Kyrie eleison!…** Wait till you hear, wait till you hear that mass."

"Look here," I said. "I shall believe you if I see Christine Daaé come out of the house on the lake and go back to it of her own accord."

"And you won't meddle any more in my affairs?"

"No."

"Very well, you shall see that tonight. Come to the masked ball. Christine and I will go and have a look round. Then you can hide in the lumber-room and you shall see Christine, who will have gone to her dressing-room, delighted to come back by the Communists' road.... And, now, be off, for I must go and do some shopping!"

To my intense astonishment, things happened as he had announced. Christine Daaé left the house on the lake and returned to it several times, without, apparently, being forced to do so. It was very difficult for me to clear my mind of Erik. However, I resolved to be extremely prudent, and did not make the mistake of returning to the shore of the lake, or of going by the Communists' road. But the idea of the secret entrance in the third cellar haunted me, and I repeatedly went and waited for hours behind a scene from the **Roi de Lahore**, which had been left there for some reason or other. At last my patience was rewarded. One day, I saw the monster come toward me, on his knees. I was certain that he could not see me. He passed between the scene behind which I stood and a set piece, went to the wall and pressed on a spring that moved a stone and afforded him an ingress. He passed through this, and the stone closed behind him.

I waited for at least thirty minutes and then pressed the spring in my turn. Everything happened as with Erik. But I was careful not to go through the hole myself, for I knew that Erik was inside. On the other hand, the idea that I might be caught by Erik suddenly made me think of the death of Joseph Buquet. I did not wish to jeopardize the advantages of so great a discovery which might be useful to many people, "to a goodly number of the human race," in Erik's words; and I left the cellars of the Opera after carefully replacing the stone.

I continued to be greatly interested in the relations between Erik and Christine Daaé, not from any morbid curiosity, but because of the terrible thought which obsessed my mind that Erik was capable of anything, if he once discovered that he was not loved for his own sake, as he imagined. I continued to wander, very cautiously, about the Opera and soon learned the truth about the monster's dreary love-affair.

He filled Christine's mind, through the terror with which he inspired her, but the dear child's heart belonged wholly to the Vicomte Raoul de Chagny. While they played about, like an innocent engaged couple, on the upper floors of the Opera, to avoid the monster, they little suspected that someone was watching over them. I was prepared to do anything: to kill the monster, if necessary, and explain to the police afterward. But Erik did not show himself; and I felt none the more comfortable for that.

I must explain my whole plan. I thought that the monster, being driven from his house by jealousy, would thus enable me to enter it, without danger, through the passage in the third cellar. It was important, for everybody's sake, that I should know exactly what was inside. One day, tired of waiting for an opportunity, I moved the stone and at once heard an astounding music: the monster was working at his **Don Juan Triumphant**, with every door in his house wide open. I knew that this was the work of his life. I was careful not to stir and remained prudently in my dark hole.

He stopped playing, for a moment, and began walking about his place, like a madman. And he said aloud, at the top of his voice:

"It must be finished **first**! Quite finished!"

This speech was not calculated to reassure me and, when the music recommenced, I closed the stone very softly.

On the day of the abduction of Christine Daaé, I did not come to the theater until rather late in the evening, trembling lest

I should hear bad news. I had spent a horrible day, for, after reading in a morning paper the announcement of a forthcoming marriage between Christine and the Vicomte de Chagny, I wondered whether, after all, I should not do better to denounce the monster. But reason returned to me, and I was persuaded that this action could only precipitate a possible catastrophe.

When my cab set me down before the Opera, I was really almost astonished to see it still standing! But I am something of a fatalist, like all good Orientals, and I entered ready for anything.

Christine Daaé's abduction in the Prison Act, which naturally surprised everybody, found me prepared. I was quite certain that she had been juggled away by Erik, that prince of conjurers. And I thought positively that this was the end of Christine and perhaps of everybody, so much so that I thought of advising all these people who were staying on at the theater to make good their escape.

I felt, however, that they would be sure to look upon me as mad and I refrained.

On the other hand, I resolved to act without further delay, as far as I was concerned. The chances were in my favor that Erik, at that moment, was thinking only of his captive. This was the moment to enter his house through the third cellar; and I resolved to take with me that poor little desperate viscount, who, at the first suggestion, accepted, with an amount of confidence in myself that touched me profoundly. I had sent my servant for my pistols. I gave one to the viscount and advised him to hold himself ready to fire, for, after all, Erik might be waiting for us behind the wall. We were to go by the Communists' road and through the trap-door.

Seeing my pistols, the little viscount asked me if we were going to fight a duel. I said:

"Yes; and what a duel!"

But, of course, I had no time to explain anything to him. The little viscount is a brave fellow, but he knew hardly anything about his adversary; and it was so much the better. My great fear was that he was already somewhere near us, preparing the Punjab lasso. No one knows better than he how to throw the Punjab lasso, for he is the king of stranglers even as he is the prince of conjurors. When he had finished making the little sultana laugh, at the time of the "rosy hours of Mazenderan," she herself used to ask him to amuse her by giving her a thrill. It was then that he introduced the sport of the Punjab lasso.

He had lived in India and acquired an incredible skill in the art of strangulation. He would make them lock him into a courtyard to which they brought a warrior – usually, a man condemned to death – armed with a long pike and broadsword. Erik had only his lasso; and it was always just when the warrior thought that he was going to fell Erik with a tremendous blow that we heard the lasso whistle through the air. With a turn of the wrist, Erik tightened the noose round his adversary's neck and, in this fashion, dragged him before the little sultana and her women, who sat looking from a window and applauding. The little sultana herself learned to wield the Punjab lasso and killed several of her women and even of the friends who visited her. But I prefer to drop this terrible subject of the rosy hours of Mazenderan. I have mentioned it only to explain why, on arriving with the Vicomte de Chagny in the cellars of the Opera, I was bound to protect my companion against the ever-threatening danger of death by strangling. My pistols could serve no purpose, for Erik was not likely to show himself; but Erik could always strangle us. I had no time to explain all this to the viscount; besides, there was nothing to be gained by complicating the position. I simply told M. de Chagny to keep his hand at the level of his eyes, with the arm bent, as though waiting for the command to fire. With his victim in this attitude, it is impossible even for the most expert strangler to throw the lasso with advantage. It catches you not only round the neck, but also round the arm or hand. This enables you easily to unloose the lasso, which then becomes harmless.

After avoiding the commissary of police, a number of door-shutters and the firemen, after meeting the rat-catcher and passing the man in the felt hat unperceived, the viscount and I arrived without obstacle in the third cellar, between the set piece and the scene from the **Roi de Lahore**. I worked the stone, and we jumped into the house which Erik had built himself in the double case of the foundation-walls of the Opera. And this was the easiest thing in the world for him to do, because Erik was one of the chief contractors under Philippe Garnier, the architect of the Opera, and continued to work by himself when the works were officially suspended, during the war, the siege of Paris and the Commune.

I knew my Erik too well to feel at all

comfortable on jumping into his house. I knew what he had made of a certain palace at Mazenderan. From being the most honest building conceivable, he soon turned it into a house of the very devil, where you could not utter a word but it was overheard or repeated by an echo. With his trap-doors the monster was responsible for endless tragedies of all kinds. He hit upon astonishing inventions. Of these, the most curious, horrible and dangerous was the so-called torture-chamber. Except in special cases, when the little sultana amused herself by inflicting suffering upon some unoffending citizen, no one was let into it but wretches condemned to death. And, even then, when these had "had enough," they were always at liberty to put an end to themselves with a Punjab lasso or bowstring, left for their use at the foot of an iron tree.

My alarm, therefore, was great when I saw that the room into which M. le Vicomte de Chagny and I had dropped was an exact copy of the torture-chamber of the rosy hours of Mazenderan. At our feet, I found the Punjab lasso which I had been dreading all the evening. I was convinced that this rope had already done duty for Joseph Buquet, who, like myself, must have caught Erik one evening working the stone in the third cellar. He probably tried it in his turn, fell into the torture-chamber and only left it hanged. I can well imagine Erik dragging the body, in order to get rid of it, to the scene from the **Roi de Lahore**, and hanging it there as an example, or to increase the superstitious terror that was to help him in guarding the approaches to his lair! Then, upon reflection, Erik went back to fetch the Punjab lasso, which is very curiously made out of catgut, and which might have set an examining magistrate thinking. This explains the disappearance of the rope.

And now I discovered the lasso, at our feet, in the torture-chamber!... I am no coward, but a cold sweat covered my forehead as I moved the little red disk of my lantern over the walls.

M. de Chagny noticed it and asked:

"What is the matter, sir?"

I made him a violent sign to be silent.

CHAPTER TWENTY TWO

In the Torture Chamber

THE PERSIAN'S NARRATIVE CONTINUED

We were in the middle of a little six-cornered room, the sides of which were covered with mirrors from top to bottom. In the corners, we could clearly see the "joins" in the glasses, the segments intended to turn on their gear; yes, I recognized them and I recognized the iron tree in the corner, at the bottom of one of those segments… the iron tree, with its iron branch, for the hanged men.

I seized my companion's arm: the Vicomte de Chagny was all a-quiver, eager to shout to his betrothed that he was bringing her help. I feared that he would not be able to contain himself.

Suddenly, we heard a noise on our left. It sounded at first like a door opening and shutting in the next room; and then there was a dull moan. I clutched M. de Chagny's arm more firmly still; and then we distinctly heard these words:

"You must make your choice! The wedding mass or the requiem mass!"

I recognized the voice of the monster.

There was another moan, followed by a long silence.

I was persuaded by now that the monster was unaware of our presence in his house, for otherwise he would certainly have managed not to let us hear him. He would only have had to close the little invisible window through which the torture-lovers look down into the torture-chamber. Besides, I was certain that, if he had known of our presence, the tortures would have begun at once.

The important thing was not to let him know; and I dreaded nothing so much as the impulsiveness of the Vicomte de Chagny, who wanted to rush through the walls to Christine Daaé, whose moans we continued to hear at intervals.

"The requiem mass is not at all gay," Erik's voice resumed, "whereas the wedding mass – you can take my word for it – is magnificent! You must take a resolution and know your own mind! I can't go on living like this, like a mole in a burrow! **Don Juan Triumphant** is finished; and now I want to live like everybody else. I want to have a wife like everybody else and to take her out on Sundays. I have invented a mask that makes me look like anybody. People will not even turn round in the streets. You will be the happiest of women. And we will sing, all by ourselves, till we swoon away with delight. You are crying! You are afraid of me! And yet I am not really wicked. Love me and you shall see! All I wanted was to be loved for myself. If you loved me I should be as gentle as a lamb; and you could do anything with me that you pleased."

Soon the moans that accompanied this sort of love's litany increased and increased. I have never heard anything more despairing; and M. de Chagny and I recognized that this terrible lamentation came from Erik himself. Christine seemed to be standing dumb with horror, without the strength to cry out, while the monster was on his knees before her.

Three times over, Erik fiercely bewailed his fate:

"You don't love me! You don't love me! You don't love me!"

And then, more gently:

"Why do you cry? You know it gives me pain to see you cry!"

A silence.

Each silence gave us fresh hope. We said to ourselves:

"Perhaps he has left Christine behind the wall."

And we thought only of the possibility of warning Christine Daaé of our presence, unknown to the monster. We were unable to leave the torture-chamber now, unless Christine opened the door to us; and it was only on this condition that we could hope to help her, for we did not even know where the door might be.

Suddenly, the silence in the next room was disturbed by the ringing of an electric bell. There was a bound on the other side of the wall and Erik's voice of thunder:

"Somebody ringing! Walk in, please!"

A sinister chuckle.

"Who has come bothering now? Wait for me here.... **I am going to tell the siren to**

open the door."

Steps moved away, a door closed. I had no time to think of the fresh horror that was preparing; I forgot that the monster was only going out perhaps to perpetrate a fresh crime; I understood but one thing: Christine was alone behind the wall!

The Vicomte de Chagny was already calling to her:

"Christine! Christine!"

As we could hear what was said in the next room, there was no reason why my companion should not be heard in his turn. Nevertheless, the viscount had to repeat his cry time after time.

At last, a faint voice reached us.

"I am dreaming!" it said.

"Christine, Christine, it is I, Raoul!"

A silence.

"But answer me, Christine!… In Heaven's name, if you are alone, answer me!"

Then Christine's voice whispered Raoul's name.

"Yes! Yes! It is I! It is not a dream!... Christine, trust me!... We are here to save you... but be prudent! When you hear the monster, warn us!"

Then Christine gave way to fear. She trembled lest Erik should discover where Raoul was hidden; she told us in a few hurried words that Erik had gone quite mad with love and that he had decided **to kill everybody and himself with everybody** if she did not consent to become his wife. He had given her till eleven o'clock the next evening for reflection. It was the last respite. She must choose, as he said, between the wedding mass and the requiem.

And Erik had then uttered a phrase which Christine did not quite understand:

"Yes or no! If your answer is no, everybody will be dead **and buried**!"

But I understood the sentence perfectly, for it corresponded in a terrible manner with my own dreadful thought.

"Can you tell us where Erik is?" I asked.

She replied that he must have left the house.

"Could you make sure?"

"No. I am fastened. I can not stir a limb."

When we heard this, M. de Chagny and I gave a yell of fury. Our safety, the safety of all three of us, depended on the girl's liberty of movement.

"But where are you?" asked Christine. "There are only two doors in my room, the Louis-Philippe room of which I told you, Raoul; a door through which Erik comes and goes, and another which he has never opened before me and which he has forbidden me ever to go through, because he says it is the most dangerous of the doors, the door of the torture-chamber!"

"Christine, that is where we are!"

"You are in the torture-chamber?"

"Yes, but we can not see the door."

"Oh, if I could only drag myself so far! I would knock at the door and that would tell you where it is."

"Is it a door with a lock to it?" I asked.

"Yes, with a lock."

"Mademoiselle," I said, "it is absolutely necessary that you should open that door to us!"

"But how?" asked the poor girl tearfully.

We heard her straining, trying to free herself from the bonds that held her.

"I know where the key is," she said, in a voice that seemed exhausted by the effort she had made. "But I am fastened so tight.... Oh, the wretch!"

And she gave a sob.

"Where is the key?" I asked, signing to M. de Chagny not to speak and to leave the business to me, for we had not a moment to lose.

"In the next room, near the organ, with another little bronze key, which he also forbade me to touch. They are both in a little leather bag which he calls the bag of life and death.... Raoul! Raoul! Fly! Everything is mysterious and terrible here, and Erik will soon have gone quite mad, and you are in the torture-chamber!… Go back by the way you came. There must be a reason why the room is called by that name!"

"Christine," said the young man, "we will go from here together or die together!"

"We must keep cool," I whispered. "Why has he fastened you, mademoiselle? You can't escape from his house; and he knows it!"

"I tried to commit suicide! The monster went out last night, after carrying me here fainting and half chloroformed. He was going **to his banker**, so he said!… When he returned he found me with my face covered with blood.… I had tried to kill myself by striking my forehead against the walls."

"Christine!" groaned Raoul; and he began to sob.

"Then he bound me.… I am not allowed to die until eleven o'clock tomorrow evening."

"Mademoiselle," I declared, "the monster

bound you... and he shall unbind you. You have only to play the necessary part! Remember that he loves you!"

"Alas!" we heard. "Am I likely to forget it!"

"Remember it and smile to him... entreat him... tell him that your bonds hurt you."

But Christine Daaé said:

"Hush!... I hear something in the wall on the lake!... It is he!... Go away! Go away! Go away!"

"We could not go away, even if we wanted to," I said, as impressively as I could. "We can not leave this! And we are in the torture-chamber!"

"Hush!" whispered Christine again.

Heavy steps sounded slowly behind the wall, then stopped and made the floor creak once more. Next came a tremendous sigh, followed by a cry of horror from Christine, and we heard Erik's voice:

"I beg your pardon for letting you see a face like this! What a state I am in, am I not? It's **the other one's fault**! Why did he ring? Do **I** ask people who pass to tell me the time? He will never ask anybody the time again! It is the siren's fault."

Another sigh, deeper, more tremendous still, came from the abysmal depths of a soul.

"Why did you cry out, Christine?"

"Because I am in pain, Erik."

"I thought I had frightened you."

"Erik, unloose my bonds.... Am I not your prisoner?"

"You will try to kill yourself again."

"You have given me till eleven o'clock tomorrow evening, Erik."

The footsteps dragged along the floor again.

"After all, as we are to die together... and I am just as eager as you... yes, I have had enough of this life, you know.... Wait, don't move, I will release you.... You have only one word to say: '**No!**' And it will at once be over **with everybody**!... You are right, you are right; why wait till eleven o'clock tomorrow evening? True, it would have been grander, finer.... But that is childish nonsense.... We should only think of ourselves in this life, of our own death... the rest doesn't matter.... **You're looking at me because I am all wet?**... Oh, my dear, it's raining cats and dogs outside!... Apart from that, Christine, I think I am subject to hallucinations.... You know, the man who rang at the siren's door just now – go and look if he's ringing at the bottom of the lake-well, he was rather like.... There, turn round... are you glad? You're free now.... Oh, my poor Christine, look at your wrists: tell me, have I hurt them?... That alone deserves death.... Talking of death, **I must sing his requiem**!"

Hearing these terrible remarks, I received an awful presentiment... I too had once rung at the monster's door... and, without knowing it, must have set some warning current in motion.... And I remembered the two arms that had emerged from the inky waters.... What poor wretch had strayed to that shore this time? Who was "the other one," the one whose requiem we now heard sung?

Erik sang like the god of thunder, sang a **Dies Irae** that enveloped us as in a storm. The elements seemed to rage around us. Suddenly, the organ and the voice ceased so suddenly that M. de Chagny sprang back, on the other side of the wall, with emotion. And the voice, changed and transformed, distinctly grated out these metallic syllables:

"**What have you done with my bag?**"

CHAPTER TWENTY THREE

The Tortures Begin

THE PERSIAN'S NARRATIVE CONTINUED

The voice repeated angrily: "What have you done with my bag? So it was to take my bag that you asked me to release you!"

We heard hurried steps, Christine running back to the Louis-Philippe room, as though to seek shelter on the other side of our wall.

"What are you running away for?" asked

the furious voice, which had followed her. "Give me back my bag, will you? Don't you know that it is the bag of life and death?"

"Listen to me, Erik," sighed the girl. "As it is settled that we are to live together... what difference can it make to you?"

"You know there are only two keys in it," said the monster. "What do you want to do?"

"I want to look at this room which I have never seen and which you have always kept from me.... It's woman's curiosity!" she said, in a tone which she tried to render playful.

But the trick was too childish for Erik to be taken in by it.

"I don't like curious women," he retorted, "and you had better remember the story of Bluebeard and be careful.... Come, give me back my bag!... Give me back my bag!... Leave the key alone, will you, you inquisitive little thing?"

And he chuckled, while Christine gave a cry of pain. Erik had evidently recovered the bag from her.

At that moment, the viscount could not help uttering an exclamation of impotent rage.

"Why, what's that?" said the monster. "Did you hear, Christine?"

"No, no," replied the poor girl. "I heard nothing."

"I thought I heard a cry."

"A cry! Are you going mad, Erik? Whom do you expect to give a cry, in this house?… I cried out, because you hurt me! I heard nothing."

"I don't like the way you said that!… You're trembling.… You're quite excited.… You're lying!… That was a cry, there was a cry!… There is someone in the torture-chamber!… Ah, I understand now!"

"There is no one there, Erik!"

"I understand!"

"No one!"

"The man you want to marry, perhaps!"

"I don't want to marry anybody, you know I don't."

Another nasty chuckle.

"Well, it won't take long to find out. Christine, my love, we need not open the door to see what is happening in the torture-chamber. Would you like to see? Would you like to see? Look here! If there is someone, if there is really someone there, you will see the invisible window light up at the top, near the ceiling. We need only draw the black curtain and put out the light in here. There, that's it.... Let's put out the light! You're not afraid of the dark, when you're with your little husband!"

Then we heard Christine's voice of anguish:

"No!... I'm frightened!... I tell you, I'm afraid of the dark!... I don't care about that room now.... You're always frightening me, like a child, with your torture-chamber!... And so I became inquisitive.... But I don't care about it now... not a bit... not a bit!"

And that which I feared above all things began, **automatically**. We were suddenly flooded with light! Yes, on our side of the wall, everything seemed aglow. The Vicomte de

Chagny was so much taken aback that he staggered. And the angry voice roared:

"I told you there was someone! Do you see the window now? The lighted window, right up there? The man behind the wall can't see it! But you shall go up the folding steps: that is what they are there for!... You have often asked me to tell you; and now you know!... They are there to give a peep into the torture-chamber... you inquisitive little thing!"

"What tortures?... Who is being tortured?... Erik, Erik, say you are only trying to frighten me!... Say it, if you love me, Erik!... There are no tortures, are there?"

"Go and look at the little window, dear!"

I do not know if the viscount heard the girl's swooning voice, for he was too much occupied by the astounding spectacle that now appeared before his distracted gaze. As for me, I had seen that sight too often, through the little window, at the time of the rosy hours of Mazenderan; and I cared only for what was being said next door, seeking for a hint how to act, what resolution to take.

"Go and peep through the little window! Tell me what he looks like!"

We heard the steps being dragged against the wall.

"Up with you!... No!... No, I will go up myself, dear!"

"Oh, very well, I will go up. Let me go!"

"Oh, my darling, my darling!... How sweet of you!... How nice of you to save me the exertion at my age!... Tell me what he looks like!"

At that moment, we distinctly heard these words above our heads:

"There is no one there, dear!"

"No one?... Are you sure there is no one?"

"Why, of course not... no one!"

"Well, that's all right!... What's the matter, Christine? You're not going to faint, are you... as there is no one there?... Here... come down... there!... Pull yourself together... as there is no one there!... **But how do you**

like the landscape?"

"Oh, very much!"

"There, that's better!... You're better now, are you not?... That's all right, you're better!... No excitement!... And what a funny house, isn't it, with landscapes like that in it?"

"Yes, it's like the Musée Grévin.... But, I say, Erik... there are no tortures in there!... What a fright you gave me!"

"Why... as there is no one there?"

"Did you design that room? It's very handsome. You're a great artist, Erik."

"Yes, a great artist, in my own line."

"But tell me, Erik, why did you call that room the torture-chamber?"

"Oh, it's very simple. First of all, what did you see?"

"I saw a forest."

"And what is in a forest?"

"Trees."

"And what is in a tree?"

"Birds."

"Did you see any birds?"

"No, I did not see any birds."

"Well, what did you see? Think! You saw branches! And what are the branches?" asked the terrible voice. "**There's a gibbet!** That is why I call my wood the torture-chamber!… You see, it's all a joke. I never express myself like other people. But I am very tired of it!… I'm sick and tired of having a forest and a torture-chamber in my house and of living like a mountebank, in a house with a false bottom!… I'm tired of it! I want to have a nice, quiet flat, with ordinary doors and windows and a wife inside it, like anybody else! A wife whom I could love and take out on Sundays and keep amused on weekdays…. Here, shall I show you some card-tricks? That will help us to pass a few minutes, while waiting for eleven o'clock tomorrow evening…. My dear little Christine!… Are you listening to me?… Tell me you love me!… No, you don't love me… but no matter, you will!…

Once, you could not look at my mask because you knew what was behind.... And now you don't mind looking at it and you forget what is behind!... One can get used to everything... if one wishes.... Plenty of young people who did not care for each other before marriage have adored each other since! Oh, I don't know what I am talking about! But you would have lots of fun with me. For instance, I am the greatest ventriloquist that ever lived, I am the first ventriloquist in the world!... You're laughing.... Perhaps you don't believe me? Listen."

The wretch, who really was the first ventriloquist in the world, was only trying to divert the child's attention from the torture-chamber; but it was a stupid scheme, for Christine thought of nothing but us! She repeatedly besought him, in the gentlest tones which she could assume:

"Put out the light in the little window!... Erik, do put out the light in the little window!"

For she saw that this light, which appeared so suddenly and of which the monster had spoken in so threatening a voice, must mean something terrible. One thing must have pacified her for a moment; and that was seeing the two of us, behind the wall, in the midst of that resplendent light, alive and well. But she would certainly have felt much easier if the light had been put out.

Meantime, the other had already begun to play the ventriloquist. He said:

"Here, I raise my mask a little.... Oh, only a little!... You see my lips, such lips as I have? They're not moving!... My mouth is closed – such mouth as I have – and yet you hear my voice.... Where will you have it? In your left ear? In your right ear? In the table? In those little ebony boxes on the mantelpiece?... Listen, dear, it's in the little box on the right of the mantelpiece: what does it say? '**Shall I turn the scorpion?**'... And now, crack! What does it say in the little box on the left? '**Shall I turn the grasshopper?**'...

And now, crack! Here it is in the little leather bag.... What does it say? '**I am the little bag of life and death!**'... And now, crack! It is in Carlotta's throat, in Carlotta's golden throat, in Carlotta's crystal throat, as I live! What does it say? It says, 'It's I, Mr. Toad, it's I singing! **I feel without alarm – co-ack – with its melody enwind me – co-ack!**'... And now, crack! It is on a chair in the ghost's box and it says, '**Madame Carlotta is singing tonight to bring the chandelier down!**'... And now, crack! Aha! Where is Erik's voice now? Listen, Christine, darling! Listen! It is behind the door of the torture-chamber! Listen! It's myself in the torture-chamber! And what do I say? I say, 'Woe to them that have a nose, a real nose, and come to look round the torture-chamber! Aha, aha, aha!'"

Oh, the ventriloquist's terrible voice! It was everywhere, everywhere. It passed through the little invisible window, through the walls. It ran around us, between us. Erik was there, speaking to us! We made a movement as though to fling ourselves upon him. But, already, swifter, more fleeting than the voice of the echo, Erik's voice had leaped back behind the wall!

Soon we heard nothing more at all, for this is what happened:

"Erik! Erik!" said Christine's voice. "You tire me with your voice. Don't go on, Erik! Isn't it very hot here?"

"Oh, yes," replied Erik's voice, "the heat is unendurable!"

"But what does this mean?... The wall is really getting quite hot!... The wall is burning!..."

"I'll tell you, Christine, dear: it is because of the forest next door."

"Well, what has that to do with it? The forest?"

"**Why, didn't you see that it was an African forest?**"

And the monster laughed so loudly and hideously that we could no longer distinguish

Christine's supplicating cries! The Vicomte de Chagny shouted and banged against the walls like a madman. I could not restrain him. But we heard nothing except the monster's laughter, and the monster himself can have heard nothing else. And then there was the sound of a body falling on the floor and being dragged along and a door slammed and then nothing, nothing more around us save the scorching silence of the south in the heart of a tropical forest!

CHAPTER TWENTY FOUR

"Barrels!... Barrels!... Any Barrels to Sell?"

THE PERSIAN'S NARRATIVE CONTINUED

I have said that the room in which M. le Vicomte de Chagny and I were imprisoned was a regular hexagon, lined entirely with mirrors. Plenty of these rooms have been seen since, mainly at exhibitions: they are called "palaces of illusion," or some such name. But the invention belongs entirely to Erik, who built the first room of this kind under my eyes, at the time of the rosy hours of Mazenderan. A decorative object, such as a column, for instance, was placed in one of the corners and immediately produced a hall of a thousand columns; for, thanks to the mirrors, the real room was multiplied by six hexagonal rooms, each of which, in its turn, was multiplied indefinitely. But the little sultana soon tired of this infantile illusion, whereupon Erik altered his invention into a "torture-chamber." For the architectural motive placed in one corner, he substituted an iron tree. This tree, with its painted leaves, was absolutely true to life and was made of iron so as to resist all the attacks of the "patient" who was locked into the torture-chamber. We shall see how the scene thus obtained was twice altered instantaneously into two successive other scenes, by means of the automatic rotation of the drums or rollers in the corners. These were divided into three sections, fitting into the angles of the mirrors and each supporting a decorative scheme that came into sight as the roller revolved upon its axis.

The walls of this strange room gave the patient nothing to lay hold of, because, apart from the solid decorative object, they were simply furnished with mirrors, thick enough to withstand any onslaught of the victim, who was flung into the chamber empty-handed and barefoot.

There was no furniture. The ceiling was capable of being lit up. An ingenious system of electric heating, which has since been imitated, allowed the temperature of the walls and room to be increased at will.

I am giving all these details of a perfectly natural invention, producing, with a few painted branches, the supernatural illusion of an equatorial forest blazing under the tropical sun, so that no one may doubt the present balance of my brain or feel entitled to say that I am mad or lying or that I take him for a fool.[11]

I now return to the facts where I left them. When the ceiling lit up and the forest became visible around us, the viscount's stupefaction was immense. That impenetrable forest, with its innumerable trunks and branches, threw him into a terrible state of consternation. He passed his hands over his forehead, as though to drive away a dream; his eyes blinked; and, for a moment, he forgot to listen.

I have already said that the sight of the forest did not surprise me at all; and therefore I listened for the two of us to what was happening next door. Lastly, my attention

---

[11] It is very natural that, at the time when the Persian was writing, he should take so many precautions against any spirit of incredulity on the part of those who were likely to read his narrative. Nowadays, when we have all seen this sort of room, his precautions would be superfluous.

was especially attracted, not so much to the scene, as to the mirrors that produced it. These mirrors were broken in parts. Yes, they were marked and scratched; they had been "starred," in spite of their solidity; and this proved to me that the torture-chamber in which we now were **had already served a purpose**.

Yes, some wretch, whose feet were not bare like those of the victims of the rosy hours of Mazenderan, had certainly fallen into this "mortal illusion" and, mad with rage, had kicked against those mirrors which, nevertheless, continued to reflect his agony. And the branch of the tree on which he had put an end to his own sufferings was arranged in such a way that, before dying, he had seen, for his last consolation, a thousand men writhing in his company.

Yes, Joseph Buquet had undoubtedly been through all this! Were we to die as he had done? I did not think so, for I knew that we had a few hours before us and that I could employ them to better purpose than Joseph Buquet was able to do. After all, I was thoroughly acquainted with most of Erik's "tricks;" and now or never was the time to turn my knowledge to account.

To begin with, I gave up every idea of returning to the passage that had brought us to that accursed chamber. I did not trouble about the possibility of working the inside stone that closed the passage; and this for the simple reason that to do so was out of the question. We had dropped from too great a height into the torture-chamber; there was no furniture to help us reach that passage; not even the branch of the iron tree, not even each other's shoulders were of any avail.

There was only one possible outlet, that opening into the Louis-Philippe room in which Erik and Christine Daaé were. But, though this outlet looked like an ordinary door on Christine's side, it was absolutely invisible to us. We must therefore try to open it without even knowing where it was.

When I was quite sure that there was no hope for us from Christine Daaé's side, when I had heard the monster dragging the poor girl from the Louis-Philippe room **lest she should interfere with our tortures**, I resolved to set to work without delay.

But I had first to calm M. de Chagny, who was already walking about like a madman, uttering incoherent cries. The snatches of conversation which he had caught between Christine and the monster had contributed not a little to drive him beside himself: add to that the shock of the magic forest and the scorching heat which was beginning to make the perspiration stream down his temples and you will have no difficulty in understanding his state of mind. He shouted Christine's name, brandished his pistol, knocked his forehead against the glass in his endeavors to run down the glades of the illusive forest. In short, the torture was beginning to work its spell upon a brain unprepared for it.

I did my best to induce the poor viscount

to listen to reason. I made him touch the mirrors and the iron tree and the branches and explained to him, by optical laws, all the luminous imagery by which we were surrounded and of which we need not allow ourselves to be the victims, like ordinary, ignorant people.

"We are in a room, a little room; that is what you must keep saying to yourself. And we shall leave the room as soon as we have found the door."

And I promised him that, if he let me act, without disturbing me by shouting and walking up and down, I would discover the trick of the door in less than an hour's time.

Then he lay flat on the floor, as one does in a wood, and declared that he would wait until I found the door of the forest, as there was nothing better to do! And he added that, from where he was, "the view was splendid!" The torture was working, in spite of all that I had said.

Myself, forgetting the forest, I tackled a

glass panel and began to finger it in every direction, hunting for the weak point on which to press in order to turn the door in accordance with Erik's system of pivots. This weak point might be a mere speck on the glass, no larger than a pea, under which the spring lay hidden. I hunted and hunted. I felt as high as my hands could reach. Erik was about the same height as myself and I thought that he would not have placed the spring higher than suited his stature.

While groping over the successive panels with the greatest care, I endeavored not to lose a minute, for I was feeling more and more overcome with the heat and we were literally roasting in that blazing forest.

I had been working like this for half an hour and had finished three panels, when, as ill-luck would have it, I turned round on hearing a muttered exclamation from the viscount.

"I am stifling," he said. "All those mirrors are sending out an infernal heat! Do you think you will find that spring soon? If you are much longer about it, we shall be roasted alive!"

I was not sorry to hear him talk like this. He had not said a word of the forest and I hoped that my companion's reason would hold out some time longer against the torture. But he added:

"What consoles me is that the monster has given Christine until eleven tomorrow evening. If we can't get out of here and go to her assistance, at least we shall be dead before her! Then Erik's mass can serve for all of us!"

And he gulped down a breath of hot air that nearly made him faint.

As I had not the same desperate reasons as M. le Vicomte for accepting death, I returned, after giving him a word of encouragement, to my panel, but I had made the mistake of taking a few steps while speaking and, in the tangle of the illusive forest, I was no longer able to find my panel for certain! I had to begin all over again, at random, feeling, fumbling, groping.

Now the fever laid hold of me in my turn... for I found nothing, absolutely nothing. In the next room, all was silence. We were quite lost in the forest, without an outlet, a compass, a guide or anything. Oh, I knew what awaited us if nobody came to our aid... or if I did not find the spring! But, look as I might, I found nothing but branches, beautiful branches that stood straight up before me, or spread gracefully over my head. But they gave no shade. And this was natural enough, as we were in an equatorial forest, with the sun right above our heads, an African forest.

M. de Chagny and I had repeatedly taken off our coats and put them on again, finding at one time that they made us feel still hotter and at another that they protected us against the heat. I was still making a moral resistance, but M. de Chagny seemed to me quite "gone." He pretended that he had been walking in that forest for three days and nights, without stopping, looking for Christine Daaé! From time to time, he thought he saw her behind the trunk of a tree, or gliding between the branches; and he called to her with words of supplication that brought the tears to my eyes. And then, at last:

"Oh, how thirsty I am!" he cried, in delirious accents.

I too was thirsty. My throat was on fire. And, yet, squatting on the floor, I went on hunting, hunting, hunting for the spring of the invisible door... especially as it was dangerous to remain in the forest as evening drew nigh. Already the shades of night were beginning to surround us. It had happened very quickly: night falls quickly in tropical countries... suddenly, with hardly any twilight.

Now night, in the forests of the equator, is always dangerous, particularly when, like ourselves, one has not the materials for a fire to keep off the beasts of prey. I did indeed try for a moment to break off the branches, which I would have lit with my dark lantern, but I knocked myself also against the mirrors and remembered, in time, that we had only images of branches to do with.

The heat did not go with the daylight; on the contrary, it was now still hotter under the blue rays of the moon. I urged the viscount to hold our weapons ready to fire and not to stray from camp, while I went on looking for my spring.

Suddenly, we heard a lion roaring a few yards away.

"Oh," whispered the viscount, "he is quite close!... Don't you see him?... There... through the trees... in that thicket!... If he roars again, I will fire!..."

And the roaring began again, louder than before. And the viscount fired, but I do not think that he hit the lion; only, he smashed a mirror, as I perceived the next morning, at daybreak. We must have covered a good distance during the night, for we suddenly found ourselves on the edge of the desert, an immense desert of sand, stones and rocks. It was really not worth while leaving the forest to come upon the desert. Tired out, I flung myself down beside the viscount, for I had had enough of looking for springs which I could not find.

I was quite surprised – and I said so to the viscount – that we had encountered no other dangerous animals during the night. Usually, after the lion came the leopard and sometimes the buzz of the tsetse fly. These were easily obtained effects; and I explained to M. de Chagny that Erik imitated the roar of a lion on a long tabour or timbrel, with an ass's skin at one end. Over this skin he tied a string of catgut, which was fastened at the middle to another similar string passing through the whole length of the tabour. Erik had only to rub this string with a glove smeared with resin and, according to the manner in which he rubbed it, he imitated to perfection the voice of the lion or the leopard, or even the buzzing of the tsetse fly.

The idea that Erik was probably in the room beside us, working his trick, made me suddenly resolve to enter into a parley with him, for we must obviously give up all thought of taking him by surprise. And by this time he must be quite aware who were the occupants of his torture-chamber. I called him: "Erik! Erik!"

I shouted as loudly as I could across the desert, but there was no answer to my voice. All around us lay the silence and the bare immensity of that stony desert. What was to become of us in the midst of that awful solitude?

We were beginning literally to die of heat, hunger and thirst... of thirst especially. At last, I saw M. de Chagny raise himself on his elbow and point to a spot on the horizon. He had discovered an oasis!

Yes, far in the distance was an oasis… an oasis with limpid water, which reflected the iron trees!… Tush, it was the scene of the mirage…. I recognized it at once… the worst of the three!… No one had been able to fight against it… no one…. I did my utmost to keep my head **and not to hope for water**, because I knew that, if a man hoped for water, the water that reflected the iron tree, and if, after hoping for water, he struck against the mirror, then there was only one thing for him to do: to hang himself on the iron tree!

So I cried to M. de Chagny:

"It's the mirage!… It's the mirage!… Don't believe in the water!… It's another trick of the mirrors!…"

Then he flatly told me to shut up, with my tricks of the mirrors, my springs, my revolving doors and my palaces of illusions! He angrily declared that I must be either blind or mad to imagine that all that water flowing over there, among those splendid, numberless trees, was not real water!... And the desert was real!... And so was the forest!... And it was no use trying to take him in... he was an old, experienced traveler... he had been all over the place!

And he dragged himself along, saying: "Water! Water!"

And his mouth was open, as though he were drinking.

And my mouth was open too, as though I were drinking.

For we not only saw the water, but **we heard it**!... We heard it flow, we heard it ripple!... Do you understand that word "ripple?"... **It is a sound which you hear with your tongue!**... You put your tongue out of your mouth to listen to it better!

Lastly – and this was the most pitiless torture of all – we heard the rain and it was not raining! This was an infernal invention.... Oh, I knew well enough how Erik obtained it! He filled with little stones a very long and narrow box, broken up inside with wooden and metal projections. The stones, in falling, struck against these projections and rebounded from one to another; and the result was a series of pattering sounds that exactly imitated a rainstorm.

Ah, you should have seen us putting out our tongues and dragging ourselves toward the rippling riverbank! Our eyes and ears were full of water, but our tongues were hard and dry as horn!

When we reached the mirror, M. de Chagny licked it… and I also licked the glass.

It was burning hot!

Then we rolled on the floor with a hoarse cry of despair. M. de Chagny put the one pistol that was still loaded to his temple; and I stared at the Punjab lasso at the foot of the iron tree. I knew why the iron tree had returned, in this third change of scene!… The iron tree was waiting for me!…

But, as I stared at the Punjab lasso, I saw a thing that made me start so violently that M. de Chagny delayed his attempt at suicide.

I took his arm. And then I caught the pistol from him... and then I dragged myself on my knees toward what I had seen.

I had discovered, near the Punjab lasso, in a groove in the floor, a black-headed nail of which I knew the use. At last I had discovered the spring! I felt the nail.... I lifted a radiant face to M. de Chagny.... The black-headed nail yielded to my pressure....

And then....

And then we saw not a door opened in the wall, but a cellar-flap released in the floor. Cool air came up to us from the black hole below. We stooped over that square of darkness as though over a limpid well. With our chins in the cool shade, we drank it in.

And we bent lower and lower over the trap-door. What could there be in that cellar which opened before us? Water? Water to drink?

I thrust my arm into the darkness and came upon a stone and another stone... a staircase... a dark staircase leading into the cellar. The viscount wanted to fling himself down the hole; but I, fearing a new trick of the monster's, stopped him, turned on my dark lantern and went down first.

The staircase was a winding one and led down into pitchy darkness. But oh, how deliciously cool were the darkness and the stairs? The lake could not be far away.

We soon reached the bottom. Our eyes were beginning to accustom themselves to the dark, to distinguish shapes around us… circular shapes… on which I turned the light of my lantern.

Barrels!

We were in Erik's cellar: it was here that he must keep his wine and perhaps his drinking-water. I knew that Erik was a great lover of good wine. Ah, there was plenty to drink here!

M. de Chagny patted the round shapes and kept on saying:

"Barrels! Barrels!… What a lot of barrels!…"

Indeed, there was quite a number of them, symmetrically arranged in two rows, one on either side of us. They were small barrels and I thought that Erik must have selected them of that size to facilitate their carriage to the house on the lake.

We examined them successively, to see if one of them had not a funnel, showing that it had been tapped at some time or another. But all the barrels were hermetically closed.

Then, after half lifting one to make sure it was full, we went on our knees and, with the blade of a small knife which I carried, I prepared to stave in the bunghole.

At that moment, I seemed to hear, coming from very far, a sort of monotonous chant which I knew well, from often hearing it in the streets of Paris:

"Barrels!... Barrels!... Any barrels to sell?..."

My hand desisted from its work. M. de Chagny had also heard. He said:

"That's funny! It sounds as if the barrel were singing!"

The song was renewed, farther away:

"Barrels!... Barrels!... Any barrels to sell?..."

"Oh, I swear," said the viscount, "that the tune dies away in the barrel!..."

We stood up and went to look behind the barrel.

"It's inside," said M. de Chagny, "it's inside!"

But we heard nothing there and were driven to accuse the bad condition of our senses. And we returned to the bunghole. M. de Chagny put his two hands together underneath it and, with a last effort, I burst the bung.

"What's this?" cried the viscount. "This isn't water!"

The viscount put his two full hands close to my lantern.... I stooped to look... and at once threw away the lantern with such violence that it broke and went out, leaving us in utter darkness.

What I had seen in M. de Chagny's hands... was gunpowder!

CHAPTER TWENTY FIVE

The Scorpion or the Grasshopper: Which?

THE PERSIAN'S NARRATIVE CONCLUDED

The discovery flung us into a state of alarm that made us forget all our past and present sufferings. We now knew all that the monster meant to convey when he said to Christine Daaé:

"Yes or no! If your answer is no, everybody will be dead **and buried**!"

Yes, buried under the ruins of the Paris Grand Opera!

The monster had given her until eleven o'clock in the evening. He had chosen his time well. There would be many people, many "members of the human race," up there, in the resplendent theater. What finer retinue could be expected for his funeral? He would go down to the tomb escorted by the whitest shoulders in the world, decked with the richest jewels.

Eleven o'clock tomorrow evening!

We were all to be blown up in the middle of the performance… if Christine Daaé said no!

Eleven o'clock tomorrow evening!…

And what else could Christine say but no? Would she not prefer to espouse death itself rather than that living corpse? She did not know that on her acceptance or refusal depended the awful fate of many members of the human race!

Eleven o'clock tomorrow evening!

And we dragged ourselves through the darkness, feeling our way to the stone steps, for the light in the trap-door overhead that led to the room of mirrors was now extinguished; and we repeated to ourselves:

"Eleven o'clock tomorrow evening!"

At last, I found the staircase. But, suddenly I drew myself up on the first step, for a terrible thought had come to my mind:

"What is the time?"

Ah, what was the time?… For, after all, eleven o'clock tomorrow evening might be now, might be this very moment! Who could tell us the time? We seemed to have been imprisoned in that hell for days and days… for years… since the beginning of the world. Perhaps we should be blown up then and there! Ah, a sound! A crack!

"Did you hear that?… There, in the corner… good heavens!… Like a sound of machinery!… Again!… Oh, for a light!…

Perhaps it's the machinery that is to blow everything up!... I tell you, a cracking sound: are you deaf?"

M. de Chagny and I began to yell like madmen. Fear spurred us on. We rushed up the treads of the staircase, stumbling as we went, anything to escape the dark, to return to the mortal light of the room of mirrors!

We found the trap-door still open, but it was now as dark in the room of mirrors as in the cellar which we had left. We dragged ourselves along the floor of the torture-chamber, the floor that separated us from the powder-magazine. What was the time? We shouted, we called: M. de Chagny to Christine, I to Erik. I reminded him that I had saved his life. But no answer, save that of our despair, of our madness: what was the time? We argued, we tried to calculate the time which we had spent there, but we were incapable of reasoning. If only we could see the face of a watch!... Mine had stopped, but M. de Chagny's was still going.... He told me that he had wound it up before dressing for the Opera.... We had not a match upon us.... And yet we must know.... M. de Chagny broke the glass of his watch and felt the two hands.... He questioned the hands of the watch with his fingertips, going by the position of the ring of the watch.... Judging by the space between the hands, he thought it might be just eleven o'clock!

But perhaps it was not the eleven o'clock of which we stood in dread. Perhaps we had still twelve hours before us!

Suddenly, I exclaimed: "Hush!"

I seemed to hear footsteps in the next room. Someone tapped against the wall. Christine Daaé's voice said:

"Raoul! Raoul!"

We were now all talking at once, on either side of the wall. Christine sobbed; she was not sure that she would find M. de Chagny alive. The monster had been terrible, it seemed, had done nothing but rave, waiting for her to give him the "yes" which she refused. And yet she had promised him that "yes," if he would take her to the torture-chamber. But he had obstinately declined, and had uttered hideous threats against all the members of the human race! At last, after hours and hours of that hell, he had that moment gone out, leaving her alone to reflect for the last time.

"Hours and hours? What is the time now? What is the time, Christine?"

"It is eleven o'clock! Eleven o'clock, all but five minutes!"

"But which eleven o'clock?"

"The eleven o'clock that is to decide life or death!... He told me so just before he went.... He is terrible.... He is quite mad: he tore off his mask and his yellow eyes shot flames!... He did nothing but laugh!... He said, 'I give you five minutes to spare your blushes! Here,' he said, taking a key from the little bag of life and death, 'here is the little bronze key that opens the two ebony caskets on the mantelpiece in the Louis-Philippe room.... In one of the caskets, you will find a scorpion, in the other, a grasshopper, both very cleverly imitated in Japanese bronze: they will say yes or no for you. If you turn the scorpion round, that will mean to me, when I return, that you have said yes. The grasshopper will mean no.' And he laughed like a drunken demon. I did nothing but beg and entreat him to give me the key of the torture-chamber, promising to be his wife if he granted me that request.... But he told me that there was no future need for that key and that he was going to throw it into the lake!... And he again laughed like a drunken demon and left me. Oh, his last words were, 'The grasshopper! Be careful of the grasshopper! A grasshopper does not only turn: it hops! It hops! And it hops jolly high!'"

The five minutes had nearly elapsed and the scorpion and the grasshopper were scratching at my brain. Nevertheless, I had sufficient lucidity left to understand that, if the grasshopper were turned, it would hop… and with it many members of the human race! There was no doubt but that the grasshopper controlled an electric current intended to blow up the powder-magazine!

M. de Chagny, who seemed to have recovered all his moral force from hearing Christine's voice, explained to her, in a few hurried words, the situation in which we and all the Opera were. He told her to turn the scorpion at once.

There was a pause.

"Christine," I cried, "where are you?"

"By the scorpion."

"Don't touch it!"

The idea had come to me – for I knew my Erik – that the monster had perhaps deceived the girl once more. Perhaps it was the scorpion that would blow everything up. After all, why wasn't he there? The five minutes were long past… and he was not back…. Perhaps he had taken shelter and was waiting for the explosion!... Why had he not returned?... He could not really expect Christine ever to consent to become his voluntary prey!... Why had he not returned?

"Don't touch the scorpion!" I said.

"Here he comes!" cried Christine. "I hear him! Here he is!"

We heard his steps approaching the Louis-Philippe room. He came up to Christine, but did not speak. Then I raised my voice:

"Erik! It is I! Do you know me?"

With extraordinary calmness, he at once replied:

"So you are not dead in there? Well, then, see that you keep quiet."

I tried to speak, but he said coldly:

"Not a word, daroga, or I shall blow everything up." And he added, "The honor rests with mademoiselle.... Mademoiselle has not touched the scorpion" – how deliberately he spoke! – "mademoiselle has not touched the grasshopper" – with that composure! – "but it is not too late to do the right thing. There, I open the caskets without a key, for I am a trap-door lover and I open and shut what I please and as I please. I open the little ebony caskets: mademoiselle, look at the little dears inside. Aren't they pretty? If you turn the grasshopper, mademoiselle, we shall all be blown up. There is enough gunpowder under our feet to blow up a whole quarter of Paris. If you turn the scorpion, mademoiselle, all that powder will be soaked and drowned. Mademoiselle, to celebrate our wedding, you shall make a very handsome present to a few hundred Parisians who are at this moment applauding a poor masterpiece of Meyerbeer's... you shall make them a present of their lives.... For, with your own fair hands, you shall turn the scorpion.... And merrily, merrily, we will be married!"

A pause; and then:

"If, in two minutes, mademoiselle, you have not turned the scorpion, I shall turn the grasshopper... and the grasshopper, I tell you, **hops jolly high**!"

The terrible silence began anew. The Vicomte de Chagny, realizing that there was nothing left to do but pray, went down on his knees and prayed. As for me, my blood beat so fiercely that I had to take my heart in both hands, lest it should burst. At last, we heard Erik's voice:

"The two minutes are past.... Goodbye, mademoiselle.... Hop, grasshopper!..."

"Erik," cried Christine, "do you swear to me, monster, do you swear to me that the scorpion is the one to turn?..."

"Yes, to hop at our wedding."

"Ah, you see! You said, to hop!"

"At our wedding, ingenuous child!... The scorpion opens the ball.... But that will do!... You won't have the scorpion? Then I turn the grasshopper!"

"Erik!"

"Enough!"

I was crying out in concert with Christine. M. de Chagny was still on his knees, praying.

"Erik! I have turned the scorpion!"

Oh, the second through which we passed! Waiting! Waiting to find ourselves in fragments, amid the roar and the ruins! Feeling something crack beneath our feet, hearing an appalling hiss through the open trap-door, a hiss like the first sound of a rocket!

It came softly, at first, then louder, then very loud. But it was not the hiss of fire. It was more like the hiss of water. And now it became a gurgling sound: "Guggle! Guggle!"

We rushed to the trap-door. All our thirst, which vanished when the terror came, now returned with the lapping of the water.

The water rose in the cellar, above the barrels, the powder-barrels – "Barrels!... Barrels!... Any barrels to sell?" – and we went down to it with parched throats. It rose to our chins, to our mouths. And we drank. We stood on the floor of the cellar and drank.

And we went up the stairs again in the dark, step by step, went up with the water.

The water came out of the cellar with us and spread over the floor of the room. If this went on, the whole house on the lake would be swamped. The floor of the torture-chamber had itself become a regular little lake, in which our feet splashed. Surely there was water enough now! Erik must turn off the tap!

"Erik! Erik! That is water enough for the gunpowder! Turn off the tap! Turn off the scorpion!"

But Erik did not reply. We heard nothing but the water rising: it was halfway to our waists!

"Christine!" cried M. de Chagny. "Christine! The water is up to our knees!"

But Christine did not reply.... We heard nothing but the water rising.

No one, no one in the next room, no one to turn the tap, no one to turn the scorpion!

We were all alone, in the dark, with the

dark water that seized us and clasped us and froze us!

"Erik! Erik!"

"Christine! Christine!"

By this time, we had lost our foothold and were spinning round in the water, carried away by an irresistible whirl, for the water turned with us and dashed us against the dark mirror, which thrust us back again; and our throats, raised above the whirlpool, roared aloud.

Were we to die here, drowned in the torture-chamber? I had never seen that. Erik, at the time of the rosy hours of Mazenderan, had never shown me that, through the little invisible window.

"Erik! Erik!" I cried. "I saved your life! Remember!... You were sentenced to death! But for me, you would be dead now!... Erik!"

We whirled around in the water like so much wreckage. But, suddenly, my straying hands seized the trunk of the iron tree! I called M. de Chagny, and we both hung to the branch of the iron tree.

And the water rose still higher.

"Oh! Oh! Can you remember? How much space is there between the branch of the tree and the dome-shaped ceiling? Do try to remember!... After all, the water may stop, it must find its level!... There, I think it is stopping!... No, no, oh, horrible!... Swim! Swim for your life!"

Our arms became entangled in the effort of swimming; we choked; we fought in the dark water; already we could hardly breathe the dark air above the dark water, the air which escaped, which we could hear escaping through some vent-hole or other.

"Oh, let us turn and turn and turn until we find the air hole and then glue our mouths to it!"

But I lost my strength; I tried to lay hold of the walls! Oh, how those glass walls slipped from under my groping fingers!... We whirled round again!... We began to sink!... One last effort!... A last cry:

"Erik!... Christine!..."

"Guggle, guggle, guggle!" in our ears. "Guggle! Guggle!" At the bottom of the dark water, our ears went, "Guggle! Guggle!"

And, before losing consciousness entirely, I seemed to hear, between two guggles:

"Barrels! Barrels! Any barrels to sell?"

CHAPTER TWENTY SIX

The End of the Ghost's Love Story

THE PREVIOUS CHAPTER MARKS the conclusion of the written narrative which the Persian left behind him.

Notwithstanding the horrors of a situation which seemed definitely to abandon them to their deaths, M. de Chagny and his companion were saved by the sublime devotion of Christine Daaé. And I had the rest of the story from the lips of the daroga himself.

When I went to see him, he was still living in his little flat in the Rue de Rivoli, opposite the Tuileries. He was very ill, and it required all my ardor as an historian pledged to the truth to persuade him to live the incredible tragedy over again for my benefit. His faithful old servant Darius showed me in to him. The daroga received me at a window overlooking the garden of the Tuileries. He still had his magnificent eyes, but his poor face looked very worn. He had shaved the whole of his head, which was usually covered with an astrakhan cap; he was dressed in a long, plain coat and amused himself by unconsciously twisting his thumbs inside the sleeves; but his mind was quite clear, and he told me his story with perfect lucidity.

It seems that, when he opened his eyes, the daroga found himself lying on a bed. M. de Chagny was on a sofa, beside the wardrobe. An angel and a devil were watching over them.

After the deceptions and illusions of the torture-chamber, the precision of the details of that quiet little middle-class room seemed to have been invented for the express purpose of puzzling the mind of the mortal rash enough to stray into that abode of living nightmare. The wooden bedstead, the waxed mahogany chairs, the chest of drawers, those brasses, the little square antimacassars carefully placed on the backs of the chairs, the clock on the mantelpiece and the harmless-looking ebony caskets at either end, lastly, the whatnot filled with shells, with red pincushions, with mother-of-pearl boats and an enormous ostrich-egg, the whole discreetly lighted by a shaded lamp standing on a small round table: this collection of ugly, peaceable, reasonable furniture, **at the bottom of the Opera cellars**, bewildered the imagination more than all the late fantastic happenings.

And the figure of the masked man seemed all the more formidable in this old-fashioned, neat and trim little frame. It bent down over the Persian and said, in his ear:

"Are you better, daroga?... You are looking at my furniture?... It is all that I have left of my poor unhappy mother."

Christine Daaé did not say a word: she moved about noiselessly, like a sister of charity, who had taken a vow of silence. She brought a cup of cordial, or of hot tea, he did not remember which. The man in the mask took it from her hands and gave it to the Persian. M. de Chagny was still sleeping.

Erik poured a drop of rum into the daroga's cup and, pointing to the viscount, said:

"He came to himself long before we knew if you were still alive, daroga. He is quite well. He is asleep. We must not wake him."

Erik left the room for a moment, and the Persian raised himself on his elbow, looked around him and saw Christine Daaé sitting by the fireside. He spoke to her, called her, but he was still very weak and fell back on his pillow. Christine came to him, laid her hand on his forehead and went away again. And the Persian remembered that, as she went, she did not give a glance at M. de Chagny, who, it is true, was sleeping peacefully; and she sat down again in her chair by the chimney-corner, silent as a sister of charity who had taken a vow of silence.

Erik returned with some little bottles which he placed on the mantelpiece. And, again in a whisper, so as not to wake M. de Chagny, he said to the Persian, after sitting down and feeling his pulse:

"You are now saved, both of you. And soon I shall take you up to the surface of the earth, **to please my wife**."

Thereupon he rose, without any further explanation, and disappeared once more.

The Persian now looked at Christine's quiet profile under the lamp. She was reading a tiny book, with gilt edges, like a religious book. There are editions of **The Imitation** that look like that. The Persian still had in his ears the natural tone in which the other had said, "to please my wife." Very gently, he called her again; but Christine was wrapped up in her book and did not hear him.

Erik returned, mixed the daroga a draft and advised him not to speak to "his wife" again nor to anyone, **because it might be very dangerous to everybody's health**.

Eventually, the Persian fell asleep, like M. de Chagny, and did not wake until he was in his own room, nursed by his faithful Darius, who told him that, on the night before, he was found propped against the door of his flat, where he had been brought by a stranger, who rang the bell before going away.

As soon as the daroga recovered his strength and his wits, he sent to Count Philippe's house to inquire after the viscount's health. The answer was that the young man had not been seen and that

Count Philippe was dead. His body was found on the bank of the Opera lake, on the Rue-Scribe side. The Persian remembered the requiem mass which he had heard from behind the wall of the torture-chamber, and had no doubt concerning the crime and the criminal. Knowing Erik as he did, he easily reconstructed the tragedy. Thinking that his brother had run away with Christine Daaé, Philippe had dashed in pursuit of him along the Brussels Road, where he knew that everything was prepared for the elopement. Failing to find the pair, he hurried back to the Opera, remembered Raoul's strange confidence about his fantastic rival and learned that the viscount had made every effort to enter the cellars of the theater and that he had disappeared, leaving his hat in the prima donna's dressing-room beside an empty pistol-case. And the count, who no longer entertained any doubt of his brother's madness, in his turn darted into that infernal underground maze. This was enough, in the Persian's eyes, to explain the discovery of the Comte de Chagny's corpse on the shore of the lake, where the siren, Erik's siren, kept watch.

The Persian did not hesitate. He determined to inform the police. Now the case was in the hands of an examining-magistrate called Faure, an incredulous, commonplace, superficial sort of person, (I write as I think), with a mind utterly unprepared to receive a confidence of this kind. M. Faure took down the daroga's depositions and proceeded to treat him as a madman.

Despairing of ever obtaining a hearing, the Persian sat down to write. As the police did not want his evidence, perhaps the press would be glad of it; and he had just written the last line of the narrative I have quoted in the preceding chapters, when Darius announced the visit of a stranger who refused his name, who would not show his face and declared simply that he did not intend to leave the place until he had spoken to the daroga.

The Persian at once felt who his singular visitor was and ordered him to be shown in. The daroga was right. It was the ghost, it was Erik!

He looked extremely weak and leaned against the wall, as though he were afraid of falling. Taking off his hat, he revealed a forehead white as wax. The rest of the horrible face was hidden by the mask.

The Persian rose to his feet as Erik entered.

"Murderer of Count Philippe, what have you done with his brother and Christine Daaé?"

Erik staggered under this direct attack, kept silent for a moment, dragged himself to a chair and heaved a deep sigh. Then, speaking in short phrases and gasping for breath between the words:

"Daroga, don't talk to me… about Count Philippe.… He was dead… by the time… I left my house… he was dead… when… the siren sang.… It was an… accident… a sad… a very sad… accident. He fell very awkwardly… but simply and naturally… into the lake!…"

"You lie!" shouted the Persian.

Erik bowed his head and said:

"I have not come here… to talk about Count Philippe… but to tell you that… I am going… to die…."

"Where are Raoul de Chagny and Christine Daaé?"

"I am going to die…."

"Raoul de Chagny and Christine Daaé?"

"Of love… daroga… I am dying… of love…. That is how it is…. I loved her so!… And I love her still… daroga… and I am dying of love for her, I… I tell you!… If you knew how beautiful she was… when she let me kiss her… alive…. It was the first… time, daroga, the first… time I ever kissed a woman…. Yes, alive…. I kissed her alive… and she looked as beautiful as if she had been dead!…"

The Persian shook Erik by the arm:

"Will you tell me if she is alive or dead."

"Why do you shake me like that?" asked Erik, making an effort to speak more connectedly. "I tell you that I am going to die.... Yes, I kissed her alive...."

"And now she is dead?"

"I tell you I kissed her just like that, on her forehead... and she did not draw back her forehead from my lips!... Oh, she is a good girl!... As to her being dead, I don't think so; but it has nothing to do with me.... No, no, she is not dead! And no one shall touch a hair of her head! She is a good, honest girl, and she saved your life, daroga, at a moment when I would not have given twopence for your Persian skin. As a matter of fact, nobody bothered about you. Why were you there with that little chap? You would have died as well as he! My word, how she entreated me for her little chap! But I told her that, as she had turned the scorpion, she had, through that very fact, and of her own free will, become engaged to me and that she did not need to have two men engaged to her, which was true enough.

"As for you, you did not exist, you had ceased to exist, I tell you, and you were going to die with the other!... Only, mark me, daroga, when you were yelling like the devil, because of the water, Christine came to me with her beautiful blue eyes wide open, and swore to me, as she hoped to be saved, that she consented to be **my living wife**!... Until then, in the depths of her eyes, daroga, I had always seen my dead wife; it was the first time I saw **my living wife** there. She was sincere, as she hoped to be saved. She would not kill herself. It was a bargain.... Half a minute later, all the water was back in the lake; and I had a hard job with you, daroga, for, upon my honor, I thought you were done for!... However!... There you were!... It was understood that I was to take you both up to the surface of the earth. When, at last, I cleared the Louis-

Philippe room of you, I came back alone…."

"What have you done with the Vicomte de Chagny?" asked the Persian, interrupting him.

"Ah, you see, daroga, I couldn't carry **him** up like that, at once…. He was a hostage…. But I could not keep him in the house on the lake either, because of Christine; so I locked him up comfortably, I chained him up nicely – a whiff of the Mazenderan scent had left him as limp as a rag – in the Communists' dungeon, which is in the most deserted and remote part of the Opera, below the fifth cellar, where no one ever comes, and where no one ever hears you. Then I came back to Christine. She was waiting for me…."

Erik here rose solemnly. Then he continued, but, as he spoke, he was overcome by all his former emotion and began to tremble like a leaf:

"Yes, she was waiting for me… waiting for me erect and alive, a real, living bride… as she hoped to be saved…. And, when I… came forward, more timid than… a little child, she did not run away… no, no… she stayed… she waited for me.… I even believe… daroga… that she put out her forehead… a little… oh, not much… just a little… like a living bride.… And… and… I… kissed her!… I!… I!… I!… And she did not die!… Oh, how good it is, daroga, to kiss somebody on the forehead!… You can't tell!… But I! I!… My mother, daroga, my poor, unhappy mother would never… let me kiss her.… She used to run away… and throw me my mask!… Nor any other woman… ever, ever!… Ah, you can understand, my happiness was so great, I cried. And I fell at her feet, crying… and I kissed her feet… her little feet… crying. You're crying, too, daroga… and she cried also… the angel cried!…"

Erik sobbed aloud and the Persian himself could not retain his tears in the presence of that masked man, who, with his shoulders shaking and his hands clutched at his chest, was moaning with pain and love by turns.

"Yes, daroga… I felt her tears flow on my forehead… on mine, mine!… They were soft… they were sweet!… They trickled under my mask… they mingled with my tears in my eyes… they flowed between my lips.… Listen, daroga, listen to what I did.… I tore off my mask so as not to lose one of her tears… and she did not run away!… And she did not die!… She remained alive, weeping over me, with me. We cried together! I have tasted all the happiness the world can offer!"

And Erik fell into a chair, choking for breath:

"Ah, I am not going to die yet… presently I shall… but let me cry!… Listen, daroga… listen to this.… While I was at her feet… I heard her say, 'Poor, unhappy Erik!'… **And she took my hand!**… I had become no more, you know, than a poor dog ready to die for her.… I mean it, daroga!… I held in my hand a ring, a plain gold ring which I had given her… which she had lost… and which I had found again… a wedding-ring, you know.... I slipped it into her little hand and said, 'There!... Take it!... Take it for you... and him!... It shall be my wedding-present... a present from your poor, unhappy Erik.... I know you love the boy... don't cry any more!'... She asked me, in a very soft voice, what I meant.... Then I made her understand that, where she was concerned, I was only a poor dog, ready to die for her... but that she could marry the young man when she pleased, because she had cried with me and mingled her tears with mine!..."

Erik's emotion was so great that he had to tell the Persian not to look at him, for he was choking and must take off his mask. The daroga went to the window and opened it. His heart was full of pity, but he took care to keep his eyes fixed on the trees in the Tuileries gardens, lest he should see the monster's face.

"I went and released the young man," Erik continued, "and told him to come with me to Christine.... They kissed before me in the Louis-Philippe room.... Christine had my ring.... I made Christine swear to come back, one night, when I was dead, crossing the lake from the Rue-Scribe side, and bury me in the greatest secrecy with the gold ring, which she was to wear until that moment.... I told her where she would find my body and what to do with it.... Then Christine kissed me, for the first time, herself, here, on the forehead – don't look, daroga! – here, on the forehead... on my forehead, mine – don't look, daroga! – and they went off together.... Christine had stopped crying.... I alone cried.... Daroga, daroga, if Christine keeps her promise, she will come back soon!..."

The Persian asked him no questions. He was quite reassured as to the fate of Raoul Chagny and Christine Daaé; no one could have doubted the word of the weeping Erik that night.

The monster resumed his mask and

collected his strength to leave the daroga. He told him that, when he felt his end to be very near at hand, he would send him, in gratitude for the kindness which the Persian had once shown him, that which he held dearest in the world: all Christine Daaé's papers, which she had written for Raoul's benefit and left with Erik, together with a few objects belonging to her, such as a pair of gloves, a shoe-buckle and two pocket-handkerchiefs. In reply to the Persian's questions, Erik told him that the two young people, as soon as they found themselves free, had resolved to go and look for a priest in some lonely spot where they could hide their happiness and that, with this object in view, they had started from "the northern railway station of the world." Lastly, Erik relied on the Persian, as soon as he received the promised relics and papers, to inform the young couple of his death and to advertise it in the **Epoque**.

That was all. The Persian saw Erik to the door of his flat, and Darius helped him down to the street. A cab was waiting for him. Erik stepped in; and the Persian, who had gone back to the window, heard him say to the driver:

"Go to the Opera."

And the cab drove off into the night.

The Persian had seen the poor, unfortunate Erik for the last time. Three weeks later, the **Epoque** published this advertisement:

"Erik is dead."

EPILOGUE

I HAVE NOW TOLD the singular, but veracious story of the Opera ghost. As I declared on the first page of this work, it is no longer possible to deny that Erik really lived. There are today so many proofs of his existence within the reach of everybody that we can follow Erik's actions logically through the whole tragedy of the Chagnys.

There is no need to repeat here how greatly the case excited the capital. The kidnapping of the artist, the death of the

Comte de Chagny under such exceptional conditions, the disappearance of his brother, the drugging of the gasman at the Opera and of his two assistants: what tragedies, what passions, what crimes had surrounded the idyll of Raoul and the sweet and charming Christine!… What had become of that wonderful, mysterious artist of whom the world was never, never to hear again?… She was represented as the victim of a rivalry between the two brothers; and nobody suspected what had really happened, nobody understood that, as Raoul and Christine had both disappeared, both had withdrawn far from the world to enjoy a happiness which they would not have cared to make public after the inexplicable death of Count Philippe.… They took the train one day from "the northern railway station of the world."… Possibly, I too shall take the train at that station, one day, and go and seek around thy lakes, O Norway, O silent Scandinavia, for the perhaps still living traces of Raoul and Christine and also of Mamma Valérius, who disappeared at the same time!... Possibly, some day, I shall hear the lonely echoes of the North repeat the singing of her who knew the Angel of Music!...

Long after the case was pigeonholed by the unintelligent care of M. le Juge d'Instruction Faure, the newspapers made efforts, at intervals, to fathom the mystery. One evening paper alone, which knew all the gossip of the theaters, said:

"We recognize the touch of the Opera ghost."

And even that was written by way of irony.

The Persian alone knew the whole truth and held the main proofs, which came to him with the pious relics promised by the ghost. It fell to my lot to complete those proofs with the aid of the daroga himself. Day by day, I kept him informed of the progress of my inquiries; and he directed them. He had not been to the Opera for years and years, but he had preserved the most accurate recollection of the building, and there was no better guide than he possible to help me discover its most secret recesses. He also told me where to gather further information, whom to ask; and he sent me to call on M. Poligny, at a moment when the poor man was nearly drawing his last breath. I had no idea that he was so very ill, and I shall never forget the effect which my questions about the ghost produced upon him. He looked at me as if I were the devil and answered only in a few incoherent sentences, which showed, however – and that was the main thing – the extent of the perturbation which O. G., in his time, had brought into that already very restless life (for M. Poligny was what people call a man of pleasure).

When I came and told the Persian of the poor result of my visit to M. Poligny, the daroga gave a faint smile and said:

"Poligny never knew how far that extraordinary blackguard of an Erik humbugged him." – The Persian, by the way, spoke of Erik sometimes as a demigod and sometimes as the lowest of the low – "Poligny was superstitious and Erik knew it. Erik knew most things about the public and private affairs of the Opera. When M. Poligny heard a mysterious voice tell him, in Box Five, of the manner in which he used to spend his time and abuse his partner's confidence, he did not wait to hear any more. Thinking at first that it was a voice from Heaven, he believed himself damned; and then, when the voice began to ask for money, he saw that he was being victimized by a shrewd blackmailer to whom Debienne himself had fallen a prey. Both of them, already tired of management for various reasons, went away without trying to investigate further into the personality of that curious O. G., who had forced such a singular memorandum-book upon them. They bequeathed the whole mystery to their successors and heaved a sigh of relief when they were rid of a business that had puzzled them without amusing them in the least."

I then spoke of the two successors and expressed my surprise that, in his **Memoirs of a Manager**, M. Moncharmin should describe the Opera ghost's behavior at such length in the first part of the book and hardly mention it at all in the second. In reply to this, the Persian, who knew the **Memoirs** as thoroughly as if he had written them himself, observed that I should find the explanation of the whole business if I would just recollect the few lines which Moncharmin devotes to the ghost in the second part aforesaid. I quote these lines, which are particularly interesting because they describe the very simple manner in which the famous incident of the twenty-thousand francs was closed:

As for O. G., some of whose curious tricks I have related in the first part of my Memoirs, I will only say that he redeemed by one spontaneous fine action all the worry which he had caused my dear friend and partner and, I am bound to say, myself. He felt, no doubt, that there are limits to a joke, especially when it is so expensive and when the commissary of police has been informed, for, at the moment when we had made an appointment in our office with M. Mifroid to tell him the whole story, a few days after the disappearance of Christine Daaé, we found, on Richard's table, a large envelope, inscribed, in red ink, "With O. G.'s compliments." It contained the large sum of money which he had succeeded in playfully extracting, for the time being, from the treasury. Richard was at once of the opinion that we must be content with that and drop the business. I agreed with Richard. All's well that ends well. What do you say, O. G.?

Of course, Moncharmin, especially after the money had been restored, continued to believe that he had, for a short while, been the butt of Richard's sense of humor, whereas Richard, on his side, was convinced that Moncharmin had amused himself by inventing the whole of the affair of the Opera ghost, in order to revenge himself for a few jokes.

I asked the Persian to tell me by what trick the ghost had taken twenty-thousand francs from Richard's pocket in spite of the safety-pin. He replied that he had not gone into this little detail, but that, if I myself cared to make an investigation on the spot, I should certainly find the solution to the riddle in the managers' office by remembering that Erik had not been nicknamed the trap-door lover for nothing. I promised the Persian to do so as soon as I had time, and I may as well tell the reader at once that the results of my investigation were perfectly satisfactory; and I hardly believed that I should ever discover so many undeniable proofs of the authenticity of the feats ascribed to the ghost.

The Persian's manuscript, Christine Daaé's papers, the statements made to me by the people who used to work under MM. Richard and Moncharmin, by little Meg herself (the worthy Madame Giry, I am sorry to say, is no more) and by Sorelli, who is now living in retirement at Louveciennes: all the documents relating to the existence of the ghost, which I propose to deposit in the archives of the Opera, have been checked and confirmed by a number of important discoveries of which I am justly proud. I have not been able to find the house on the lake, Erik having blocked up all the secret entrances.[12] On the other hand, I have discovered the secret passage of

---

[12] Even so, I am convinced that it would be easy to reach it by draining the lake, as I have repeatedly requested the Ministry of Fine Arts to do. I was speaking about it to M. Dujardin-Beaumetz, the undersecretary for fine arts, only forty-eight hours before the publication of this book. Who knows but that the score of Don Juan Triumphant might yet be discovered in the house on the lake?

the Communists, the planking of which is falling to pieces in parts, and also the trap-door through which Raoul and the Persian penetrated into the cellars of the opera-house. In the Communists' dungeon, I noticed numbers of initials traced on the walls by the unfortunate people confined in it; and among these were an "R" and a "C." R. C.: Raoul de Chagny. The letters are there to this day.

If the reader will visit the Opera one morning and ask leave to stroll where he pleases, without being accompanied by a stupid guide, let him go to Box Five and knock with his fist or stick on the enormous column that separates this from the stage-box. He will find that the column sounds hollow. After that, do not be astonished by the suggestion that it was occupied by the voice of the ghost: there is room inside the column for two men. If you are surprised that, when the various incidents occurred, no one turned round to look at the column, you must remember that it presented the appearance of solid marble, and that the voice contained in it seemed rather to come from the opposite side, for, as we have seen, the ghost was an expert ventriloquist. The column was elaborately carved and decorated with the sculptor's chisel; and I do not despair of one day discovering the ornament that could be raised or lowered at will, so as to admit of the ghost's mysterious correspondence with Mame Giry and of his generosity.

However, all these discoveries are nothing, to my mind, compared with that which I was able to make, in the presence of the acting-manager, in the managers' office, within a couple of inches from the desk-chair, and which consisted of a trap-door, the width of a board in the flooring and the length of a man's forearm and no longer; a trap-door that falls back like the lid of a box; a trap-door through which I can see a hand come and dexterously fumble at the pocket of a swallowtail coat.

That is the way the forty-thousand francs went!... And that also is the way by which, through some trick or other, they were returned.

Speaking about this to the Persian, I said:

"So we may take it, as the forty-thousand francs were returned, that Erik was simply amusing himself with that memorandum-book of his?"

"Don't you believe it!" he replied. "Erik wanted money. Thinking himself without the pale of humanity, he was restrained by no scruples and he employed his extraordinary gifts of dexterity and imagination, which he had received by way of compensation for his extraordinary ugliness, to prey upon his fellow-men. His reason for restoring the forty-thousand francs, of his own accord, was that he no longer wanted it. He had relinquished his marriage with Christine Daaé. He had relinquished everything above the surface of the earth."

According to the Persian's account, Erik was born in a small town not far from Rouen. He was the son of a master-mason. He ran away at an early age from his father's house, where his ugliness was a subject of horror and terror to his parents. For a time, he frequented the fairs, where a showman exhibited him as the "living corpse." He seems to have crossed the whole of Europe, from fair to fair, and to have completed his strange education as an artist and magician at the very fountainhead of art and magic, among the Gipsies. A period of Erik's life remained quite obscure. He was seen at the fair of Nijni-Novgorod, where he displayed himself in all his hideous glory. He already sang as nobody on this earth had ever sung before; he practised ventriloquism and gave displays of legerdemain so extraordinary that the caravans returning to Asia talked about it during the whole length of their journey. In this way, his reputation penetrated the walls of the palace at Mazenderan, where the little sultana, the favorite of the Shah-in-Shah, was boring herself to death. A dealer in furs, returning to Samarkand from Nijni-Novgorod, told of the marvels which he had seen performed in Erik's tent. The trader was summoned to the palace and the daroga of Mazenderan was told to question him. Next the daroga was instructed to go and find Erik. He brought him to Persia, where for some months Erik's will was law. He was guilty of not a few horrors, for he seemed not to know the difference between good and evil. He took part calmly in a number of political assassinations; and he turned his diabolical inventive powers against the Emir of Afghanistan, who was at war with the Persian empire. The Shah took a liking to him.

This was the time of the rosy hours of Mazenderan, of which the daroga's narrative has given us a glimpse. Erik had very original ideas on the subject of architecture and thought out a palace much as a conjuror contrives a trick-casket. The Shah ordered him to construct an edifice of this kind. Erik did so; and the building appears to have been so ingenious that His Majesty was able to move about in it unseen and to disappear without a possibility of the trick's being discovered. When the Shah-in-Shah found himself the possessor of this gem, he ordered Erik's yellow eyes to be put out. But he reflected that, even when blind, Erik would still be able to build so remarkable a house for another sovereign; and also that, as long as Erik was alive, someone would know the secret of the wonderful palace. Erik's death was decided upon, together with that of all the laborers who had worked under his orders. The execution of this abominable decree devolved upon the daroga of Mazenderan. Erik had shown him some slight services and procured him many a hearty laugh. He saved Erik by providing him with the means of escape, but nearly paid with his head for his generous indulgence.

Fortunately for the daroga, a corpse, half-eaten by the birds of prey, was found on the shore of the Caspian Sea, and was taken for Erik's body, because the daroga's friends had dressed the remains in clothing that belonged to Erik. The daroga was let off with the loss of the imperial favor, the confiscation of his property and an order of perpetual banishment. As a member of the Royal House, however, he continued to receive a monthly pension of a few hundred francs from the Persian treasury; and on this he came to live in Paris.

As for Erik, he went to Asia Minor and thence to Constantinople, where he entered the Sultan's employment. In explanation of the services which he was able to render a monarch haunted by perpetual terrors, I need only say that it was Erik who constructed all the famous trap-doors and secret chambers and mysterious strongboxes which were found at Yildiz-

Kiosk after the last Turkish revolution. He also invented those automata, dressed like the Sultan and resembling the Sultan in all respects,[13] which made people believe that the Commander of the Faithful was awake at one place, when, in reality, he was asleep elsewhere.

Of course, he had to leave the Sultan's service for the same reasons that made him fly from Persia: he knew too much. Then, tired of his adventurous, formidable and monstrous life, he longed to be someone "like everybody else." And he became a contractor, like any ordinary contractor, building ordinary houses with ordinary bricks. He tendered for part of the foundations in the Opera. His estimate was accepted. When he found himself in the cellars of the enormous playhouse, his

---

[13] See the interview of the special correspondent of the Matin, with Mohammed-Ali Bey, on the day after the entry of the Salonika troops into Constantinople.

artistic, fantastic, wizard nature resumed the upper hand. Besides, was he not as ugly as ever? He dreamed of creating for his own use a dwelling unknown to the rest of the earth, where he could hide from men's eyes for all time.

The reader knows and guesses the rest. It is all in keeping with this incredible and yet veracious story. Poor, unhappy Erik! Shall we pity him? Shall we curse him? He asked only to be "someone," like everybody else. But he was too ugly! And he had to hide his genius **or use it to play tricks with**, when, with an ordinary face, he would have been one of the most distinguished of mankind! He had a heart that could have held the empire of the world; and, in the end, he had to content himself with a cellar. Ah, yes, we must needs pity the Opera ghost.

I have prayed over his mortal remains, that God might show him mercy notwithstanding his crimes. Yes, I am sure, quite sure that I prayed beside his body, the other day, when they took it from the spot where they were burying the phonographic records. It was his skeleton. I did not recognize it by the ugliness of the head, for all men are ugly when they have been dead as long as that, but by the plain gold ring which he wore and which Christine Daaé had certainly slipped on his finger, when she came to bury him in accordance with her promise.

The skeleton was lying near the little well, in the place where the Angel of Music first held Christine Daaé fainting in his trembling arms, on the night when he carried her down to the cellars of the opera-house.

And, now, what do they mean to do with that skeleton? Surely they will not bury it in the common grave!... I say that the place of the skeleton of the Opera ghost is in the archives of the National Academy of Music. It is no ordinary skeleton.

www.ingramcontent.com/pod-product-compliance
Lightning Source LLC
Chambersburg PA
CBHW020918310726
48980CB00011B/949/J

* 9 7 8 1 8 3 4 1 2 2 8 6 1 *